THE MAN WITH THE AXE

MAURICE SMITH

◆ FriesenPress

One Printers Way
Altona, MB
R0G 0B0
Canada

www.friesenpress.com

ISBN
978-1-03-832542-6 (Hardcover)
978-1-03-832541-9 (Paperback)
978-1-03-832543-3 (eBook)

1. FIC050000   FICTION, CRIME

Distributed to the trade by The Ingram Book Company

CHAPTER 1

It was one a.m., so it was time for the last game. We always played dealer-choice poker from seven p.m. until one a.m. once a month. The six of us rotated from one player's residence to another. This month it was my turn. Me? I'm Mitch Watson, a private investigator. I work mostly for lawyers, sometimes for insurance companies.

I had inherited the bungalow we were in. The basement was finished, and there was a nice room there where we played. It was furnished with a sofa, two recliners, six dining-room chairs, a TV, a fridge, and a cabinet with a microwave on top. We had a rectangular table that was perfect for us—two on each side and one at each end. There was a small washroom in another part of the basement.

I looked around the table at my poker buddies. We were all in our late thirties or early forties. All of us always in casual clothes: T-shirts or golf shirts, sometimes a sweater in the colder weather. Casual pants. No one seemed to wear jeans anymore. It was the middle of October, and the weather was unusually mild.

I was at one end of the table. On my right was my best friend, Jack Hornby. We had known each other for over twenty years. Jack had coached the football team at the university and then become a personal trainer at a gym. He also had a few private customers. Jack and I had bowled together, played golf together, and sometimes went to the racetrack together. Jack got divorced many years ago and lived with his twenty-year-old son Brad, whom he adored. Jack was around my height, six feet, and near the same weight, about 180 lbs. His brown hair had streaks of gray. So far, I was not seeing any of my own.

Next to Jack was Tony Marino, who was an artist. He'd had a tough time getting started, but he had just signed a contract with a large company to supply paintings for their boardroom and conference rooms. Tony had a thin face, was small boned, and had long, dark hair. He looked like an artist.

At the other end of the table sat Henry Miller, a friend of Tony's. We called Henry Farmer Boy because he used to be a dairy farmer. His parents were killed in a car accident, and a couple of years later he sold the farm and bought an old-fashioned house, complete with a wood stove in the living room. We often said that you could take Henry out of the country, but you couldn't take the country out of Henry. He was a good-natured guy but completely naïve about city life. He had a workshop in his basement and made tables and furniture to sell to customers. He had married a much younger woman, Julie, just over a year ago. I didn't think it would last, but so far so good as far as I knew. I could see Julie falling for him for two reasons. He was rich and handsome. Henry was a big man with a square face, light-brown hair, and a warm smile. Everyone liked Henry.

On the side to my left was the odd couple, Greg Dillon and Doug Hamilton. They were good friends but completely opposite in many ways. Greg was a computer-systems analyst and a very sharp person—sharp in his ways and in the way he talked and dressed. He had wavy black hair, sideburns, a thin pencil mustache, and a small black goatee. If they ever remade *The Three Musketeers,* he would be a natural. He was single and loved the ladies. The feeling was mutual most of the time.

Doug was an auto mechanic. He had an army-style crew cut.

While Greg was the best dresser, Doug was the worst. He rarely varied from an old T-shirt and an old pair of pants. Actually, anything seemed to look old on Doug. So, why were they friends? Two reasons—sports and gambling. They both followed all sports and had season tickets for the football and hockey teams. They enjoyed a day at the horse races and an occasional trip to the casino. While watching a football game they would sometimes bet on what the next play would be. Doug was married and had two children, probably something that would never happen with Greg.

So, that was our group, a strange combination of guys with different styles of living. However, we all loved poker, and apart from an occasional moment of someone being cheesed off for some reason, we were a good group with lots of humor. We had all come together one way or another and had progressed to the point where we could insult each other and laugh about it. Well, most of the time.

For the last game, it had come around to me to deal. "The Axe," I announced. It was our favorite game. We had taken it from an old seven-card stud game that we played as teenagers. One-eyed jacks and the man with the axe were wild, and a pair of sevens took all. We'd dropped the one-eyed jacks because we didn't like a lot of wild cards. We kept the man with the axe, the king of diamonds, and a pair of sevens. We had actually taken a vote on whether to keep the sevens. Greg, Doug, and I voted for it while Jack, Tony, and Henry voted against it. It was a tie, so we agreed that wherever we played we would play the way the host voted. I was beginning to have my doubts about it because it seemed that a pair of sevens was coming up too often. Initially, I thought it added something to the game, but sometimes it didn't seem fair.

We were not high rollers by any means. Bets were two or three dollars at any time, with five bucks optional on the last card. If the ax was dealt face up, the player had to put a fiver in or fold. If he stayed in, he could bet five. Up to three raises were allowed on each round of cards dealt.

I dealt the first two rounds face down and the next one face up. I dealt Greg the seven of diamonds, Doug the jack of spades, Henry the ace of spades, Tony the queen of spades, Jack the four of hearts, and myself the seven of clubs. I had the queen of clubs and the three of diamonds down. Getting the seven meant I had to stay in until the last card in case I got a pair. Henry was high so he threw in a buck, and we all followed. No one raised.

Next round, Greg got the ten of diamonds, Doug the nine of hearts, and Henry the ace of clubs, so that was two aces for Henry. Tony got the four of diamonds, Jack got the five of hearts, and I got the three of clubs. So, a pair of threes for me, but I was counting on another seven. Henry, with a pair of aces, was high, so he bet two bucks. Tony folded, and the rest of us called the two bucks.

In the fifth round, Greg got the ten of hearts, so that was two pairs for him. Doug got the eight of hearts and Henry the jack of clubs. Jack got the six of clubs, and I got the two of diamonds. Henry bet two bucks again, and we all called.

In the sixth round, Greg got the nine of clubs, Doug the five of diamonds, Henry the four of spades, and Jack the king of diamonds—the axe! Jack wasted no time and threw in a fiver. I dealt myself the queen of hearts. So, two pairs for me and still a chance for a pair of sevens. Henry was still high on board with his pair of aces. He hesitated. I felt that he didn't know whether to bet two or five or fold. I think he just had the ace pair. Finally, he bet two bucks. Jack raised it five; maybe he already had the straight. I stayed in and hoped for a seven. Doug folded, followed by Henry. So, just Greg, Jack, and I were left, with one card to go, face down. I dealt Greg, then Jack, and then me. I gingerly turned up one corner of the card. It was the six of clubs. Close but no cigar. Too bad. A pair of sevens would have been nice on the last hand. I didn't think my two pairs would win.

Greg was high on the board with a pair of tens and bet five. Jack raised it five, and I folded. Greg was laughing as he threw in five and turned his cards over. He had two sevens. "Pair of sevens, Jack," he said, waving them in the air.

"You prick," Jack snarled. "You could have shown them sooner."

Greg was still laughing. "I got the second seven on the last card. And besides, I could have raised you again at the end, but I saved you five bucks because I'm a good guy."

"Bullshit," Jack snorted.

"Okay, that's it." I said. "I'm changing my vote, so we won't play that again with the sevens."

Greg looked at me. "Sticking up for your buddy, Mitch?"

"No," I replied. "It's just a crummy way to win. Anyway, let's forget it. Next month we're at your place, Greg."

"Yes, and I'll be ready for you soft touches." He laughed as he went out the door.

Jack had already left, and the rest followed.

I looked around the room. Apart from a few empty beer bottles, it looked okay. We had chili at eleven o'clock that I had cooked earlier. The guys had put their bowls in the dishwasher in my small kitchen downstairs. So, with not much for me to do, I turned out the lights and headed upstairs. Time to pack it in.

I was asleep right away. I dreamed I was on a boat. Why I was on a boat I didn't know, but the ship's bell kept ringing. It had a melodious sound, but it kept ringing. I looked everywhere for the ship's captain, but I couldn't see him or anyone else. I found the bell and smashed it with my fist. But it was not the bell; it was the headboard of my bed. It woke me right up.

Still hearing the ringing, I looked around. It was my cell phone. I had forgotten to turn it off. That happens a lot. I checked the name: Henry Miller. He must have hung up every time it went to voicemail and dialed again. I checked the time. It was two a.m.

I grabbed my phone and stabbed the "answer" button, "It's two in the morning, not two in the afternoon Henry," I snarled.

"Mitch," he said hoarsely, and I could tell something was wrong. "Mitch," he said again. "It's Julie." Then he was sobbing heavily into the phone.

"Henry, what is it?" I asked. I waited a minute while he pulled himself together.

"Julie has been killed!" Another long pause. "With my axe!"

CHAPTER 2

I tried to calm him down as much as possible. He was somewhat in shock. I did get from him that when he'd returned home, he had called out for her and found that she was not in the house. So, then he went outside and discovered her in the backyard with an axe buried in her throat and blood everywhere.

I told him not to do anything and not to touch anything, and I would leave right away and get there as fast as possible.

Usually, it is about forty-five minutes from my house to his. At two a.m. I was able to do it in thirty-five. On the way, I thought of all I had to tell him. What was going to happen, how to respond to the police, how the whole property would become a crime scene. It must have been tough for Henry to see Julie that way, but the next twenty-four hours would be a nightmare as well.

The house was mostly red brick with a porch all the way across the front. There were some flowers just below the porch and two large areas of grass and weeds on each side of the paved walkway to the front door. There was a two-car garage and a long, wide driveway.

His house and driveway would be a crime scene and would be taped off. I didn't want to be caught in it, so I parked outside the house next door. I walked up Henry's front path and used the knocker on his dark mahogany door.

Henry opened it and put his arms around me, sobbing all the while.

I said that we should go to his living room, sit down, and talk about what had to be done. It was going to be difficult. At the moment, it was a disaster for Henry. He couldn't think straight, and we would have to call the police soon.

I told him that when the police came, it would probably be a patrol car, the detectives, and then a forensics team and someone from the coroner's office, but not necessarily in that order. Our city was called Cairnford, and we were smackdab in the middle of Middle America. In our city, the police were in "divisions," not precincts, but it was the same thing, really, just different terminology. The buildings were still referred to as police stations. The main forensics office was downtown, but we had a satellite forensics unit in the north part of the city as well. Detectives used to complain about how long they always had to wait for a forensics team to arrive. Anything requiring more detailed analysis was still done downtown. Anyway, Henry was in the 9th Division area, and the forensics team would come from the satellite office.

I told Henry that areas would be photographed and dusted for fingerprints. Evidence markers would be put in the appropriate places. Yellow police tape would be placed across the driveway and around the house. He would be questioned in the house and then taken to the division and questioned again. He might have to write out a statement. He wouldn't be allowed to return for several days. Therefore, he better start thinking about where to stay and what to pack. That is, if they would allow him to pack.

I knew all this from former cases, and I was sure most of it, if not all of it, would apply. Henry didn't say anything, seemingly still shaken up from the worst thing that had happened in his life. I told him to just sit there, and I would go into the backyard to see Julie. I said her name rather than "the dead body." I didn't want Henry to break down altogether.

I went to my car and got a flashlight. There was no moon, just a dark night. The gate to the backyard was open. It was a big backyard, and I didn't see anything at first, so swinging the flashlight back and forth, I ventured farther in. Then I saw her, nearly in the middle of a large grassy area. She was lying on her back with the blade of the ax lodged deep in her throat. There was a lot of blood on her and all around. I didn't go close, because I didn't want to be accused of compromising a crime scene.

I went in the house and told him that we had to call the police. He asked me to do it. I called 911, identified myself, and said I was a friend of Henry Miller, who had just found his wife killed in the backyard. "He is very distraught," I mentioned. I gave the address, and then I was instructed not to touch anything, that officers were on the way.

I told Henry and then asked him to pull himself together so that he could talk intelligently and coherently to the police when they arrived.

I had a longtime friend in the police division, Detective Frank Dobson, whom I had been involved with in other cases in the past. We had become very good friends. I hoped he would be one of the detectives assigned to the case.

Before they arrived, I asked Henry if he wanted me to take on the case. I hated to use the word "case." I could see Henry was thinking Julie was now a "case" instead of a person. I went on quickly. "Henry, I'm between jobs right now. I can get sometimes three hundred and fifty dollars a day from lawyers and insurance companies. I would never charge you that, but I will need something to get by on. How about half, a hundred and seventy-five dollars a day, and I'll waive expenses? I knew Henry had the money and I did need something to keep me going, so I didn't feel too bad about it.

Henry said, "Okay whatever you want."

I asked Henry for the names and addresses of Julie's closest friends and associates. I needed to start interviewing before the police did. Whoever got there first would get the most information. People didn't like saying all the same things over again. The second time around they were more likely to leave things out. The dreaded words for me were, "I already told the police."

Henry said that Julie kept them all in her cell phone. He thought it would be in her purse in her bedroom.

I told him we would have to leave it. Henry didn't use his cell phone much and had numbers and addresses in his address book that was on the side table by his recliner. He was able to give me three numbers and addresses out of his book - Julie's sister, her best friend Susan, and the place where Julie worked. Henry also said her best friend, Susan Long, knew all Julie's friends and associates and knew more about Julie than anyone else.

At that moment I heard steps on the porch, and I knew the police were there. I braced myself, mostly for what Henry would have to go through. He didn't know it, but he would instantly be regarded as the main suspect. In cases like this, the spouse is always number one until another suspect becomes apparent.

I answered the door just as they knocked. Two uniformed officers, a male and female. Apparently, the female was the senior of the two. They were about the same height, maybe around five foot eight, and other than that I couldn't tell much about them with their head gear, dark-blue uniforms, and black boots.

The female asked if I was the one who had called it in. I told her I was. She introduced herself as Officer Irene Kirby and her partner as Officer Drew Simpson.

I asked them in, told them my name, and introduced Henry as the husband of the victim. Kirby asked if we had touched anything, and I said no. She asked where the victim was, and I told her. They went into the back and came back a few minutes later. Then the conversations began. The questions and answers would be asked again and again, first by the uniformed officers, then by the detectives, and again at the police station.

Kirby started with Henry as Simpson pulled out his notebook. "What time did you discover your wife?"

"It was around two o'clock."

"Were you not both in bed at the same time earlier?"

"No. I was at a poker game at Mitch's place until just after one, and I got home at around two."

"What did you do when you got home?"

"I went up to her bedroom to see if she was asleep, but she was not in bed, so I looked in every room in the house and then went outside with a flashlight and found her in the back."

At that point Henry started tearing up again, but Kirby kept on with the questioning. "After you found your wife, what did you do?"

"I came in, sat down, and tried to make sense of it. It was so horrible. I guess I just sat there crying for a while. I couldn't help it."

"You didn't think to phone the police?"

"No. I couldn't think of anything."

"So, did you call your friend, Mitch?"

"Yes. He told me not to touch anything and that he would be right up as soon as he could."

"What time did you call him?"

"I don't know. Must have been a bit after two a.m."

"Then you just sat there until he came?"

"Yes."

She turned to me. "What time did you get here?"

"Between two forty-five and three a.m. I think."

She checked her phone. "The call to us came in at three-twenty. What took so long? What were you doing?"

"I had to calm Henry down. He was nearly incoherent. As you can see, he is much better now but still not in a good way."

She gave me a hard look, but then the front door opened, and there stood the two detectives.

♦

CHAPTER 3

♦

One was tall with black hair streaked with gray. He was wearing a dark-blue suit with a light-blue shirt and tie. He had a lined face and dark-gray eyes with a steely look about them. He looked lean and mean. He looked like a detective. His partner was entirely different. He was younger, bigger, and heavier, wearing a dark-brown blazer, khaki pants, and brown shoes. He didn't look like a detective. Even though his name was Green, I thought of him as Brownie.

The older one introduced himself as Detective Rick Surmansky, his partner being Ben Green.

Apparently, Surmansky knew the uniformed officers and asked them to come out on the porch with Green and him.

I could see from the living room window that they were going over what was known so far. Also, Surmansky asked to see Officer Simpson's notes. Surmansky asked questions about some of the items in the notes. Then they all went into the backyard, the officers showing the way with their flashlights.

After a few minutes, they returned to the house. Before the detectives started with us, Surmansky asked the officers to get started putting the crime-scene tape around the house. He told them the whole property was a crime scene, and they needed to tape it all off. The forensics crew could duck underneath it when they arrived.

I knew the detectives would start asking questions, some the same as before. They looked for inconsistencies and pounced on them. As Surmansky turned to us, Brownie took out his notebook.

Surmansky asked "Who is the victim's husband?"

"I am," Henry replied.

Okay, I thought, *here we go. I hope Henry can retain his composure.*

"When did you last see your wife?"

"At around six o'clock when I left for Mitch's place."

"Where were you and your wife at the time?"

"In our backyard."

"What were you doing there?"

"Julie was planting flowers. I just went to say goodbye."

"At six in the evening? That's a strange time to be planting flowers."

"They were tulip bulbs. Julie wanted to get them in before it got dark."

"Why would she do it and not you?"

"Julie works in a flower shop. She likes working with flowers."

"What time did you get to the poker game?"

"Oh, sometime between six-forty-five and seven o'clock."

"What time did you leave the game?"

"A bit after one a.m."

Surmansky went on with what time Henry got home and what he did then. Henry told him and I knew what was coming next.

"Why did you not call the police right away?"

"I was too upset, I couldn't think straight."

The detective took a hard look at Henry, trying to detect any signs of lying.

Then we were interrupted by noise from outside. The forensics team and the medical examiner had arrived. It was an eerie scene. They all wore headlamps, and they all had them on. They were dressed in their lab gear, all except the medical examiner, who wore a black suit and plastic gloves and carried a black case. The detectives took them all outside into the back. At least two were carrying photography equipment, and one was carrying what looked like a case of evidence markers. Fingerprint personnel would be the rest.

Henry and I sat inside the house in silence most of the time. The detectives came back first.

Surmansky looked at me. "What time did you arrive here?"

"I don't know. I don't keep looking at my watch but it must have been between two forty-five and three."

"The call was not made to 911 until three-twenty. What were you doing in the meantime?"

"I was just trying to calm Henry down. I went into the back to see what had happened, and then I came in and made the call. To answer your next question, I never went anywhere else in the house."

Surmansky turned to Henry. "Is anything missing?"

Henry thought for a moment. "Mitch told me not to touch anything, so I stayed here, so I don't know."

Surmansky was sharp. "You said when you came home you looked in every room in the house, looking for your wife. So, I repeat the question. Did you notice anything missing?"

Henry was finally getting it together. "I was only looking for Julie; I wasn't taking an inventory."

That was something I might have said. Good for Henry.

Surmansky turned to Brownie. "Take him upstairs. Don't let him touch anything, but check the bedrooms to see if anything is missing." Then, turning to Henry, he said, "Does your wife have a computer, laptop, cellphone, and purse? If so, where will they be?"

Henry thought for a moment. "She has all of those, and they should all be in her bedroom. The cell phone should be in her purse at the side of the bed. I have a cell phone but nothing else."

With that, Henry and Brownie left the room.

The medical examiner came in. I didn't notice earlier because I hadn't been looking at the person, but then I saw who it was, and I recognized her from the past. She was a large African American,

Janene Mani. Some people called her Jan, and others called her Janman. She had a large, happy, smiling face—unusual considering her line of work. She was known for her wicked sense of humor and could banter with anyone. Political correctness was nowhere to be found in anything she said. I liked her a lot.

She spotted me. "Well, if it isn't the world's greatest PI—in his own mind, of course."

I smiled back. "Hi, Jan. I haven't seen you lately."

I valued her as a good friend, someone I thought I could say almost anything to.

"Hi, Mitch. What are you doing here?"

Surmansky, getting impatient, replied for me. "He's a friend of the husband, so now can we have the prelim?"

"If there was something other than the obvious, I would have to tell you in private, but I can tell you the obvious: the victim died from bleeding out from a wound caused by an ax that pretty near decapitated her. Death would have occurred roughly about ten hours ago. Let's see, what time is it now?"

"Four-fifteen," Surmansky replied.

The medical examiner thought and then said, "So, the death occurred sometime between five p.m. and seven p.m. last night about as good as I can make it. When forensics is finished outside, she can be taken to the office."

The "office" was the term used by forensics for the examination area next to the small morgue in the forensics building.

Jan turned to the detective and said she wanted to talk to me privately about a couple of other cases I have had and asked if we could go out on the porch. He nodded. We went outside.

"What cases?" I asked.

She looked at me with a smile on her face. "That was just a ruse for Surmansky, so I could talk to you privately. I don't like him at all. He is a really good detective, but I don't like his attitude. I can't stand him. I hope he gets taken off the case. I hope that you can solve this one before him, but you'll need our help. You know that we're not supposed to do this. However, maybe I can give you some information after I've done the autopsy. I would be putting my career on the line if it were found out, so you have to be very careful and not tell anyone else, or it could get back to me.

Wow, I thought. I hated for someone to go that far for me, and I hardly knew her, although we had taken an early liking to each other when we first met on a case some time ago. "Jan," I said, "I really appreciate that, and whatever it is, it will stay with me. If there is anything I can ever do for you, please let me know. Anyway, if I can solve this thing, we'll go out and celebrate."

Then, on impulse, I reached out and gave her a big hug. It was a big hug because she was big, and there was lots to hug.

We went back inside before Surmansky sent out a search party for us. Just then, Henry and Brownie came back down from upstairs.

Brownie spoke first. "Mr. Miller noticed that a blue jewelry box was missing from the top of his wife's dresser. He said nothing else was missing. The computer, laptop, cell phone, and purse are all there."

Surmansky looked around the living room, taking in every detail. He turned to Henry. "That door on my left, does that go to the dining room?"

"Yes," Henry replied. "The kitchen goes on from there."

Surmansky looked at Brownie and Henry. "Burglars don't usually bother with dining rooms and kitchens, but let's take a look to see if anything is missing or out of place."

Off they went, leaving me alone. The uniformed officers were still taping off the property, and forensics were still in the backyard.

Henry and the detectives returned shortly, and I looked at Henry. He anticipated the question. "Everything seems normal," he said.

Just then, the head of forensics, Dave Whitehead, who had been with the police force longer than I could remember, entered the room. He was a big man with a head of hair that matched his name.

He noticed Surmansky and turned to him. "We're almost finished outside, we'll have to come back tomorrow. Even with the headlamps we could have missed something. Anyway, we need to look at the area in the daylight."

Surmansky thought for a moment. "Okay, I'll tell the officers to stay until the end of their shift and then have someone on scene for twenty-four hours a day for the next couple of days at least."

At that moment, the uniformed officers returned, and Kirby told the detectives that the property was taped off. Surmansky told them to stay on site and then called the station to advise them of the situation and the need for on-site personnel. He turned to Henry. "Are your car and your wife's car in the garage?"

Henry nodded.

The detective asked Henry for the keys to both cars. Henry took his out, and Whitehead put them in an evidence bag. Henry said that Julie's keys would be in her purse.

Surmansky looked at everyone and said, "We will be taking the witnesses to the station." He turned to Whitehead. "The victim's computer, laptop, purse, and cellphone are in the bedroom upstairs. So, take them and also Mr. Miller's cell phone." With that, he stuck out his hand to Henry, who gave him his cell phone, which went into another evidence bag.

Surmansky looked at Henry and me. "We are going to the station, and you will be questioned separately. Watson, you will be first, then Miller. All being well, after your questioning you will leave the station, so you will not see your friend. Therefore, if there is anything you wish to say to him, do it now."

"Henry, where will you stay?"

He thought for a moment. "At my brother's house."

"Okay," I said. "First chance, phone your brother, and tell him what happened. They will allow you that call from the station. When you see him, phone your sister. During questioning, just tell the truth, exactly what happened, and everything will be okay. Tell me your brother's phone number, and I'll call you tonight."

Henry did, and I wrote it down.

I had one question for the detective. "Can I follow you down to the station in my car? I parked outside the crime scene."

"Is that your Mustang outside?" he asked.

"Yep, that's my baby."

"I thought it was. Okay, but if you're not at the station within five minutes of us, I will send out an APB."

I looked to see if he was smiling. He was not.

CHAPTER 4

It took about fifteen minutes to drive to the station. Henry and I were placed in separate interrogation rooms. The two detectives sat across from me at an oval table. The room was sparse—a table and four chairs. There were drawers on the detectives side of the room.

Surmansky pushed a couple of buttons at the edge of the table, saying that the interview would be recorded. He mentioned the date, the subject, and who was present. Then he asked me for the record to state my name, address, and what I was employed at, then state all my involvement in the case so far.

I tried to remember the times and what I had previously stated and added nothing new.

Surmansky had a few new questions, such as:

"Does Henry have a temper?"

"How did he get on with his wife?"

"What did he tell you about his wife?"

Actually, all his new questions were about Henry. I had no trouble answering any of them.

Then the detective opened a drawer and pulled out a legal pad. He asked me to write a statement about what had happened that night and then sign it.

No problem. It took a while, and I made sure that I kept everything the same as what I had stated.

Afterwards, he read it through, had no more questions, and said I could go. They would be in touch.

I raced out of there and then stood outside, feeling a huge sense of relief. That part was all over with. I checked my watch. It was almost six a.m. What to do?

First go home and have a shower. I was hungry, but I didn't feel like cooking, so I'd go to McDonald's for a bacon-and-egg McMuffin with a hash brown and coffee. Boy, did that sound good!

By the time I drove home, had a shower, changed my clothes, drove to McDonald's, and was sitting in a booth with my breakfast and my newspaper, it was close to seven a.m. I ate quickly, then read the paper and sat there, thinking of the order in which to do things.

I felt that there were three interviews I had to do that day to beat the detectives there. They were Julie's sister, the flower shop, and Julie's girlfriend, Susan Long. I hoped Henry had been able to call his sister. I thought that I should give him more time. I did not want to be the one to break the news.

When I got back home I checked the website for A&A Flowers. A&A were Arthur and Alice Bundheim. They were German immigrants who had come over in the nineties to start a new life and had opened the flower shop in a small strip plaza in a residential area about twenty minutes away from Henry and Julie. The store was open at nine a.m. I would go there first.

I was looking forward to meeting the girlfriend later because Henry said she knew everything about Julie and all her secrets. I thought it a bit telling that Henry didn't seem to know any of Julie's secrets.

What was I going to be opening up? I had no idea, but I felt that there would be a lot of surprises and that I would be meeting a lot of new people from various walks of life.

◆

[HAPTEK 5

◆

A&A Flowers was in an old plaza with a bakery, a dry cleaner, a computer sales and service store, a liquor store, a pet grooming place, and a convenience store. I walked in and noticed all kinds of flowers, bushes, and plants. As it was the middle of October, there weren't many flowers, but there were a lot of chrysanthemums. Those I recognized. Flowers were not my strong suit, and I had no idea what most of everything else was.

There was a long counter down one side of the room with various collections of all kinds from their stock. A young man was behind the counter, looking through a sheaf of orders.

He called out, "Hey, can I help you?" He was in his late twenties and had a few days of stubble on his face. It looked like either he was undecided whether to grow a beard or was too lazy to shave.

There were two glass-enclosed offices on platforms at the end of the room, and I saw a woman in one of them. "Is that one of the A's?" I asked Stubbleface.

"Yep. That is Mrs. Bundheim. You want to see her?"

I ignored him and went right up to the office.

She saw me coming and opened the door as I got there. She looked me up and down and then asked, "Can I help you?"

Alice Bundheim was tall and thin with gray hair tied back in a bun. She had dark-blue eyes that seemed to look right through me.

I introduced myself, said I was a private investigator, and that it was about Julie.

She invited me in, but I noticed concern in her manner and eyes when I mentioned Julie. "What about Julie?" she asked. "Is she alright?"

There was no easy way to do it. "No. I'm sorry to tell you she is not alright." I paused. "Last night her husband found her in their backyard." Another pause. "She was dead. She had been killed."

Mrs. Bundheim looked at me in disbelief. Her hands went to her face. "No, no, it can't be! That's terrible!" she screamed at me. Then a suspicious look came in her eyes. "How do you know?" she asked.

I told her that Henry was a friend of mine and that he had been playing cards at my place. When he returned home at about two a.m., he had found her in the backyard with a wound in her neck. She was dead. "He called me. I went there, and then I called the police for him." I mentioned that Henry had asked me to investigate the case and that the police would also likely be visiting her within the next few days.

She realized then that this was the truth, and it hit her hard. She started crying and trying to speak at the same time.

I just waited—there was nothing else I could do.

Finally, she tried to regain her composure. "You said there was a wound in her neck. From what? Also, Julie was a lovely person. Who would do such a thing?"

How could I tell her that a person she liked a lot had almost been decapitated with an ax? "It appears that the weapon was an axe that Henry had in the backyard."

It took a moment for that to sink in, and when it did, it made it worse than before. Again her hands flew to her face. "Oh, that's horrible, simply horrible. I feel faint and sick."

I hated to be in such situations. I said quietly, "Is there anything I can get you or do for you?"

She shook her head, so I continued. "I do not know how it happened or who was involved. That's why I'm investigating for Henry, and the police are already investigating."

Mrs. Bundheim's eyes were red and teary, and her face was white. She did look like she was either going to be sick or faint. I was thinking of giving her a break and going down to question Stubbleface when she asked, "What happens now?"

I told her that I needed to ask questions of everyone who knew Julie to get some idea of what she was like and see if there was a motive to be found, so I started it off. "What was Julie like here at the store? And what did she do?"

"Julie did most of the arrangements. She had a knack for it. She was a lovely, wonderful person, and we all got along well together."

"Did Julie have any arguments with any of the customers?"

"Oh, no. No one here has any arguments with customers. They know what they want, and we know how to please them."

"Did Julie seem different in any way, lately?"

"No, I don't think so. She was always cheerful and outgoing."

I couldn't think of much more to ask her, so I said I would talk to the young man at the counter. I asked what his name was and what he did. She said his name was Ronnie Ramsden, and he was the driver. Sometimes he helped with arrangements.

I walked back down to the counter.

He looked up at me. "Hey, what was all that fuss about up there? You tell her bad news? Mrs. A looked like she was going to puke."

I told him what had happened. His response was what I expected from him.

"Wow, that's tough. I'm going to miss her. I liked looking at her every day. I'll have to cross her off my fantasy list."

I couldn't imagine how Julie could have worked alongside that jerk. I asked him the usual question: how did they both get along?

"Oh, fine," he said.

Then I thought of something else. "Did you ever deliver flowers to her home?"

He looked at me, wondering what I was getting at. "Why would I?"

"Oh, I don't know. Maybe she was taking some items home, and you were going her way, so you said you would drop them off for her. That's possible, isn't it?"

He didn't get the point of my question, which was to see if he knew where Julie lived.

He came back with, "Yes, it's possible, but it never happened."

Just then, a tall, thin man came into the store. I asked Ramsden if that was Mr. A and he said, "Yep, that old geezer is Mr. A."

I thought maybe I should tell Mr. A what his driver had said.

Arthur Bundheim looked at us both and then walked up to his office.

I followed him up.

He turned around and looked at me. I looked at him and his wife. They could have been twins. Both of them were tall and thin with long faces and long noses. They were both rather unattractive. Maybe that was why they were married. They couldn't attract anybody else.

He was dressed in a burgundy windbreaker and light-gray pants. He wore a black tie under his jacket. Smart casual, but I thought he would have worn a suit since he was representing a business.

I told him who I was and what I did and that I had already talked to his wife and that she could tell him why I was there. He looked at his wife and could tell that she was still in distress. She told him everything I had said.

His response was much more composed, to say the least. "Wow, I'm sorry to hear that. Julie was a very nice person and a good worker. We will have to get someone else."

Oh, what a warm, wonderful human being he was. It amazed me that Julie was able to work with him and dumbass Stubbleface. I would have to ask Julie's girlfriend, Susan, about all that. I wanted to get out of there as soon as possible.

"Mr. Bundheim," I said, "as your wife has mentioned, Henry Miller has hired me to investigate, so I just want to ask you a few questions to get further insight into Julie, and then I will be on my way. How well did you know Julie?"

"I'm out of the building a lot, so I didn't know much about her personal life. When I did talk to her here, I found her very personable and likable. She always did a good job with the flower arrangements."

I tried to make the next question as general as possible. "Did you ever deliver flowers yourself to Julie's house, and did you ever meet Henry?"

He hesitated. "Yes, there was one time when Julie was having a party there for her university friends and was going to take up a lot of flowers, and I told her I was going up that way and could deliver them if Henry was home. She was okay with that, and I met Henry for just a minute or two, so nothing of interest there. Another time we both went to the university together to deliver several arrangements. It was their fiftieth anniversary. Ronnie had a lot of deliveries, so we both made the trip."

That led to more questions. "During that trip, what did Julie talk about? Did she mention Henry?"

"You know, I don't remember much about our conversations, but I don't think she mentioned Henry."

"Did she appear concerned or worried about anything over the last week or two?"

They looked at each other, then he shook his head, "I don't think so."

I tried to think of what else to ask, but I just wanted to get out of that place. I dropped two of my cards on Mrs. A's desk and asked them to call me if they could think of anything else.

When I got outside, I looked back and thought that flowers

smelled nice, but it was people who stunk up the world.

So, next it would be either Julie's sister or girlfriend. Either way it would be an improvement over A&A and Stubbleface.

CHAPTER 6

I thought about calling Henry to see if he was up yet but then decided to give him a bit more time. I would go home, make myself some lunch, wait a while, then call him at around two p.m. He would be up by then. He was next of kin, so he should be the one calling Julie's sister and her girlfriend.

I phoned his brother at two o'clock.

"He is just getting up now. I'll have him call you."

"No," I said. "I need to talk to him now. I don't care if he has his pants on or not."

I waited a few minutes, then Henry's sleep-addled voice came on the line. "Yeah, Mitch?"

"Henry, before you do anything else, phone Julie's sister and girlfriend. Tell them what happened, that you have hired me to investigate, and that I will call them, asking to come over. Do it now, then call me right back to confirm. I'll wait fifteen minutes, and if I haven't heard from you, I'll call you back. Got it?"

"Okay," he said, and we both hung up.

Fifteen minutes later Henry called back. "Mitch, they are shocked and are very upset, but they are interested in talking to you."

"Thanks, Henry," I said, then hung up.

I thought I would call Julie's sister first. Then I realized something. All the times that Henry and I had mentioned Julie's sister, he had never said her name. It was always "Julie's sister." I would have to ask her what her name was.

I called the number that Henry had given me, and a clearly shaken woman's voice answered. I told her who I was and that I was extremely sorry for her loss, then asked if I could come over. She said yes and gave me her address. It was on the other side of town. I told her I would be there in thirty to forty minutes.

Another thing Henry had never told me—and which I had never asked—was if Julie's sister was married and if they had any children. I was about to find out.

The house was in an upscale part of town in a fairly recent development. A nice-looking, two-story building with a double garage and a porch running the length of the front of the house. Not a lot in the way of bushes but a weed-free, well-kept lawn gave the house a neat look.

I rang the doorbell, and a slightly heavier version of Julie opened it. Brown hair, brown eyes, and pleasant facial features. She was wearing a white blouse and a navy-blue skirt. I guessed there might be children, as she was wider around the hips than Julie was.

"Hi. Are you Mr. Watson?"

"Yes, but please call me Mitch. What should I call you?"

"Since my name is Jennifer, everyone calls me Jenny, so you can too."

With that she invited me inside. We walked down a carpeted hallway and into a living room covered in a white shag carpet. *Lush but hard to keep clean,* I thought. So, I asked her about it. "Wow, how often do you get the carpet cleaned?"

"Twice a year. Yes, it's expensive, but William loves shag carpet and especially white shag carpet. If he had his way, every room in the house would have it. Even the bathroom."

So, she was married. "What does your husband do for a living?" I asked.

"He is a lawyer in a very successful law firm."

"Do you work too?"

"No, since the children were born, I've been a typical housewife."

While we were talking, she gestured to the black leather sofa that occupied one side of the room. She chose to sit in an armchair facing me.

"Where are your husband and children?" I asked.

"They're in the backyard, raking leaves. I think they're raking them into a pile, so they can jump in them. Anyway, I thought it best if we did this privately."

"Okay, Jenny, let's get started then. I am very sorry for your loss. I didn't really get to know Julie, but I know she was a lovely person and well loved by you and Henry and probably everyone who knew her."

Wiping a tear from her eye, she said quietly, "Yes, she was all of that. I still can't believe that she's gone."

It was time to get to the nitty gritty. "Tell me, in no particular order, what she was like, what she liked, who her friends were, where she worked, about her marriage, and about anybody you can think of who could have committed this horrible thing."

"Julie was outgoing, had a lot of energy, was very likable, very smart, and everything you would want a sister to be." With that last remark, the tears came.

I felt my eyes getting a little misty too.

She wiped her eyes, composed herself fairly quickly and said, "Sorry about that; I couldn't help it."

I told her I completely understood.

I could see Jenny thinking about what I had asked for in my questions. I was going to prompt her when she said, "Julie loved exciting things, and there are not many exciting things around here."

This was a good prompt for me. "Henry was not an exciting person; he was happy with peace and quiet, so that makes me wonder about their marriage."

Jenny thought for a moment then said, "Yes, sometimes I wondered too. I know Henry was very fond of Julie, but I thought there was something lacking the other way around. They never argued or said anything disparaging to each other, but I detected a lack of warmth or you could say a lack of interest, especially from Julie to Henry. What they were like in their home, I don't know."

It was time for me to think for a moment, and then I decided to bring up another area for discussion. "What about her job? How did she like it there? I was at the flower shop earlier, and I was not impressed by either of the males there."

Jenny nodded. "I know what you mean, but Julie loved flowers so much; she said they brightened up everyone's lives. Besides, she said the guys were out of the store most of the time. Anyway, she never said either of them actually bothered her. I'm sure there were sexist remarks made though."

I thought of another area to explore. "What about her girlfriend, Susan Long? Did they go out together? If so, what did they do?"

Jenny thought about the best way to answer. "They went out every Tuesday, I believe, drinking and dancing—anything else you would have to ask Susan. I know Julie kept quiet about that part of her life. Susan knows a lot more than me."

"So, other than that and when she went out with Henry, she was home the rest of the time?"

"No. She was taking a travel agency course on Wednesdays and a hotel management course on Thursdays."

"So, she was planning on leaving the flower shop?"

"Yes, eventually."

"Taking those courses would be expensive. She wouldn't be paid that much from the flower shop, so how did she manage it?"

"I think Henry might have been paying for them. But again, you would have to ask Susan or Henry."

We talked a bit more in general. She asked me about the cases I had been on, especially the murder ones. She was quite interested. We must have spent as much time talking about that as we did about Julie.

Afterwards, I told her I would like to speak to her husband in private to get a man's perspective on Julie.

So, Jenny and William changed places, with Jenny going out in the backyard and William coming in.

The lawyer was a big man with a big square face, brown hair, and a ruddy complexion. He was dressed in a beige sweater and black pants. He greeted me with a firm handshake.

I asked him what he thought of Julie—her manner and her actions. Did she seem happy?

He mostly echoed what Jenny had said, that Julie seemed like a fun-loving person but that something was lacking between her and Henry. He said that as a lawyer he delved into people's lives, but he had no intention of delving into their lives.

No, I thought, *I'm the one who has to do that now.*

I thanked him and asked him to send Jenny back in. I thanked Jenny for her time and information and told her I would be in touch.

I left the house feeling that I was going to get a lot more information from Susan, and it would paint a different picture of Julie.

CHAPTER 7

I called Susan Long, told her who I was, and asked if I could come over. She asked if I knew her address. I said I did, and she told me to buzz her apartment from the entranceway in the front of the building, and she would buzz me up. She lived in a four-story apartment building in a middle-class section in the west end of town. She was on the fourth floor in apartment 404.

She met me at the door. Susan was what we call a redhead. Actually, it really is a ginger color, but we always call them redheads. She had the remnants of freckles on her face. They made her look rather pretty, but I'm sure she was teased about them in her school years. She wore lipstick that matched her hair and was dressed in a green sweater and khaki jeans. She looked sharp and smart and above all else, just plain nice.

"Mr. Watson, right?" she asked.

"Yes, but please call me Mitch," I said. "What may I call you?"

"My name is Susan, but I get Sue, Suze, and Susie. I never told anyone that they could call me any of those names, but that is what I get. I prefer Susan."

"Okay," I said. "Then that is what I will call you."

It was a one-bedroom apartment, tastefully furnished, although nothing elaborate. She motioned me to an armchair, and she sat on the small sofa. She started off the conversation. "Mitch, I am completely shocked at what's happened. I'm still having a hard time believing that all of this is true. I know that you will want to know everything that I know to help you find out who did this. I'm sure that Jenny has already told you that she thinks I know more than she does, and she's right."

"I have a feeling that some of what you are about to tell me will be difficult for you," I replied "but you're right, if we're going to get to the bottom of this I need to know everything." I let that sink in and waited.

Susan looked at me for a moment. "Some of this will paint a rather bad picture of Julie, and I think that is unfair, but anyway, here goes. Julie was in a failed marriage. She is a free spirit. Okay, *was* a free spirit, I can't get used to the past tense with Julie."

She paused and collected her thoughts. "She thought it was time she settled down, and she met Henry, a rich, handsome man who fell head over heels with her. He was kind and generous, a really good guy. She thought, 'If I'm going to get married, then this is the guy. What could go wrong?' Well, just about everything.

"His and her lifestyles were entirely different. Henry was quiet, passive, and placid, and that became quite boring for Julie. She wanted to change herself for him, but she couldn't. So, to try to put some excitement back in her life, she started going out with me every Tuesday. We went to bars and clubs where there was drinking and dancing. Sometimes downtown, sometimes in the C Section."

I will explain the C Section shortly. To do this I have to explain a fair bit about my city of Cairnford, and that will take a while. For now, let's just say the C Section is what some people would say is the bad part of the city.

Susan continued. "Julie liked to flirt with guys; it was her way of having fun, nothing serious. Drinking, dancing, and flirting once a week. Great release, great fun. Julie parked at my place, then we would take an Uber to wherever we were going, and then take one back to my place later. She told Henry that if she didn't come home on a Tuesday night, it was because she had had too much to drink and was staying at my place."

Susan paused for a moment, and I realized that the difficult part was coming. She gazed at me with a sad look in her eyes. Then she shook her head. "When we started doing this, Julie didn't intend to actually have an affair or anything like that. It first happened when we went to a male strip club, of all places. Just for fun, of course. One of the stars was Mike, an ex-football player. He was huge, about six feet six and around two hundred and eighty pounds. The guy was not only huge but also had charisma and put on a good show. Julie liked him a lot. I heard her murmur to herself, 'This would be a nice change.'

"It just so happened that when we left the place, he was also coming out, and Julie looked up at him and smiled. He asked her if she liked the show, and she told him she liked his part very much. He told us he was going to a diner a block away and asked if we wanted to join him. Before I could say no, Julie said yes. After some chit chat and with Julie still looking him up and down and giving him big smiles, he asked if we would like to go to his place. He was parked nearby and would drive us there and later drive us home or get us an Uber. I said no and hoped Julie would do the same. However, Julie couldn't resist and simply said okay."

"Did Julie say what happened?" I asked. As soon as I said it, I realized I should not have asked; I really didn't want to know.

"Julie said that lovemaking was an art, and Mike was no Picasso."

Somehow, for some reason I felt pleased.

"Were there others?" I asked.

Susan thought for a moment and then said, "I can think of two others."

"Did Julie wear her ring on Tuesday nights?"

"No. She took it off before we went out."

I thought of Henry and said, "That's a crappy thing to do, making guys think she's single."

Susan looked at me sharply. "So, Julie was not perfect. None of us are, but she was still a wonderful person in just about every other way."

I was beginning to have my doubts, but I let it go. "So, tell me about the other ones."

"There was Alan—he was really nice. He had everything. He was a great dancer, which Julie liked. Also, he had a great sense of humor, was good looking, outgoing, and a perfect match for Julie. The first night we met him they were together most of the night. However, she didn't leave with him.

"The next Tuesday we went to the same club, and again they were together most of the night. I might as well not have been there. Then when the club was closing, she told me she was going to his place. After that night she said she was never going back to that club again. I thought something bad must have happened, but she said she liked him so much that if she saw him again, she couldn't help herself, and she would get serious with him, but she couldn't do that because she still needed her space, so we never went back to that club again."

"Did you see him anywhere else?" I asked.

"No. You know, I never got his last name. Guys don't always give them anyway."

Yes, I thought, *and some women are that way as well.* "So, who else?" I asked.

"Steve Kowinski. He did give his last name. He seemed proud of his heritage for some reason. She regretted that one after. He was okay as a guy, but she did it for spite, seeing that she'd had an argument with Henry that day. She and Henry didn't have that many arguments; they just didn't talk much about their differences. There was a party that she wanted both of them to go to, and Henry didn't, so they didn't go. Anyway, the next week when I saw her, she said she felt sorry for Henry and really regretted that night. That's all I can think of, and it didn't happen that often during all the times we went out."

No, I thought, *but once is enough. Then it opens the door for other times.* Then I asked her if there were any guys Julie had said no to who became troublesome.

She said just one. "Yuri Moldev. He couldn't take no for an answer. He started calling her a slut and other bad names, and then I got hold of security, and they escorted him out."

So, that made we wonder. "Did you ever see him again?"

"Yes, a couple of different times at the same club, but he never came near us again."

"So, if that is all about Tuesday nights, did Julie have other girlfriends that she saw occasionally?"

Susan thought for a moment. "She had a friend from university who's a female stripper, and to answer your next question, yes, she quit university after two years. I think she got tired of studying and wanted to make some money."

I tried to take that all in. "What's her name?"

Susan had a smile on her face, as she said, "Her stage name is Bonny Boom Boom Bountiful, which actually is very close to her real name, which is Bonny Bounty. She's performing now at the Sizzle Saloon in the C Section.

"Then there are three university friends who got together with Julie once a season, every three months, and went out for a night on the town. They rotate as a designated driver each time. I will give you their names and phone numbers. I think that's it."

I thought for a moment. I had one more question, but I didn't know how to put it. It was awkward asking a woman who I didn't really know.

"Susan, I have a question that is somewhat embarrassing, but I have to ask. When Julie was intimate with those men, I would think she would use protection of some kind—did she ever say?"

Susan looked at me directly. "It's okay, and yes, absolutely, she always used protection. She carried condoms in her purse and was adamant that they be used. She said it would be terrible if she got pregnant and that would never happen." Then she said, "I have a question for you now. What will I tell the police when they come?"

Tough one, I thought. I didn't want them getting to possible suspects before I had a chance to see and talk to them. "Susan, don't lie to them. Just don't add any information. There is no need to say anything unless you're asked. That is what I suggest. Do what you think is best for you."

"Okay," she said. "Now I have another question. What are you going to do with all this information?"

I thought about it. "I'm going to try to see the four guys you mentioned. I'm not interested in what happened in their bedrooms, but I am interested in their attitudes, what they thought of Julie, what she talked about, if they seem to be lying, and they are worth investigating further. Right now they are persons of interest. Any or all of them could become suspects.

"So, this is where I need your help. I will try to see Mike the stripper outside the club. I don't want to go inside. For the other three, would you be willing to go with me to the clubs where you and Julie met them and point them out to me? I could sure use your assistance."

Susan pondered her fingernails, then looked up at me. "Okay, the next few Tuesday nights we have a date." She smiled as she spoke.

I smiled back. "Susan, I will pick you up on Tuesday at nine o'clock, and we will go to the club where you first met Alan."

She said, "Okay," and so I left.

CHAPTER 8

So, what to do now? I wondered. It was late afternoon, and I was feeling bushed. *When did I sleep last? Let's see, it must have been Thursday night, and now it's getting to be Saturday night. Okay then, get a bite to eat, head over to where Henry is staying, bring him up to date, and then pack it in for the day.* After a hot beef sandwich and two cups of coffee at a family restaurant, I felt better and headed over to see Henry.

He had told me one time that his brother was called Edward. Their parents wanted their children named after kings. Since America had no kings—unless you called Elvis a king—they decided to pick ones from England. William and George come immediately to mind, but Henry and Edward were the ones they chose.

Edward was an accountant and his wife Audrey worked in the supermarket as a cashier. They had two children, a boy and a girl, who both worked during their summers to help pay their way to an out-of-state university. Edward was older than Henry and he and Audrey had their children early in their marriage.

They lived in a townhouse in a suburban development, nothing fancy but seemingly a nice, comfortable place to live. Edward answered the door and ushered me into a large living room—large for that type of building. It was furnished with a sofa and two armchairs, all in a neutral shade of brown. The walls were a soft beige. I was going to fall asleep there unless the conversation was bright and cheerful.

It was not. I sat on the sofa along with Henry. Edward and Audrey were in the armchairs.

I brought Henry up to date on what I had done, whom I had seen, and what they had said. I left out the part about the one-night stands. Henry had enough misery for the time being. He stared at the floor the whole time, having trouble taking it all in. Nobody asked any questions, which I found hard to believe.

Finally, Henry said, "What happens next?"

I told him that I would be interviewing the neighbors to see if they had heard or seen anything. Then I had other friends of Julie's to see. Also, I would be checking with the police to see what they had discovered. Edward asked me if the police would divulge any information. I told him that I thought that I could get them to work with me a bit.

There didn't seem to be too much else to say. Edward started talking about their neighborhood and how he thought it was going downhill. Then he complained about City Hall and what they were doing or not doing. He talked about how the city was not cleaning up all the leaves that had been falling lately. He said they should have had a plan at the beginning of October. Audrey echoed almost everything he said.

Henry said he didn't care, and that made two of us. I had to get out of there. I could just picture Julie and Henry going over for an evening of cards with these two. A good one-night stand would seem rather appealing after that. I wouldn't have minded one myself at that moment. I told them I would keep in touch, and then I left.

The air outside was crisp and cool, but it felt great. I needed that. I headed home. As soon as I got in, I took off my shoes and jacket, headed for my bedroom, threw myself on my bed, and was out like a light.

◆

[HAPTER 9

◆

I woke up in the middle of the night and then turned over and dozed until the sun started to fill in the cracks between the curtains. After a shower and breakfast, I read the newspaper. The police had released information on Julie's death. They didn't say much, only that her husband had found her in their backyard with a deep wound in her neck and that she had probably bled to death. There were no suspects, and it was an ongoing investigation. After that I started to plan the day. It was Sunday, so people would be home and not working—a good day to see Henry's neighbors.

Oh, I just remembered. I was going to explain the C Section of Cairnford and how it came about. So, here goes.

The city of Cairnford sits in the middle of Middle America. The nearest big city is Kansas City, which is about an hour's drive away.

We have a busy downtown with office buildings, banks, drug stores, restaurants, and all the other usual services. Just outside downtown to the east, we have the area now called the C Section. Beyond that are the residential suburbs.

On the west side is a big lake. It's not Lake Superior, but it is a fair size. There are areas for swimming, fishing, and boating.

In the residential suburbs are parks and tennis courts. There are golf courses beyond the suburbs. Beyond that are cornfields, and forest areas in the distance. Generally speaking, Cairnford is a nice city.

I love Middle America. The people are hard-working, honest, and down to earth, and they tell it like it is. However, would many Americans want to take their vacations here? In my opinion, probably not.

When you think vacations, you think coastal areas. Florida and California and, of course, Hawaii instantly come to mind. If you love big cities, then New York, Miami, New Orleans, Las Vegas, San Francisco, and Los Angeles are my favorites. A lot of other people probably have them in their top ten too.

New England is a lovely place in the fall. Colorado and adjoining states are great for winter sports. So, where does all this leave Middle America, and specifically Cairnford, when it comes to where people want to spend their holidays? The answer is nowhere. That is my opinion. I'm sure that some people will find something to argue about, but I guess we all have our opinions.

Anyway, the city councilors about eight years ago seemed to agree with me and decided to do something about it. The area just east of the downtown core was mostly old industrial buildings that had been around for ages. The city owned a lot of the property in the area and decided to own all of it and create an area that would bring people into the city.

They would create a three-block section running north and south and across it a three-block section running west and east. Think of nine blocks like tic tac toe. Actually, the streets were already there. Where they ran through those blocks they would be renamed with male and female names. Remember, this was around eight years ago. I don't think that would happen today.

So, running west to east we had Charles, Cameron, Connor, and Curtis streets. Running north to south through that area we had Cindy, Catherine, Celine, and Cassandra streets. So, for example, if you walked down Cindy Street from Charles to Curtis, you would be walking three blocks.

High-end retailers would be sought to open stores in the area. Flashy but classy bars and nightclubs would become part of the area. Gourmet restaurants would be established. A concert theater would be set up with standup comedians invited as well as other artistic performers.

Along the northern perimeter would be an amusement park, complete with a roller coaster, Ferris wheel, merry-go-round, bumper cars, tilt-a-whirl, and other rides. Also, there would be a midway with dubious games of chance.

At the eastern end there would be a tower with a revolving restaurant at the top. Originally, it was planned to have an observation deck at the top, but seeing that there was a Ferris wheel and also the revolving restaurant, that idea was shelved. The last item planned was a casino near the amusement park.

All the operators of these establishments were given five-year leases and verbally guaranteed that people would flock to the area. You know the saying, "Build it, and they will come."

The area would be advertised on radio, TV, and the newspapers, spread across the state, and hopefully find its way to other parts of the country. The advertising would be:

Come to the Cairnford C Zone
C stands for Class, Cheer, Comedy, Concerts, and Casino

There would be appropriate artistry, depicting people having fun in the activities suggested.

The first year, people did come, mainly because it was a novelty. The second year, business started to dry up. Leases were high, so operators had to charge high prices to make ends meet. However, area people were not high-enders.

The amusement park, the revolving restaurant, and the casino were reasonably successful. All the other businesses started to fail in the second year. By the time the third year came, they had formed their own kind of union and hired a legal firm to help break their leases. They said they had been guaranteed that there would be continuing business and there was not. They were willing to pay a small penalty, but that was all. It never got to court. Penalties were negotiated, and then they all left.

The city was desperate, with no income from all those properties. A commercial real estate company was hired to find businesses to replace the ones who left. As it turned out, any business was welcome.

So, we had a couple of KWIK CASH 4U stores that charged ridiculous interest rates. Pawnbrokers set up business near the casino. Massage therapists turned out to be massage parlors. Then there were adult video stores, strip clubs, both male and female, and other types of low-class interest.

This naturally brought in all the low-class individuals that thrive in these areas. We now had pickpockets, muggers, ladies of the evening who were no ladies, and drugs, along with drug dealers, which we had never had before.

The whole C Zone had become the opposite of what it was intended to be. Citizens started to call it the C Section rather than the C Zone. The joke was that if a young woman went into the C Section alone at night, in nine months she might need a C Section. From one C Section to another, so to speak.

Finally, there was some good news coming. It was an election year at City Hall for the councilors, and they were going crazy, wondering how to fix this mess, which was basically their own creation. They came up with a great idea. They would get rid of all the sleaze and build condominium towers. They would be popular with all the communities around the area. First of all, it would save commuting time for those who worked downtown. Many farmers and other people in the suburbs were tired of cutting grass and shoveling snow. Young married couples couldn't afford the price of houses. So, with all of this, condos would be a sure-fire success. They should have thought of that in the first place.

Specialized restaurants such as Italian, Chinese, and Japanese would be sought after. Bakeries would be another good idea. The motion was voted on last month and was passed unanimously. So, now there was something to look forward to. Unfortunately for me, at the moment, the C Section was still there and this coming week I would have to take my investigation to the heart of the area. Time to wear my jockstrap and my gun.

CHAPTER 10

It was Sunday. A good day to check in on Henry's neighbors. They would be home and not working. I would wait until around nine-thirty a.m. and take about thirty-five minutes to get up there. The traffic would be light.

At nine-fifteen my phone rang. I didn't recognize the number. I answered, and a female voice inquired, "Is that Mr. Watson?"

I said it was.

She went on. "Good morning, Mr. Watson. This is Detective Beth Puccillo from the 9th Division. My partner, Detective Patrick Finnegan, and I have been assigned to the Julie Miller case. We would like to talk to you. Will you be home?"

I said I would be.

She said they would be there within the hour. *Okay,* I thought, *maybe I'll check with the neighbors in the afternoon.*

As I sat around, waiting for their arrival, I was thinking an Italian woman and an Irish man; what kind of a pairing would that be? How would they get along working together? I would soon find out.

At around ten, they arrived. They were a smart and attractive couple. She was the second redhead I had seen in two days. She had hazel eyes, a round, smiling face, and was wearing a smart, knee-length beige suit.

Her partner was about the same height, had dark-brown hair

cut in a military style brush cut, and a square face with a jaw that stuck out a bit. He was wearing a navy blazer and gray pants. They announced themselves and extended their hands, which I shook.

Detective Puccillo spoke first. "We have all the reports from Detective Surmansky and the uniformed officers. I know you must have gone over your involvement several times already, but could you do it one more time for us?"

I said I would, and I did. Both detectives checked their notebooks as I spoke.

When I was finished, Detective Finnegan said that it all corresponded with what they had, and then he asked me what I had been doing since I was interviewed at the station. Did I have any information?

I liked that they both were asking questions. They seemed like a real partnership. Maybe one was a bit more senior, but it didn't show. This, however, was a critical time. I wanted to know what they knew as much as they wanted to know what I knew. Trying to get them to tell me anything might be difficult. Also, how much did I want to tell them?

I thought this over and said, "I can tell you what I have found out, which is not much, but this should be more than a one-way street. We're all working toward the same goal. We can help each other if we cooperate. I know there may be some things that you may not want to disclose right away, but I think there must be some general information that you can divulge."

They looked at each other. Detective Puccillo spoke first. "Withholding information from the police during a criminal investigation can be regarded as an obstruction of justice, so we expect you to be forthright with us. If there is any information that we can and wish to divulge, we will."

That was probably as good as I would get, so I figured I might as well be as friendly and cooperative as possible to get the best results.

I told them about my meetings with the staff at the flower shop and my meeting with Julie's sister and with her sister's husband. I also told them about my meeting with Susan Long, but I left out the part about the one-night stands. I mentioned that Susan had said Julie's marriage was not working and that she intended to get a divorce sometime in the future when she had a new job and more money.

Detective Finnegan said, "So, what was your overall feeling about Julie and her state of mind? And also, how did Mr. Miller perceive things?"

I thought for a moment, trying to find the right things to say. "Julie was an outgoing person who craved excitement. She didn't get it from her marriage, but Henry was naïve and had little idea of what was happening. The marriage should never have happened."

I thought it was their turn. "So, I know it's early in the investigation, but can I ask if anything has been uncovered and what are you working on?"

They looked at each other again. Then Detective Puccillo answered. "Too early for anything to surface, but we are checking databases, and we have interviewed the neighbors, who basically said they saw nothing and heard nothing."

"Which databases are you looking at?" I asked.

Detective Finnegan replied. "Ax murders and also recent burglaries in the neighborhood."

I didn't want to sound critical but I couldn't help myself. "A waste of time in both cases, and before you ask why, I'll tell you. The perp didn't go there with the intent to kill; he didn't bring his own ax. As for burglaries, it wasn't one. She was outside, and he met her outside. The jewel case was taken to make it look like a burglary. No burglar takes just one item and doesn't mess around with anything else."

It was Detective Puccillo's turn. "You know we have to look at every possibility. You don't know for sure that your statements are one hundred percent correct."

I thought that was a nice way of saying it. So far, I rather liked these two detectives. I wished we could use first names. I tried. "Detectives, I wonder when we are informally together like this, can we use first names? I hate being called Mister Watson even though 'Mister' is a sign of respect. Mitch is good every time for me. Saying 'Detective' first is also a sign of respect, but I do respect both of you and what you do. We may have many conversations in the future, and I would really like to use first names."

They looked at each other again. It was a toss-up who would speak first. Detective Finnegan won. "Okay, Mitch." He smiled as he said it. "You are a material witness in the case. You were at the crime scene before the police were. So, it wouldn't be appropriate for us to be seen as being friends with a material witness. However, I think in meetings like this and over the phone we can use first names, but if there is anyone else with us, then the respectful terminology must be used."

"Thanks Patrick," I said, smiling.

We talked a bit about our backgrounds and a few other general topics, then they said they would be on their way. They gave me their cards, and I gave them mine. We all said we would keep in touch, then they left.

I thought about what to do next. They said they had talked to the neighbors but got no information. Maybe they didn't ask the right questions. I would go up in the afternoon. I didn't want to go there when the neighbors were either making or eating lunch.

Around two o'clock I drove onto Henry's street. The tape was still around his property. It would probably be there for a few more days. I planned to visit the next two houses on each side of Henry's house. Also, the three right opposite him. The houses in the area were farther apart than in most neighborhoods, so it was doubtful that anyone had heard or seen anything in any houses beyond the ones I chose.

The houses were pretty much the same. The developer had a plan and stuck to it. I knocked on the door of the first house to Henry's right.

The door was answered by a teenage girl and a little shih tzu with an old sock in his mouth. "Hi, can I help you?" she said. "Muffin, put that sock down." The dog ran off. "Muffin thinks everyone has come to play with him."

I had not, so I explained who I was and what I wanted to know.

She said that her folks were on vacation and she was looking after the house while they were away. As for seeing anything or hearing anything at the approximate time of the crime, well she would have been watching TV and not have heard or noticed anything. I thanked her, said goodbye, then went to the house next to hers.

An elderly lady answered and said the police had already been around and that she would tell me the same thing she told them. She and her husband knew nothing.

I was going to say that I was sorry to interrupt her from what she was doing, but she closed the door before I could. I was batting a thousand so far, but it was more or less what I had expected.

I went to the first house to the left of Henry's house, knocked on the door, and got a pleasant surprise. It was a young woman who looked rather plain at first sight because she was wearing absolutely no makeup. However, she had a pretty face with a nice facial structure and a pert little nose. She had brown hair in waves down to her shoulders and was wearing a snug green sweater and even snugger white pants.

When I finished looking, I told her who I was and why I was there. She said the police had already been there but to come in anyway. It was the best offer I had gotten that day, so in I went.

The living room had a hardwood floor and attractive area rugs with a burgundy pattern on a dark-green color scheme. A small sofa was burgundy, and there were two dark brown armchairs and a beige recliner. There were pictures on the walls of mostly forest-like scenes. The end result was a very warm and relaxing atmosphere. I loved it.

She introduced herself as Mindy Lamont. She said she lived with her father, John Lamont.

I asked what her occupation was, and she said she was a librarian. Just then her father came into the room. He was a big man, all muscle and no fat, not much hair either but a big, clean-shaven, smiling face. He was wearing a plaid shirt and an old pair of pants. Mindy introduced me to her father and told him who I was and what I did.

I asked him what his occupation was, and he said he was a fireman. Then he corrected himself and said, "firefighter." He said there were some good women on the job these days.

I wondered if there was a Mrs. Lamont. If so, where was she? I wondered if it was rude to ask. I decided to take a chance. "Um, is there a Mrs. Lamont? "I asked, smiling.

They looked at each other. Finally, he said, "We're divorced. She has an alcohol problem, and Mindy decided to stay with me."

What could I say to that? "Oh, I see. Yes, I understand. By the way, I would like to be called Mitch. May I call you John and Mindy?"

"Of course," they replied in unison.

Mindy asked if I would like something to drink. I told her coffee, double cream if she had it. She said she would be right back and then went to the kitchen.

In the meantime, John asked me about my work, and I told him the kinds of cases I worked on. Mindy came in with a tray with a mug of coffee and some cookies. It was a nice gesture, and the coffee and cookies hit the spot. I could have stayed there for a while and looked at Mindy but not with her dad watching me.

Finally, I got down to business. "Did either of you hear or see anything next door between five and seven on Friday night?"

John answered first. "I was at the fire hall. What about you, Mindy?"

Mindy said that she would have been making dinner and then eating it around that time, but she hadn't heard or seen anything.

I asked what kind of neighbors Henry and Julie were and if they ever heard or saw them arguing. They both said that they didn't have that much to do with them—most people on the street pretty much minded their own business. They had never heard or seen them argue.

John and Mindy seemed very nice, what I would call good people, so I decided to try to get social, especially with Mindy. "Did you go to university to get a degree to become a librarian?" I asked.

She smiled. "You don't need a degree, but it helps. Yes, I did go, studied international history among other subjects, and I did get my degree. I love reading, I love helping people, and I love being a librarian."

Yes, I thought, and in her line of work she would deal with a much better class of people than I would in my line of work.

Mindy asked me what kind of books I liked to read. A tough question because I didn't get to read many books when I was working. I told her spy stories and detective stories. She told me she would look out for any new books of that kind for me. I thanked her and thought that it would be a good opportunity to see her again.

The three of us talked a bit more about general stuff, and then I said that I would be on my way. John shook my hand and said it was good to meet me. Mindy went with me to the door and smiled and told me to keep in touch. I said I would, gave her my card, and asked for her phone number, which she gave me. As I drove away, I saw her waving at the front door.

You know, after that I didn't feel like bothering with any other neighbors. *Oh well,* I thought. I could return the next day and check the ones across the road from Henry's house. I didn't see the point of bothering with any more on Henry's side. I was thinking it was a waste of time.

It wasn't, and that was because I'd met Mindy.

CHAPTER 11

So, where to now? I wondered. I had not talked to my detective friend Frank Dobson yet. We had known each other since high school, and I think of Jack and Frank as my two closest friends. The thing with Frank was I never knew when he was working. He could be on any shift. His days off were not always the same. However, he usually answered his cell when he could.

I called him. It was late afternoon. I hoped it was a day off. I was in luck. He picked up.

"Hello"

"Hey, Frank, this is the one detective that never gives you a hard time."

"Yeah, well, I hear you're working on the Miller case, so I think that 'one detective thing' is about to be over."

"Frank, are you off today?"

"Yes. What's on your mind?"

"How about we go out for dinner?"

"Okay, where do you have in mind?"

"How about a steakhouse? A good, old-fashioned man's dinner, jumbo shrimp, a juicy filet washed down with a couple of beers, and anything else we fancy."

"Okay, Mitch, you had me at 'steakhouse.' What do you think, Casa Seville?"

That was a steakhouse started by a Spanish family several years ago and was in a suburban plaza about twenty minutes away from me.

"Good, Frank, see you there at six o'clock." And we both hung up.

I was thinking I had accomplished nothing that day, but it was a Sunday, and not much happened then anyway. I had a website on which I advertised my services. I didn't include my phone number. I didn't want people calling all the time, so on the website I gave them my email address. So, I decided to check my email to see how many job offers I had. The downside was, even if there were job offers, it would be difficult to accept any and continue this investigation at the same time. Anyway, I would go home and check on my computer, even though I could get it on my phone. I don't like sitting in my car and looking at my phone all day.

I went home, turned on the computer, and checked my website. The only offering was an adultery case. The man wanted me to follow his wife on a couple of nights she said she was staying with a girlfriend. I had to decline. I thought my nights were going to be full going downtown and to the C Section in search of Julie's evening friends.

I had a shower and changed my clothes. I know I was just having dinner with a male friend, but when I spend a lot of time sitting in your car, I get to feel a little sweaty and tired. A shower and a change of clothes perks me up.

Frank was waiting for me when I arrived. He was wearing a light-blue turtleneck sweater and navy pants. I was wearing a red shirt, a red windbreaker, and black pants. We looked like a couple of sharp dudes.

It was dark inside, with the long bar illuminated and lights at all the booths. The walls were all mahogany paneling. The floor was carpeted in a rich red-and-black pattern. *I'd better not fall down,* I thought. *I might get mistaken for part of the carpet and get trod on.*

The servers were all females dressed in black tops that showed their cleavage and short black skirts. There were not as many such places as there used to be, but I enjoyed the atmosphere of the ones that were still around. A hostess showed us to a booth near the end of a long row. She was wearing a similar top as the servers but with a long dress with long slits up both sides.

Our server was a cute Chinese girl named Lisa who said everything with a smile. I can tell you that Frank and I didn't always agree on the same things, but that day we agreed on everything. Two jumbo shrimp, two filets—medium rare—two baked potatoes, and two Buds.

The Buds came first. We clinked glasses, then took a couple of swigs. Frank opened the conversation. "So, Mitch, do you want to start picking my brain now?"

"No, Frank, I didn't come here for that. We haven't seen each other for some time, so I thought it was about time."

"I couldn't tell you anything significant about the investigation anyway. You're a material witness. The police aren't supposed to get too cozy with them. You're lucky I'm here today."

"Has anything of significance happened with the investigation so far?"

"No. It's too early."

"What about the autopsy report, has that come out?"

"I have not seen it, Mitch."

"That doesn't answer my question. It could have come out whether you saw it or not."

"I do not know if it is out yet. Satisfied now?"

Just then, the shrimp came, so we stopped talking for a few minutes. Big, juicy shrimp. I could have eaten twice as many as were draped around the glass.

I resumed the conversation. "I need your opinion on something, Frank. I was thinking of getting a list from Henry of what he thinks was in that jewelry box that was taken. Then I was going to visit the pawnbroker's tomorrow. Do you think that's too early? Would the perp want to dispose of them right away or wait until the investigation dies down?"

Frank thought for a minute. "I think he wouldn't want that thing lying around anywhere near him. I think he would want to get rid of it right away, probably before the cops start sniffing around."

It was my turn to think. "Okay, then I will head to the C Section tomorrow afternoon. The pawnbrokers would have been closed on Sunday. I want to visit them after the perp but before you guys get there."

"You always want to be one step ahead of us, don't you?"

"Well, yes. If you guys are not going to tell me anything, then I have to be one step ahead. Tell me about Detectives Puccillo and Finnegan. They visited me earlier today. They seem like a good fit for each other. How are they viewed at the station?"

Frank smiled. "You're just thinking about Puccillo, I know. Yes, she is one good-looking detective. They're both quite smart and work well together. We're a happy family in the Ninth Division."

Our steaks came, and we shut up for a while again. The steaks were juicy and tasty, and even better when washed down with a Bud. I know fine diners would have chosen a wine instead, but we were not fine diners. We did know what we liked, though. Afterwards, we had another beer and talked about general things. Then we went our separate ways, agreeing to keep in touch more often.

There was nothing left for me to do that day, so I went home and checked my email. There were more offers for me to check out adultery situations. It seemed there was a lot of that going on in our city. Unfortunately, I couldn't see myself investigating those cases and working on the Miller case at the same time. They all required night work. So, I declined their offers and called it a day.

CHAPTER 12

Monday dawned sunny and cold. I would have to wear a warmer windbreaker. I wear a suit if I'm meeting a lawyer or an insurance executive or anywhere else it may seem appropriate. For most other, less formal, times, it's a windbreaker and a sharp pair of pants, color coordinated. In other words, smart casual.

I thought about how I would plan my day. That morning I would phone the company that was running the travel and hotel courses that Julie was taking. Hopefully, I would get to see the instructor. That afternoon I would visit the pawn shops.

My thoughts were interrupted by my phone ringing. It was Jan, the medical examiner.

"Hi, Jan. Nice to hear your voice. How are you?"

"Good morning, Mitch. I'm good, as usual. By the way, are you wearing socks?"

"That's a strange question, but yes I am. Why do you ask?"

"Because I have news that is going to knock your socks off!"

What could that be? The only thing I could think of was the autopsy report, but that should have been straightforward. "I don't think it can be about the autopsy report," I said, "so what is it?"

"It is about the autopsy report," she replied. She didn't say anything else, so all I could think of were smartass questions. That was my strong point. "So, was she poisoned or killed from a drug overdose or have something else in her?"

Jan chuckled. "She definitely had something else in her. She was two months pregnant!"

"Whaaaat?" I screamed into the phone. "How can that be?"

As soon as I said that, I realized that this would qualify as the most stupid question of the day and probably the week. Also, I knew that Jan would rib me about it.

"Well, Mitch, do you think that maybe, just maybe, she was screwed? This one should not be too complicated, even for you. Give it some thought."

"No Jan, it's just that . . ." I stopped. Did I want to reveal what Susan Long had told me?

Before I could go on, Jan continued. "Is it that you need more time to figure it out, Mitch? Maybe you should call me back when you have the answer."

I made up my mind. "Jan, it's that her best friend, who said that Julie told her everything, told me that she was adamant that if she was intimate with anyone, he would have to wear a condom. She absolutely didn't want a baby under any circumstances."

We were both quiet for a few moments. Then Jan spoke. "Then there are only three answers. Either something went wrong with that plan, Julie didn't tell her friend everything, or she was raped. That's all it could be."

"Maybe we should switch jobs," I said, "you be the detective and I be the medical examiner, because you're right on; it has to be one of those three answers."

Jan laughed. "First of all, you couldn't do my job. You would probably puke into the cadaver during your first post-mortem exam. Anyway, I'm happy here. So, now that we have narrowed this down to three possibilities, what are you going to do?"

"I'm going to have to sit down and think of the best way to proceed and which of these three scenarios is the most likely."

"Mitch." Jan sounded dead serious. "You didn't hear any of this from me. If it comes out that you heard it from me, I could lose my job. Please be very careful."

"Sure, Jan. Of course I will. Do you think the detectives will let Henry know? And do you think they will make it public?"

"I think they should tell Henry. After all, he is Julie's husband. As far as making it public, that's up to the chief."

"Okay. Thanks a lot for all this. When I have solved the case and it's all over, we will go out and celebrate big time."

Jan laughed. "I'm counting on it."

We said our goodbyes and then hung up. Wow, lots to think about.

I thought about the three possibilities and which was the most likely. Then I realized there was a fourth possibility. Maybe Susan had not told me everything she knew. I would have to see her again. I was going to see her tomorrow, but I didn't want to wait. I had to see which way I should proceed.

Before that I needed to talk to Henry to see if the detectives had given him the news. If so, I could tell Susan I got the news from Henry. Besides, before I visited the pawn shops I needed a list from him on the jewelry that was taken.

First things first. I would phone the company that was responsible for the travel and hotel courses Julie was taking. Maybe I could visit their premises and talk to the instructor. Susan had given me the name of the business, the Career Education Centre (CEC). The instructor for both courses was Tom Duncan.

I called the number and got a recorded message. "The Career Education Centre is closed Saturday, Sunday, and Monday. Office hours are Tuesday through Friday from eleven a.m. to seven p.m. Courses take place from Tuesday through Friday from seven p.m. to ten p.m. Thank you for calling the CEC."

Nuts! I had not counted on that. Now I had nothing to do until the afternoon. I spent the rest of the morning thinking about the four possibilities.

◆

CHAPTER 13

◆

At two p.m. I called Henry and asked for a list of the items that he thought were in the jewelry box. I told him to think of all the times Julie had worn earrings, necklaces, any rings other than her wedding rings, and any watches she might have kept in there. Henry said he would call me back. I told him half an hour at the most. Also, I asked him if he had received any updates from the detectives. He said he had not.

A half hour later, he called me back and gave me a list that he said was the best he could do. There were six sets of earrings, three necklaces, and a watch. He described the colors of the earrings and the necklaces. I felt there should be more, but Henry couldn't think of everything, so I would just use what he gave me.

I wrote everything down as I was talking to him and then after I hung up, I typed an email to myself, listing everything. I was ready for the pawnbrokers.

I knew of four: two were in the C Section and two were downtown. I visited all four, going to the ones in the C Section first, as they were on the way to downtown. It took me all afternoon, and I had nothing to show for it. None of them had seen the jewelry box or the items. I told them if they showed up, to call me right away.

They all asked about the police. I said okay, call them too, but I told them to call me first and to get a good description of the person.

It took so long because in each case there was only one person behind the counter, and they all had more than one customer. I think it was a wasted afternoon. Oh well; you never know.

After that I didn't feel like cooking, so when I got home, I ordered a pizza—medium with pepperoni, mushrooms, and green olives. I had lots of Bud Lights in the house, so the day wouldn't be a complete loss.

I thought that Edward and Audrey would be home, so that if I phoned, one of them would answer instead of Henry. That way I could ask if the detectives had called or seen Henry that day.

Audrey answered, so I asked her. She said that the detectives had called, and Henry was in a bad mood after and didn't want to talk about it. I asked if it was okay if I came over, and she said sure.

All three were in the living room when I arrived, watching TV. I told Henry I wanted to talk to him for a couple of minutes. We went into the dining room on the other side of the hall.

I had to start off strong. "Henry, you heard from the detectives today. I have to know everything they said. If I'm going to find out who killed Julie, I need every detail. The cops are competing with me, so they won't tell me everything, but I have to know. Now, what did they tell you today? The autopsy was due, so was that it?"

Henry looked down at the floor and didn't answer for a few moments. Then he looked up at me and said in a quiet voice, "They said Julie was two months pregnant. How could that be, Mitch? How could that be?"

I had thought Henry might say that, but I still couldn't think of a good reply. I didn't want to give Henry Jan's answer.

"I don't know, Henry, but I'll find out. I'll get back to you as soon as I can. Try to relax. There's an answer to everything, and we will get all the answers." That was rather lame, but I couldn't think of anything better. I said my goodbyes and quickly left.

When I was in my car, I called Susan Long. I told her I had new information and that even though I was seeing her the next day, I needed to see her right away. She said to come over.

When I arrived, she buzzed me right up. She was wearing a red sweater and tight black pants. Red and black were often my colors. She filled them out better than I did. I took my place in the armchair, and she sat on the sofa, as before. She asked if I wanted anything to drink, and I said, "No, thanks."

She started the conversation. "So, what is this breaking news that couldn't wait an extra day?"

I thought about the best way to tell her, and I decided to just tell it like it was. "Susan, the autopsy report said that Julie was two months pregnant."

Her mouth gaped open, and her eyes widened in shock. "Mitch, how can that be?"

My question to Jan didn't seem that stupid after all, since everyone else was asking the same thing. I told her the four possibilities.

Her eyes clouded over, and she looked at the wall as if it were far away. "Mitch, I told you everything I know except for one thing, and on that one I do not know what happened, and Julie didn't want to talk about it, so I left it alone."

I had no idea what this was about, so I waited for her to elaborate.

"There was one other person she went off with, but I don't know if they were intimate or not. His name was Brad."

"Brad!" I shouted. "What was his last name?"

She shook her head. "He did say it, but I forget. Why? Do you know someone called Brad?"

I had to stay calm; I hadn't expected this. "Yes, I do know someone called Brad. Describe the Brad you saw."

Susan described Brad Hornby, Jack's son. She mentioned that he had been there with two other university students and that Julie and Brad had taken a liking to each other. Susan talked about how Brad looked like such a bright, innocent, clean-cut, young man.

Julie asked Brad if he would like to go with her and that she had a place in mind.

I asked Susan if she knew what the place was. She didn't, but she thought it might have been a hotel. Susan went on. "In any case, she would have not been intimate with him unless he wore a condom, so I don't see what difference this all makes anyway."

There was silence for a few minutes as we digested all that we had said. I was thinking about the four possibilities, and I decided to tell Susan what I was thinking. "As for the four possibilities, the one that stands out is that Julie didn't tell you everything. She didn't tell you all about Brad, and she didn't tell you about getting pregnant."

"Mitch, I don't know what to think. She didn't want a baby under any circumstances. I do not understand this at all."

That made two of us.

I tried another possibility. "What about the possibility of Julie being raped?"

Susan shook her head. "When? Tuesdays I have told you about. Wednesdays and Thursdays she was taking those courses. Friday after work she did shopping for groceries for the coming week. Saturdays and Sundays, she and Henry were either at Julie's sister and her husband's place or Henry's brother's place or any of them were at Julie's place. On Mondays after work Julie did the house cleaning and the laundry. So, when, Mitch? When did she have time to be raped?"

I shook my head. "So many questions, so few answers. Actually, there are no answers right now."

Susan looked at me. "So, what do we do, Mitch? What can we do?"

I answered as best I could. "Tomorrow I'll talk to Brad first thing, and then I'll call the place where Julie was taking those courses. In the evening—well, better make that night—we will go check out Alan. We will get some answers. It will all fall into place."

I could see she was not convinced. I'm not sure I was. I had had enough for the day. I would sleep on it and then get to work in the morning. I told Susan I would see her at nine o'clock tomorrow night, then I headed home.

CHAPTER 14

I was up early the next morning and thought about the best way to see Brad without Jack knowing. The problem with getting to talk to Brad was that he was taking several courses at the university. They were at different times of the day, and they could be at different times from one week to another. One day he might have four classes, the next day only two. I didn't know what his schedule was.

I knew that Jack worked on Tuesdays at a seniors' center where he gave a physical exercise course. He would go out at about nine-thirty a.m. Brad took two buses to get to the university, so depending on his classes that day, he could go out before or after Jack.

My plan was to park way down the street. If Brad left first, I would let him get near the bus stop, then I would race up to him and tell him I would give him a lift. If Jack left first, I would wait until Jack drove away and then go knock on the door.

I parked on the street at eight o'clock. Fifteen minutes later, Brad came out, wearing a black windbreaker and black jeans, his long blond hair contrasting sharply. I figured he must have a class at nine o'clock. The university was on the west edge of the city by the lake, so it would take him about forty-five minutes to get there with two buses.

I didn't see a bus coming in the rearview mirror, so I waited until he was at the end of the street at the bus stop. I drove along, rolled down the passenger window, and called out, "Hey, Brad, want a lift to the university?"

He said, "Sure, thanks," and hopped in.

Brad asked why I was going to the university, and I told him that I just wanted to talk to him. He asked what about. I said we should wait until we got to the parking lot.

We didn't talk much on the way there. I asked him how his classes were going. He told me they were interesting and a bit about them.

We arrived at the parking lot. It was not very busy at that time of the morning. I found a spot with no other cars around. Then came the tough part. I hated asking Brad the questions I would have to ask, but I had to do it. I got right to it.

"Brad, you must have seen on the news or read in the newspaper that Julie Miller was killed Friday night. I know you had a night out with her some time ago. Her husband, Henry, hired me to investigate her murder."

Brad's face went white, then red. He didn't look at me or say anything, so I continued.

"I know that you didn't know she was married, you didn't know that she was married to Henry, and actually, you didn't know her at all. You did nothing wrong, but I have to ask you a few very personal questions. Did you have sex with Julie?"

Then it all came out. Once he started, he couldn't stop.

"Oh, Mitch, I was so excited and nervous. She said we could get a room next door at a small hotel. It was a crummy hotel, but it had a bed, and I guess that's all you need. Anyway, I was so nervous, but Julie urged me on, and it was over so fast, but I couldn't help myself. Then she said a strange thing. She said, 'I'm sorry, Brad.' I wondered what she meant by that. I thought we were going to be there all night, but she told me to wash up, then she would, and we would leave. She would get an Uber for each of us. I asked her why, and she said that she didn't want my dad to see me with her.

I had mentioned I lived with my dad. So, we were in the hotel for only a short time. I suggested that maybe she could get her money back. She said that we used the bed, the soap, and the towels and to just forget it. We didn't talk much on the way home. It was all very strange. I thought it would be different."

"Brad," I said, "Julie probably regretted that in a way she had violated the innocence of such a clean-cut young man. Julie was not perfect by any means, but she did have feelings for people. Sometimes she regretted the things she did. Now I have to ask you a really personal question. Did you or she use any type of protection?"

"Absolutely," Brad said. "I told Julie that I didn't want to be a father, and she said that in no way did she want to be a mother. She said that she never wanted to have children, but then she said maybe not ever, but anyway, not for a long time. So, she gave me a condom to put on."

I felt much better after he said that. So, it was not a big thing after all. Actually, it was just a happening and for me a dead end. Most dead ends are depressing, but I was overjoyed at this one.

Brad said he never told his dad and asked me not to. I said I would not. I told him only Julie, he, and I knew, and Julie was gone, so the secret was ours. Even Susan Long didn't know what had happened. I told Brad not to worry, to just forget about it and get on with his life. We said goodbye, then Brad left for his first class.

What should I do now? I wondered. It was almost nine o'clock. I wanted to call the place where Julie had been taking those courses, but since the office didn't open until eleven o'clock, there was no point. Since I hadn't had breakfast, I decided it was time to go to McDonald's.

CHAPTER 15

After breakfast I went home and checked my email. At eleven o'clock I called Career Education Courses and received a cheery response: "Welcome to CEC Career Education Courses. My name is Wendy. How can I help?"

I told her I wanted to speak to Tom Duncan. She said that he gave courses on Wednesday and Thursday from seven p.m. to eleven p.m. and came in at six o'clock on those days to brush up on the night's course. I told her who I was and that I was a private investigator and I would come in at six o'clock tomorrow. She tried to put me off, saying that Mr. Duncan didn't like being disturbed while he was preparing to teach. I told her that this was a murder investigation and that I would be there tomorrow at six. Then I hung up.

Next on my list was the detectives. I called the number they had given me, said who I was, and asked for Detective Puccillo.

She came on the line. "Mr. Watson I presume?"

"My, you are a great detective," I replied. "This is an honor."

"Okay, Mitch, let's cut the crap," she said. "What's on your mind?"

I asked her if there was anything new since the last time we talked. She said there was nothing new. I started to get angry. "Is the chief in?" I asked.

She seemed startled. "You mean Chief Mountford?"

"Since that is the only chief you have at the division, I guess so."

"Why do you want to speak to him?"

"Beth, put me through, and it will all become clear."

Chief Lawrence (Larry) Mountford had come up the hard way. He had started as a foot-patrol officer, then a mobile-patrol officer, then a detective, and finally made division chief. After twenty-five years, he was respected by everyone on the force.

Each division had a division chief. There were three Cairnford deputy police chiefs downtown, with responsibilities for violent crimes, white-collar crimes, and drugs. In turn they reported to the Cairnford chief of police, and he reported to the police commissioner, who was appointed by city council. So, everybody had a boss.

"Mountford here," a voice said on the phone.

I told him who I was and what I was doing and that I wanted a few minutes of his time, along with the two detectives. He told me that all three of them would be there for the next hour. I said I would be there in thirty minutes.

Thirty-five minutes later, I walked onto the second floor where all the detectives and the chief hung their hats. You can never account for traffic. I spotted the detectives first and then the chief in his corner office. I caught the gaze of the detectives, pointed to the chief's office, and headed that way.

The detectives and I arrived there at the same time. The chief always had the door open unless he was talking to someone. He motioned us in. I went in last and closed the door. Fortunately, three chairs were arranged around the front of his desk. The detectives took the farthest two. Before I sat down I stuck out my hand over the desk and said, "Chief, I'm Mitch Watson, PI. Glad to meet you."

The chief was in his early fifties with gray hair, a square face, and slight bulge around the stomach but generally looked to be in good health. He shook my hand warmly. "Yes, I have heard a lot about you, Mr. Watson. What can I do for you today?"

"It's about the investigation into the death of Julie Miller. The detectives—who, by the way, I have a lot of respect for—and I have the same goal in mind, and that is to find the person responsible for Mrs. Miller's death. We can help each other, but we are not doing that. Yesterday, I had to find out from Henry Miller that the victim was two months pregnant. Earlier this morning I asked Detective Puccillo if there was anything new in the case and she said no, nothing.

"In my position I can do things that your division cannot because of police protocol and because you have other cases to work on. I only have this case. I won't take another case until this one is closed. However, you have advantages in that you can consult databases for many things that I have no access to. Therefore, it would seem to be a no-brainer that we cooperate with each other.

"As I just said, I respect Detectives Puccillo and Finnegan and can only assume that Detective Puccillo was following some police protocol when she said there was nothing new. I guess we could all go our own ways, but that would seem to be much less efficient than working together in some respect."

I waited for some reaction from the chief. The detectives remained quiet. The chief was looking at the ceiling in thought, then he looked at the detectives, then at me. Finally he said, "Mr. Watson, everything you said is true, but what you didn't say is just as important."

Okay, I thought, *what did I not say?*

"You didn't say that you're a material witness and you're also a close personal friend of the only possible suspect we have at the moment. I don't think we have ever given any information out to a person under those circumstances. How do you think it would look if news of that got out?"

"Well, Chief, to counter that, it can also be said to anyone that I'm helping the police catch the person responsible, so it makes sense to assist me where possible."

The detectives remained silent. I didn't know what they were thinking.

The chief was looking up at the ceiling again. Then he turned his gaze back to me. "What you said can account for some information that we can give you if we think it will help all of us. I can go that far, and I will leave it to the discretion of the detectives. However, I will not guarantee that everything we know will be made available to you."

I knew that was as good as I would get. I wanted to leave on good terms. "Thanks for that, Chief, and thanks for your time. I will do my best to do my part and assist the detectives with any knowledge that I come by." As I got up, I stuck my hand out, and he shook it warmly again. I looked at the detectives, not sure how to proceed. "Are we okay, guys and girls?" I asked. "I promise I will never go over your heads again." I smiled as I stuck out my hand.

Detective Finnegan had a firm grip, and Detective Puccillo had a soft, warm, hand.

"Bye folks," I said, then I left.

I wasn't sure if I'd made much headway, but some was better than nothing.

CHAPTER 16

There wasn't much left to do in the day except for that night when I would pick up Susan and head downtown to try to find Alan, whom Julie had a two-night stand with.

Then I had an idea. On my computer I had an Excel program. I would create a spreadsheet with all the persons that Julie had known either directly or indirectly. I would run them down the left side and then put headings at the top.

Going down the left side, I started with Henry and then the poker players. I thought they were barely possible due to the time and them being on the way to my place for poker. I would have ruled them all out, but I was going to include everybody. So, I included Doug's wife and also Brad, even though that was a dead end.

Who else? There was Julie's sister and her husband, Henry's brother and his wife, and Susan Long. Yeah, I know, ridiculous, but I said I was including everyone. There were also the three people at the flower shop and Tom Duncan, the person teaching the travel and hotel courses. The men who'd had a one-night stand with Julie included Mike, Alan, and Steve. The man who'd argued with her was Yuri. There was also her girlfriend, Bonnie, and the three university students, whom I had yet to meet. Actually, I had yet to meet about half the people on the list. Oh yes, and the neighbors—John and Mindy.

The headings at the top were: ALIBI, MOTIVE, KNEW JULIE'S ADDRESS, PERCENTAGE. That last one would mean the percentage out of a hundred that the person was likely guilty. On most of them it would be zero or one percent. If it was zero, why would I have them on the list? Because it included anybody who knew Julie or knew of Julie.

As I filled in the alibi column, I realized I had not asked anyone yet. It was difficult for anyone other than the police to ask this question. Most people would say I had no right to ask that. But I would ask from now on, and I would ask the detectives about the people in the flower shop. The detectives would have asked them. For the poker players I just put in PG, which stood for "poker game."

For motive, no one seemed to have any motive. I had to leave it blank.

For those who knew the address, I put in a Y for "yes." That included all the poker players, Julie's sister and husband, Henry's brother and his wife, Susan Long, the flower shop people, and Tom Duncan. I didn't know about the one-night standers, her girlfriend Bonnie, the three university students, Doug's wife, or Brad. I was ruling out the last two anyway.

On the percentage column I wrote zero for all the poker players, Doug's wife, Brad, Julie's sister and husband, Henry's brother and his wife, Susan Long, and I wrote one for the neighbors, who I didn't know well enough yet.

I wrote twenty for the driver at the flower shop, thirty for Mr. A, and one for Mrs. A. Everyone else whom I had not met yet, I left blank. When I had met everyone, then I would know whom to concentrate on after I had it all filled in.

There was nothing else to do, so I settled down for a snooze and set my alarm for six o'clock. When I got up I would make myself dinner and then wait until it was time to pick up Susan to go downtown.

After dinner, Henry called, wanting to know if there was any news. I told him about all the people I had seen, including Julie's sister and her husband, the flower shop group, Susan Long, and the neighbors. Also, I mentioned that I had been to the pawnbrokers and none of Julie's jewelry had turned up yet. I told him that I had been to see the chief to try to get the detectives to give me any new information. I said I thought that things would be a bit better with getting information.

Henry wondered when he could go home and also when he'd get his and Julie's car back. I told him that the next time I talked to the detectives, I would ask them. I didn't want to guess and give him wrong information.

He said another thing to ask about was when Julie's body would be released for burial. He said that his brother, Julie's sister, and he would be planning the funeral, but he would need to tell the funeral parlor when they could pick her up. I promised Henry that I would try to find out everything this week. After I hung up, I wondered a bit why Henry couldn't have done that himself.

CHAPTER 17

I put on a white golf shirt, black pants, and a red windbreaker and headed out to pick up Susan. She met me in the lobby of her apartment building at nine o'clock. She was wearing a dark-blue jacket over a light-blue sweater and tight dark-blue pants. It seemed that everything she wore was tight. I wondered if she wore tight pajamas or if she even wore pajamas. Then I wondered, since she was so sharp looking, why she didn't seem to have any boyfriends. So, I asked her on the way downtown.

She said that she'd had boyfriends in the past, but they were either after only one thing or they were completely boring. She was taking a break from them for a while. I could imagine her and Julie walking into the clubs. All the guys would be straining their necks to look at them.

The club where they had met Alan was called Nightlife. *Not too original,* I thought. Being downtown instead of in the C Section it was somewhat classier.

We entered and I looked around the floor. There was a small stage for a band— that was on weekend nights. It was a Tuesday, so there was a disc jockey. In front of him was a small dance floor. A bar extended halfway down one wall with banquettes running down the other half. Along the other wall were alcoves, some for two people and some for four.

The hostess was a pleasant-looking woman in her thirties wearing a shimmering red dress. I asked her for an alcove for two. She showed us the way and said our server would be right over.

I looked around the room. The walls were covered in dark oak paneling with no pictures or anything on them. The carpeting was black with flecks of red. It was kind of classy.

It being Tuesday the place was half empty. I asked Susan to look around to see if she could see Alan. She did so and said he was not there.

Just then our server came over. He was a dark-haired young man in his thirties with a nametag: Herb. Susan ordered a glass of the house red, and I ordered a Bud Light. That was what I often had at lunchtime, but I didn't know how long we would be there, and because the expenses were on me, I decided to keep it light.

When Herb came back with the drinks, I asked him if he knew of a regular customer named Alan. He said he didn't, but if we could describe him, maybe he might know. I asked Susan to describe him. She did, and Herb knew right away. He said that Alan was taking a course on Tuesday nights and was coming in on Thursdays. I thanked him and said I would pay for the drinks rather than run a tab.

After he left, I suggested to Susan that we leave before the DJ came back on. Apparently, he was on a short break. She said this was a bummer coming all the way downtown, and we didn't get to see Alan. I thought for a moment. I had an idea.

"Susan, what about the others—Steve and Yuri. Can we see either of them here, or are they at other clubs?"

She said that Steve would be in the C Section and was closer than Yuri. I said that we would finish our drinks and then go there.

The club where Susan and Julie saw Steve Kowinski was called the Coral Club. No one met us at the door, which I thought was odd. Since the layout was similar to the Nightlife club, we made our way to a small alcove on one side of the room.

There was no paneling. Actually, it looked like the walls were drywall painted a medium blue. However, there were pictures on the walls of the great coral reefs around Australia.

A young woman named Lisa appeared as our server. She was only in her early twenties, but she already had a street-smart look about her. That was what the C Section did to some people. We ordered the same drinks as before.

I asked Susan to look around to see if she could see Steve Kowinski. She noticed he was sitting by himself at a table near the back of the room. The place was only half full, like the other place. I asked Susan if she would join me to meet him. She thought about it. I was not so sure myself if it was a good idea.

I was not interested in what went on in the bedrooms in these one-night stands. What I wanted to hear was what they thought of Julie, what she talked about, if they have an alibi for the night of the crime, and if they know her address. Also, I wanted to look them in the eye and observe their actions to see if they were lying.

As we approached Steve, he noticed us, and I could tell he recognized Susan. He said hello. I introduced myself, showed him my license, and told him that I had been hired to investigate Julie's death.

Steve had a dark complexion with facial hair running in thin lines down both sides of his face and meeting under the chin. He had a thin, pencil mustache. He reminded me of Greg. However, whereas Greg was slim, Steve was on the heavy, muscular side. I figured he must work out.

I asked him if he was Polish, and he said he was. He asked me if I knew because of his name. I said that was it. He said that his parents had emigrated from Poland and bought a farm many years ago and that he'd been born on the farm. He said he had never really liked the farm and had moved to the city where he worked as a programmer in an insurance company.

It was time to get down to business. I laid out the ground rules first.

"Steve, I know you and Julie went off together the night she saw you here. I do not want to know about any intimate action that occurred. I do want to know what you thought of Julie and what she talked about, anything except the bedroom."

"Well, Mitch, is it?"

I nodded.

"Julie seemed a bit stressed out, like something was bothering her, but she never mentioned anything. I noticed the impression of a wedding ring on her finger, but she didn't say she was married. I figured maybe she was just separated. If I had known she was married, there was no way I would have invited her to my place. I don't do that.

"She talked about traveling and how she wanted to take a long holiday and was taking some courses. She never mentioned any other person, male or female."

Susan piped in. "Yes, Julie did mention traveling and taking courses when we were together here."

Steve continued. "She seemed a bit obsessed with that and talked about it some more. It was as if she couldn't wait until it all came through."

I was looking at him all the time he was talking, and he seemed to be telling it like it was, no holding back. My next two questions would test him. "Steve, how did Julie get home that night?"

"I called an Uber for her. I told her I would pay for it."

"So, she gave you her address?"

"Yes, of course. Oh, wait a minute, I see what you're getting at. I never kept it, and I do not remember it."

"Steve, I have to ask, do you have an alibi for last Friday night between five and seven p.m.?"

"Um, I live alone, and I would have been making dinner and

eating it at around that time, so the answer is no. So, I knew her address, and I have no alibi. Are you going to have me locked up?"

"No, I couldn't do that, and anyway, I believe you. I have to warn you, though, the police may be asking these questions, so be prepared."

"I didn't do anything to hurt her, so I should have nothing to worry about, right?"

"Yes, that's right." I wondered, though. The police were in need of suspects, but I hoped they would view Steve as I did.

I asked Susan if she had any questions. She said no, so I thanked Steve, and we went back to our table. The DJ had started a set, and it was getting loud. I asked Susan to hurry up with her drink. I would finish mine, then we would get out of there.

Back at her place, she asked if I wanted to come in for a coffee or a drink. I said okay to a coffee. I took my usual seat on the sofa and waited while she went into the kitchen. She came out about five minutes later with a tray with two mugs of coffee, milk and sugar, and some cookies. Actually, it all seemed rather nice. I thought it was too bad that Susan had not found the right guy yet. If a man treated her decently and was creative in taking her places, it would be a nice relationship for both of them. It didn't seem like a right fit for me, but I did like talking to her, and looking at her.

Susan broke into my thoughts. "So, what now, Mitch? What happens next?"

"Tomorrow I will talk to the man who taught those courses to Julie. Then I'm going to wait outside the male strip club and wait for Mike whatever-his-name-is to come out. I will let you know the outcome."

With that, I thanked her and wished her goodnight.

CHAPTER 18

I got up later than usual Wednesday morning. I had nothing planned until the evening. It was October 24, 2018. In one week it would be Halloween. Sometimes I would be home, in which case I would leave the light on. If I was out on a job, I would leave the light off. This year I didn't know which one it would be.

I spent the morning reading my emails and replying where necessary. Also, I filled in the columns on my spreadsheet where I had an answer. In most cases I had to leave things blank. It made me think more about the case.

Nothing seemed to make sense. A burglary that wasn't, at least in my opinion. A murder that wasn't—again, in my opinion. The perp hadn't been armed. He (or she) wouldn't have known there was an ax there. Something had happened, and the result, in my opinion, was manslaughter.

I could have been wrong about everything, but I didn't think so. I had no answers, only dead ends. I was hoping that some of the men whom Julie had gone out with would lead to something, but that had not happened. I was conducting the investigation the right way, but so far, no results. However, it was only five days since the crime, and it usually took much longer than that to find all the answers.

I needed to talk to someone about it. I didn't want to talk to Henry. I knew Jack was working, as were Doug and Greg. When I wanted to talk with someone about a case, I usually went to see Jack or called my police friend, Frank. That day I had a different idea. I would call Tony. I hadn't talked to him since the poker game. He was an artist, and his home was his studio, or the other way around.

I gave him a call. He said to come over in the afternoon; it would be a good break for him. Tony lived in a two-bedroom apartment in a middle-class part of the city about twenty minutes from my place. He used the second bedroom as his studio.

I got there at around two o'clock. I beeped his room from the lobby, and he buzzed me up. He was on the top floor of a three-story building. There was an elevator. Sometimes they don't have one. He was waiting for me and opened the door, and we shook hands.

One thing about Tony: he would never be fat. He had a thin face and a thin frame. He looked good, and he said he was fine, though he was very upset about what had happened to Julie. He and Henry were good friends, and Tony might have known Julie better than any of us.

We went into his living room. It was sparsely furnished. The walls were painted beige, and there was a dark-brown sofa and an armchair another shade of brown. There was a coffee table, two end tables, a TV, and that was about it. Oh yes, three pictures he had painted were hung on the walls. Each one featured a different type of scenery: mountains, seaside, and a forest.

He asked if I wanted a drink. I told him I'd have some coffee, so he went into the kitchen. A few minutes later, he came out with a tray with two mugs of coffee, cream and sugar, and cheese and crackers. All very nice. Just like Tony.

I told him everything I knew except about the pregnancy and one-night stands. He said he didn't know why anyone would hurt Julie. He was very upset for Henry, who was his best friend. He said he thought Henry was suffering from depression and should get help. Then he said something that had me concerned. He said he was going to start investigating and help me find out who was responsible for Julie's death.

I told him that could be dangerous and that he had no experience with that sort of thing. He said he thought he was smart enough to do the job and take care of himself. I tried to persuade him to not do it, but he said he was going to do it for Henry. I didn't like that idea at all. Finally, he said he wanted to show me his artwork in his studio.

We went into the second bedroom, where he had several pictures all framed and ready for delivery. Some showed kids playing in the sand at the beach. There were jungle pictures, some with animals; mountains partly covered in clouds, and others of a scenic nature. He said his style was high realism, and it was. He was a genius at what he did. He would soon be very well known.

I told him what I thought of his work and then stressed again to think twice about doing any investigation into Julie's death. I could see that he wasn't going to change his mind, so I thanked him for the coffee and cheese and crackers, and we said our goodbyes.

CHAPTER 19

There was still a long time until my visit to see the course instructor, so I decided to go home, check my email, have a nap, and, of course, think about the case.

After all that and then dinner, I headed back out to midtown where in the middle of a small plaza I found Career Education Courses. I was there at six o'clock.

When I entered through the front door, I saw a small lobby with a front desk with a fat, middle-aged lady behind it and a tall, thin man in his late thirties leaning on the desk, talking to her.

I went over and said, "You must be Wendy, and you must be Tom Duncan."

"And you must be the private detective that Wendy told me about," the man replied.

I said that I was and then asked if we could go into a small room for a few minutes to talk about Julie.

He told me sure, but his time was tight. I assured him it would not take long.

The room at the back of the building seemed like a break room. There were vending machines against the walls with chips and chocolate bars and others with cold or hot drinks. Tables and chairs were strewn around the room. I asked him to briefly tell me about himself.

He said that working there was a part-time job. He was a programmer and worked full-time downtown. He said that this was the last year they were having the travel-agency course, so he would probably quit when it was over.

I asked him what he thought about Julie.

He said that Julie was a pretty, outgoing young woman who was very eager to learn everything about travel and hotels. He said she asked more questions than anyone else. I asked him if she ever seemed overly upset about anything. He said not that he knew. I asked him if she had made any friends there or gotten into any arguments with anyone.

He said that during classes there was no time for that. During breaks they either went into that room or to the washroom. The breaks were short, so there was not much time for social stuff. The bottom line was he was not aware of any friendships or problems with anyone.

Finally, I had to ask him, "Do you have an alibi for Friday night between five p.m. and seven p.m.?"

He seemed surprised that I would ask him that, but he said, "I have a girlfriend who I see every Friday. We go to a movie, or she makes me dinner, and I stay there for a while. It makes a nice break after working the long hours on Wednesday and Thursday."

"Tom," I said, "if you could call her now and she can verify that with me, I'll be on my way."

Tom speed-dialed her number. She picked up right away. Tom didn't waste time. "Nona, I have an investigator here investigating the death of that student who was murdered last Friday. Would you please tell the investigator about that night?" With that he handed me the phone.

"Hi, Nona. This is Mitch Watson. I have been hired to investigate the death of Julie Miller. Would you please tell me if you know the whereabouts of Tom Duncan last Friday between five p.m. and seven p.m.?"

"Hi, Mr. Watson. Tom got to my place at about five-thirty. He works downtown until five. I was making dinner. It was pork chops in a mushroom and onion sauce. We had dinner, and Tom was with me until well past seven o'clock."

I thanked her, gave the phone back to Tom, thanked him, and then left. I was happy for them, but for me, it was just another dead end.

I had about five hours before I would go to the men's strip club and wait outside for Mike. I thought about going to the casino to play some blackjack, but five hours was too long. In the end I would lose. I might lose anyway in a shorter time, but the longer I was there, the greater the chance I would lose.

I called Jack to see if he was home. He said he was and told me to come over. I went over and found Jack in the kitchen, making coffee. Brad was there too, tying up the garbage.

I asked an obvious question. "Garbage day tomorrow, guys?"

"Yes, Brad always looks after the garbage, the dishes, the dusting, and the vacuuming, and sometimes the shopping and the cooking."

"Then what do you do, Jack?"

"I work so that we can both live here. What do you think of that?"

"Not much, Jack. You don't work that hard." We both laughed.

I saw Brad struggling with the garbage, trying to push it down into one bag. Jack noticed him. "Use another bag, Brad."

"No, I got it," Brad replied as he was able to bring the drawstrings together and tie it up.

"Good job, Brad," I said.

Brad smiled and went to his room to work on his computer. Jack and I went to the living room.

"So, you want to talk about the case, Mitch?" Jack started off.

"Yes, but I don't know what to say. There's not much new. Every-thing seems to pan out, but that only leaves dead ends. No real follow-up required. Frustrating."

"Do you have a handle on everyone Julie knew?"

"Yes, and I get to talk to everyone, but there are no motives, nothing really, except, of course, if I'm missing anything."

"Well, it's only been a few days. Maybe a break will come."

We played two-handed euchre for a while. First one who won five games was the champion. I won five games to four. Then we played cribbage. We won two games each.

"Goodnight, folks," Brad called as he went to bed. We both wished him goodnight.

I figured it was getting time for me to head down to the C Section. I was not looking forward to it. I said goodnight to Jack and headed out. I had a bit of time left, so I headed for the casino. It was a modest place, nothing gaudy like Vegas, but they had all the latest slot machines, craps, roulette, and blackjack tables.

I was best at blackjack but all the tables were filled. Quite busy for a Tuesday night. So, I took a shot at a slot machine. No jackpot for me, just twenty bucks down the drain. I watched some blackjack for a while, and then I went over and watched a roulette wheel where there was a crowd. A person could lose their money fast there. The odds were more against a player than at blackjack. I had played roulette a long time ago and learned my lesson. I always seemed to have to learn the hard way. I headed a couple of blocks over to the strip club to wait in the parking lot.

CHAPTER 20

I got there at about eleven-thirty. Susan had said they'd met Mike outside just after midnight. I picked a spot in the lot where I could see anyone coming out the back entrance. It was a cold night. I kept turning the ignition and the heat on and off.

At about twelve-fifteen I saw the big man coming out. He was really big. I would say six feet four inches and around 280 pounds. He was barrel chested, and his arms were bigger than my legs. Needless to say, he had a large face. It was topped with a high brush cut.

I got out of my car and reached him right before he got into his car.

"You're Mike, right?" I asked.

"Who wants to know?" he said.

I showed him my ID. "I'm Mitch Watson. I was hired to investigate the death of Julie Miller, whom you knew. I'm not interested in anything that happened at your place, but I do want to know what you thought of Julie, what she talked about, and what her attitude was like. I'm trying to get a general picture, then along with everything else, I hope it will lead somewhere. I'm asking these questions of everyone who knew Julie at all. Is there someplace around here where we can sit and talk for a few minutes?"

He smiled at me. "I don't think there is much I can tell you that will be of help, but there is a diner over at the corner of Conner and Celine, known as Dick's Diner. We can go there for a few minutes.

"Okay," I said. "I'll follow you over. I'll pay for whatever you have, but don't have dinner."

He laughed. "See you over there."

Dick's Diner turned out to be a small, nondescript diner with a counter, barstools, and booths running down one side. Behind the counter stood a man in his fifties, with gray hair and a gaunt face. If that was Dick, why would he want to work the night shift? I decided to ask him.

Mike and I sat in a booth, and Mike asked if I was having coffee and anything else.

I told him just coffee.

Mike hollered out, "Hey, Dick, two coffees and a slice of apple pie and ice cream."

"Coming right up," was the reply.

Mike started the conversation. "Julie's girlfriend must have told you about us."

"Yes, she did. She has been a good source of information so far."

"Listen, Mitch, I didn't know she was married. If I had known, I would not have gone with her. You may not believe this, but that was the first and only time I went with a customer. The club frowns on it, and I don't want to get involved anyway. You have to understand that Julie was quite aggressive. Actually, she was quite aggressive all the way."

Just then, Dick came with the coffees and the pie.

I said, "Hey, Dick, if you own the place. Why would you work the night shift?"

He looked at me for a moment, smiled, and said, "It's because right now I can't get anyone to work this shift. I get housewives most of the time during the day, university students on weekends, but it is difficult getting anyone for this shift. If you want to buy this joint, just name your price."

I laughed. "No thanks, I have enough problems of my own right now."

He smiled and walked back to the counter.

I turned to Mike. "So, you were saying Julie was aggressive. What did she talk about during the time she was you?"

"Mostly her future. She told me all these places she wanted to travel to. She was even taking some kind of courses to help her. She also said she sure didn't want any kids for a long time. Julie was quite outgoing; she didn't seem to be married, just a young woman out for a good time. I don't know why anyone would want to hurt her."

"Well, Mike, right now, neither do I, but I'll find out. By the way, I never got your last name."

"Do you want my real name or my stage name?"

"Real name. I'm really not interested in what you do."

"Hutchinson. That's why I need a stage name." He laughed.

"So, Mike, how did she get home that night?"

"She said that she would get an Uber. I said that I would pay for it, so I ordered it."

I was starting to see a trend. What Mike was saying pretty near matched everything Steve had said. I thought his next answer would probably also be the same as Steve's.

"Mike, one last question. Do not feel bad or annoyed about this. I'm asking everyone the same question. Can you account for your whereabouts last Friday night between five p.m. and seven p.m.?"

"Yes, I can, but unfortunately, there is no one to verify it. I live alone. At about five-thirty I would start making my dinner. At about six I would start eating my dinner, and at about six-thirty I would be on my way to the club. So, no alibi."

I thought that with all these guys it would be pretty much the same thing. All single, living alone, and six o'clock would be their dinnertime. Nothing strange about that. It didn't help me at all, though. Just seemed like another dead end. I finished my coffee and reached into my wallet for a ten-dollar bill. I put it on the table. I asked Mike if that would cover everything, including the tip. He said it would.

I shook his hand, thanked him for his time and information, and wished him good luck in the future. He said that he hoped I caught the person responsible, and I told him I would. With that, I left the diner, only too happy to get out of the C Section.

It was after one a.m. when I got home. I wanted to think about tomorrow and plan my day before I packed it in. I thought I would see if I could meet again with the detectives on a friendlier basis, and we could all go over what we had found out, which from my point of view was not much.

I would also find out when Henry could return home and get his car and cell phone back. I figured I should go to see Henry and cheer him up a little. Then tomorrow night go with Susan I would try to see the mysterious Alan, whatever his last name was.

CHAPTER 21

The morning was cloudy, and it looked like it was going to rain. It was also getting colder. I decided that after breakfast I would call the detectives to see if I could come to the division, and we'd all get together and bring each other up to date.

About nine o'clock I called and asked the desk sergeant if I could speak to either Detective Puccillo or Detective Finnegan. He said they were both in, who did I want? I thought I would try Finnegan first this time.

His voice came clear on the line. "Detective Finnegan here."

I mentioned that I would like to have a good, productive talk with them and asked if I could come up to the division. He told me to wait a minute and he'd check with his partner. A moment later he said that they were just heading out, but I was sort of on the way, so they would stop at my place. They would be there within the hour.

About forty-five minutes later, they knocked on my front door.

I opened up with a cheery, "Hi, folks. Good to see you both. Come on in."

They were both wearing topcoats over their suits. It was the end of October, so it was the time of year to wear more stuff.

I took their coats and asked them if they wanted coffee, and they both said no. I asked them to please use first names at my place. They nodded and Patrick said, "Okay, you called the meeting, so what's on your mind?"

I told them about my visit to the pawn shops, following up with the neighbors, the meeting with Tom Duncan, and my chats with Steve and Mike. I said that Susan had said that she and Julie had conversations with them at the clubs. I didn't say they were one-night stands. I didn't mention Brad at all.

The detectives seemed interested in everything I told them. Patrick even took a few notes. I explained everything in detail, so there were few follow-up questions.

Then I told them I had several questions for them. I started with the databases. "Did you get anything from the databases?"

Beth replied, "Nothing worthwhile at all."

"Did you get anything from forensics, like fingerprints?"

"Only Henry's and hers," Beth said. "Any others were old and smudged. Strange thing, though, his prints were not in her bedroom, and her prints were not in his bedroom. I can't see that couple making love on the kitchen floor."

I knew the answer. "I'm sure it was a long time since the last time, and Julie did a lot of dusting and vacuuming, so I'm sure they would all be gone by now. Beth and Patrick, did you find out if anyone at the flower shop had alibis? I never asked them."

"No real alibis," Patrick said. "Mrs. Bundheim said she was home making dinner. Mr. Bundheim arrived home at about six-forty-five p.m., late from an appointment. We checked where he was, and that part was true, but he still would have had time to go to the Millers' and get home. It would have been a rush, but it was possible. The driver was home alone, having dinner."

I said that this was the problem; it was a regular dinnertime, so the neighbors would not be looking out their windows, and possible suspects living alone would be eating their dinner.

"When do you think Henry can go home? And when can he get his car and cell phone back?" I asked. "What about Julie's cell phone and computer? When can all these items go back to Henry, and did you find anything significant on any of them?"

The detectives looked at each other and then Beth answered. "We were thinking of Saturday for the tapes to be removed and the two cars and Henry's cell phone to be returned. We might keep Julie's computer and cell phone a bit longer. We didn't find any information on any of that equipment that would have anything to do with what happened. However, it was significant in a way that there were no phone calls, texts, or emails about Julie's nights out with her girlfriend, Susan. Why did she keep it all quiet? I suppose she didn't want Henry to accidentally find out."

You are right on with that, Beth, I thought.

"Tell me, are you going to make it public about the pregnancy?" I asked. "In some cases when I'm interviewing someone, it might be helpful to mention this and get their reaction."

"We'll have to check with the chief on that one, although since you and Henry Miller already know, I don't see that it makes much difference," Beth said.

"Just before you go, what are your gut thoughts on this case?" I looked at both of them as I said it.

Patrick replied, "We are fifty-fifty on it being a burglary. We think there is still a possibility of that. By the way, there was a burglary in our division area on Monday night. We're on our way downtown to check with the pawnbrokers. We'll also see if there is anything new on the Miller jewelry. You might like to know that the burglary was similar to the Miller case. Although in this case, the married couple slept together in the main bedroom, and the burglar only took jewelry from the woman's dresser. As far as the Miller case being a murder, we think it probably is, although there's a chance an accident could have happened. The only suspect we have is Henry Miller, but we have no actual evidence, so we're still looking for suspects. Finally, we appreciate your help so far."

I looked at them both and smiled. "I appreciate your help as well. I'll tell Henry that he will likely get some things back this weekend and can return home. Thanks for coming around." With that we said our goodbyes, and they left.

I don't think any of us were any further ahead, but at least we were cooperating in an amiable way. I decided to go over to see Henry and give him some good news. I took a chance that he was still at his brother's place, so I didn't bother phoning.

Sure enough, Henry was there by himself. He still looked depressed. He just opened the door and walked back into the living room. I went in and sat on the sofa, and Henry sat on one of the armchairs. He looked up at me and said, "So, have you solved the case yet?"

"No, Henry, but I do have some good news for you. This weekend you should be getting your phone and cars back, and you will be able to go home."

I mistakenly thought he might have jumped for joy, but he just said, "Well, that's something."

I wondered if we would ever get back to the real Henry. It was tough talking to him when he was so depressed. Maybe he should get grief counseling. I didn't think me telling him would go over that well. Then I thought that I should get Tony to try. They were close friends. Maybe Henry might listen to Tony.

I told Henry about my meeting with the detectives and most of what was said. His only comment was, "So, we're no further ahead?"

I told him no, but we were all doing the best we could.

Henry started talking about Julie being pregnant. "Mitch, she must have been raped and didn't want to tell anyone. It must have happened on Tuesday night when she was out with her girlfriend. It's strange that Susan knows nothing about it. Julie told her everything. Are you sure that Susan doesn't know about this?"

"Henry, she was as shocked as you were when I told her. She wondered, like you, how this could have happened."

"It must have happened on a Tuesday," he said, "one of those nights when she said she was staying over at Susan's place. Every other day and night are accounted for."

For some reason I didn't want to talk any more about it with Henry. The main reason was probably because I had no answers to any questions. I tried to talk about other things, but Henry was not interested. I was getting depressed just talking to him.

I asked him if he wanted to go out for lunch. He said no. I felt relieved. I told him I would keep in touch and then I left.

I felt like having a sub for lunch, so I went and got myself a heated pizza sub, then went home and ate it, washing it down with a Bud Light. I thought I'd better not drink that much because I was going to the club with Susan that night to finally meet Alan. There would be some drinking done there.

I thought I might as well check my email and have a snooze while I waited for the evening.

CHAPTER 22

It was close enough to Halloween, so I wore an orange golf shirt with dark-brown pants and a brown suede-leather windbreaker. Susan was wearing what she'd worn one of the first times I saw her—a green sweater and khaki pants with an olive-colored jacket. We looked like a cool couple, as usual.

We arrived at the club at around nine-thirty, and Susan looked around for Alan. She saw him on the far side of the room. He was in an alcove with another man, who looked a bit like him. A relative perhaps?

They both were wearing red windbreakers. Alan was also wearing a white sports shirt and black pants. The other man was wearing a gray shirt and gray pants. They both had what I call dirty-blond hair, light-brown hair with lighter streaks. They wore it fairly long, down to their shoulders. Their faces were tanned, and were both handsome. I could see Julie falling for Alan.

Susan and I took a booth on the other side of the room. I was trying to figure out how to do this. He might not want to talk to me with Susan or his friend there. Then I had an idea.

"Susan," I said, "I'll go over and introduce myself and mention that he and I should talk in private. I'll give you the keys to my car and ask you to wait for me there. I'll text you when Alan and I have finished talking. Okay with you?"

"That's okay with me," she said, "but shouldn't we order first?"

We saw a server heading our way. I hailed him. Susan ordered the house red, as usual. I ordered bourbon on the rocks. If it went well with Alan, I might order another one.

When our drinks came, we both took a sip, then I gave Susan my car keys. She went out, and I left our drinks and went over to see Alan.

He looked up as I neared the alcove. I smiled and introduced myself. I told him that I was investigating the death of Julie Miller, and my plan was to talk to absolutely everyone she had talked to over the last few months. I also said I was not interested in any intimate details; I just wanted to get a picture of Julie from the way other people saw her. What did she talk about? Was she happy? Did she seem concerned? "All the little details help," I said. I told him I was alone on the other side of the bar and that Susan was with me, but she would wait in my car. I asked him to come over. He said okay, but first he introduced me to his brother, Adrian. I shook hands with Alan and Adrian and then Alan followed me over.

First, I asked him what his last name was. He told me it was Wilson. Then I started it off by simply saying, "Tell me about Julie."

He was looking at the table, and he didn't look me in the eye right away. He said, "That was absolutely horrifying what happened to her. I didn't know she was married until I read about it in the paper. I would never go out with a married woman."

He looked up at me and then back down again. I asked him what Julie talked about, what her attitude was like, and if she had showed any concern over anything. "What was the feeling between both of you as you said goodbye the second night?"

He looked up at the ceiling, then down at the floor, but never directly at me. "Julie was a wonderful and lovely person. She seemed so caring and compassionate and at the same time very outgoing. She was ambitious, always talking about the future, how she wanted to see the world. I never even thought she could be married.

"When we said goodbye the second time, I thought we would meet at the club the next week, and we would be getting serious, but she never came back. I suppose it was because she was married. When I read the horrible news, I was so confused. Who in the world would do such a terrible thing?"

As he talked, I watched his eyes and his body motions. Then I realized he was acting. He said things that he thought whoever he was talking to wanted to hear. He would make a good con man. However, I could see how women could think he was great. He was good looking, and he could definitely talk the talk.

I instinctively took a dislike to him. I like people who tell it like it is, as most Middle Americans do. I had a couple more questions to ask him. They were the ones I'd asked all of Julie's one-nighters.

"How did she get home from your place those nights?"

I got the usual answer.

"Oh, I arranged for an Uber for her."

So, he knew her address like the others. Question number two.

"I'm asking all of Julie's acquaintances, do you have an alibi for that Friday night?"

He looked pained. "I was hoping you wouldn't ask me that. No, I do not. The newspaper said between five and seven p.m., and I would have been home by myself eating dinner."

Yes, I suspected that would be the answer. I asked him if he could think of anything else to add to what he had told me. He said he couldn't think of anything. I thanked him for talking to me. He said it was his pleasure, then he headed back to his brother. I decided I would get the detectives to put all of the men whom Julie met at the clubs through their databases. I had one more to go—Yuri Moldev, I would see him next Tuesday.

I texted Susan and told her to come back. She came in, sat down, and the first thing she said was, "Isn't he a nice guy?"

"No, he is not," I replied.

Startled, Susan looked at me. "What do you mean?"

"He is an actor. He says things that he thinks you want to hear. He is very good at it. I can understand why you and Julie liked him."

I felt like there was nothing left to do, so I said, "Susan, let's go home, okay?"

She nodded, and we left. We drove to her place in silence. Then she asked me to come in for a coffee; she wanted to talk about the way things were going. I said that was fine with me.

I sat in the armchair as before, she made coffee, brought it in, and then settled on the sofa. "Mitch," she said. "Where are we at? It seems that we are getting nowhere."

"It has only been six days," I said. "Murders do not get solved that early all the time. I'll have the detectives put all these guys, including Yuri, in their databases to see if there is anything there to follow up on. Now, are you sure you have told me everything Julie told you?"

Susan said she thought so. She was starting to look depressed, so I tried to cheer her up. "We will get to the end of this. We will find out who is responsible."

She smiled. "Thanks, Mitch."

We talked a little more, and then I left.

♦

CHAPTER 23

♦

Friday was cloudy and cool. I didn't have much on the agenda. I was going to see Julie's stripper girlfriend Bonnie, but that would be tonight. I felt like talking the case over with someone to help me with my thinking and even to think of something I had missed.

I called my favorite medical examiner, Jan, and asked if she could spare some time. She said she was up to her neck in cadavers, but she had an idea. How would I like to come to her place for dinner, and we could talk about everything?

I jumped at the chance and told her I would love that. "Let's have dinner first and talk afterwards," I said. She was okay with that, and I asked her what time. She said about six o'clock, and then she gave me the address. I told her I would be there.

I was not sure what to do next. It was coming to a time when leads were few and far between. Less and less time was required to follow any leads. The problem was, I couldn't take another job while working on this one.

It amazed me that in novels where the main character was a private detective, there was something to do throughout every day. Often it was being chased or chasing someone. Usually, it turned into violent action. In those stories, the first incident often led to drug rings, prostitution rings, or other multi-layered criminal activities. The case involving Julie led to none of those situations.

All the leads led to virtually nothing.

Julie's time seemed to be all accounted for except for Tuesday nights, although Susan had told me what went on those nights.

I figured that I could stay on the case for a couple of weeks longer, but if there were no further developments that led anywhere, I would have to close my files, tell Henry, and then pick up another job.

I thought I would spend the day with Henry. Maybe we could have lunch together and go to the casino to cheer him up a little. First, I had to call him to see if he was okay with that.

I called him, and he said, "Fine, come on over." I was glad to hear that. Sometimes a depressed person just wants to be left alone.

I arrived there at about eleven-thirty. Henry seemed a bit more like his old self and surprised me by saying he would make us a pizza for lunch. He said he had the dough, tomato sauce, mozzarella cheese, pepperoni, red peppers, and green olives. I found it hard to believe that Henry could and would do that.

He did, and it turned out great. A bottle of Coors hit the spot, and I told Henry he'd done a great job. I saw him smile for the first time since he'd last seen Julie.

After lunch we sat in the living room, and I updated him on everything, although I still didn't tell him about the one-night stands. I thought that maybe Henry had figured that out anyway. He kept saying that Julie must have been raped on a Tuesday night. There were no other times possible. I didn't argue with him because at the moment it seemed like the most likely possibility.

I still had my doubts about that, but I had no other answer. Nothing fit, so I was looking forward to what Jan might have to say and also to see if Julie had given any secrets to her friend, Bonnie.

Henry and I went to the casino at about two-thirty. I told him that we could stay until four-thirty, and then I would have to drive him back home. I told him I was going to see Jan to get her take on everything. I didn't tell him about Bonnie.

The casino was fairly busy, but I was able to get a seat at a black-jack table. Henry went to his favorite roulette table. I got as high as being up $150, then everything went bad. None of my double-downs worked. I never got the right cards after splitting pairs, and the dealer always seemed to be at least one card better than me. So, when I got back down to being even, I quit.

I saw Henry over at a slot machine. I told him we had to go. He cashed out what he had left on the machine, and we walked out. I asked him how much he had won. He said he was down about $200, mostly on roulette. He seemed quite happy about it. The action had been good for him. I had never seen a happier loser.

CHAPTER 24

After I dropped Henry off at his brother's place, I headed off to see Jan. She lived in one of the few condos in Cairnford. It was on one of the main streets heading out of the west end of the city.

Jan rented a one-bedroom unit on the third floor of a ten-story building. She was waiting in the lobby for me when I arrived. She said they were having problems with the buzzer in the lobby. We took the elevator up to the third floor and then walked down to the end of the hall. She opened the door to 312 and invited me in.

What I noticed at once was that it was a very colorful living area. The living room had a small, dark-red, two-seat sofa. There was a dark-brown lazy boy and a forest-green armchair. The wall-to-wall carpet was a blend of dark orange and dark brown. The drapes had a pattern of red, orange, and pink flowers. The room was bright and cheerful, just like Jan.

She asked me if I wanted a beer before dinner. I said no, but I might want one with dinner. She said I sure would. Then she excused herself and headed to the kitchen.

From her living room window, I could see the lake. There were very few people around. It was starting to get too cool for most of the activities in that area. However, the weather in Cairnford was hard to predict. Often after a cooling period, we could get a few warm days with systems coming up from the Gulf.

I stood at the window for a while. It was a nice view. Most places in the city had a boring view of their neighborhood. There were very few high-rise buildings. That would all change when they finally demolished the C Section, and new condos were built. I thought that they would fill up fairly quickly.

My thoughts were interrupted by Jan calling me to come for dinner. The dining area was an extension of the living room, forming an L shape. There was a rectangular table with six chairs. Jan had placed two bowls on the table across from each other. I sat where there was a bowl, assuming that was the plan.

Jan came in with a large pot which she put on a mat on the table. Then she went back to the kitchen to get spoons. She came back with two large spoons for us and a larger one for the pot. She said that this was her version of burning Mexican chili. She told me it contained ground beef, kidney beans, brown beans, garlic, salsa, chili powder, and cilantro leaves. She asked me, "Now do you want a beer?"

I said, "Oh, yes."

She brought me a bottle of Miller beer. So, Coors for lunch and Miller for dinner. I was good with that. I found it a bit ironic that I was drinking Miller while I was going to be asking Jan about the Miller case. Oh well, different cases.

The chili was hot, spicy, and tasty. I had seconds, then another beer. I felt good. It had been a good day so far, and I still had to see Bonnie.

We settled with our coffees in the living room. I told Jan everything I knew about the case, but I left out the part about Brad. As far as I was concerned, that was over and done with. I was thinking that some of the rest of it was going to be that way too.

So, I went over the burglary issue again. I told Jan that I was still not convinced, even though there had been a similar burglary in the neighborhood with no violence. I went over the timing of Julie's schedule. Friday through Monday mostly at home with Henry or with him and his brother's family or with her sister and her family. Monday through Friday working at the flower shop, and Wednesday and Thursday evenings taking courses.

Jan said, "So, Tuesday seems to be the day when whatever happened, happened."

I looked at her and I asked, "Do you think she was raped on a Tuesday night?"

She thought for a minute and then said, "Well, it has to be that, or something went wrong with one of those one-nighters."

It was my turn to think for a minute. Jan's suggestions begged another question, which I raised. "If either of those is the case, then why didn't Julie tell Susan? She told Susan everything."

"These are very personal things, Mitch. There are times when you don't tell anyone anything."

"Okay then, if you're right, and right now I don't have a better answer, how do I go about getting to the truth?"

"I think it would be someone she knew in either situation, so why don't you follow up with the most likely person?"

While I was still thinking this over, she startled me by saying, "Do you have the dates when these one-nighters occurred?"

I felt ashamed of myself. I had never thought to ask Susan that simple question. Of course, maybe we could narrow it down that way. I thought for a moment then said, "Jan, is it exactly two months since Julie was impregnated to the day you discovered the fetus?"

"The science is not that exact, Mitch. Every fetus doesn't grow exactly the same. However, I would say two weeks either way is the most latitude I would give."

I thought this over and felt that I didn't want to talk about it any longer. Not much point until I talked to Susan. So, how could I tell Jan that I was leaving her and going to a strip club? I realized I couldn't. So, we talked for a while about a few other things, mostly about her work. Then I told her that I had not slept much lately and was feeling bushed. I was very sorry, but I had to go.

Jan looked put out and suggested I could get a few hours' sleep on her sofa. I knew that would happen. I told her I would take a raincheck, but I would be back for a visit when I was up to speed. I thanked her for a great dinner and her ideas and somewhat reluctantly let myself out.

When I got in my car, I pulled out my cell phone and called Susan. She answered on the first ring. "Susan," I said, "I need the dates that Julie had those one-night stands. I'll give you time to think about it because we have to get it right. Will you please call me tomorrow?"

She said she would and we both hung up.

Maybe Jan had come up with the right answer, and we could at least narrow the pregnancy thing down. It might lead us to the person responsible for what had happened a week ago.

CHAPTER 25

I was on my way down to the C Section, specifically the Sizzle Saloon, to see Bonnie Boom Boom Bountiful, one of Julie's girlfriends from the university. The Sizzle Saloon was on Cameron at the corner of Celine. The male strip club was one block over on the corner of Cameron and Catherine.

It was Friday night, so the C Section was busy. The parking lot behind the Sizzle Saloon was full. I decided to try the one at Mike's club. There was one last space, so I took it. It was an okay night for a short walk.

I was halfway there when I heard steps behind me, and an attractive young woman bumped into my right hip. She looked up at me and said sorry, but at the same time, I felt the slightest touch on my left side. I whirled around and lashed out with my right foot at the man who was trying to pick my back pocket.

I caught him flush on his left kneecap, and he screamed and fell to the ground in a fetal position, holding his knee. "You son of a bitch!" his accomplice yelled at me. "Why did you do that?"

I looked at her with no sympathy. "When pickpockets use the distraction technique, I always use the kick to the knee. Maybe it will persuade them to try something else."

He was still on the ground, holding his knee. She went over and tried to comfort him. Then she looked up at me. "You didn't have to do that. We didn't physically attack you. What you did to him was an assault."

She was right, and people were starting to gather around. I said, "Call the police if you like. Ask for Detectives Puccillo and Finnegan. Tell them that the detective that is helping them solve a murder just stopped a couple of pickpockets. They will be mighty pleased." With that I turned and walked away. I had taken some liberty using the detectives' names but I thought that would stop them from calling it in.

I kept on walking until I reached the strip club. I hoped I could get a seat. There were seats all around the stage. On the floor there were tables for two and tables for four. There was a sort of balcony with five tiered rows, mostly with tables for two people. However, I thought some of the tables might be strung together.

Downstairs looked quite full, so I decided to try the balcony. I saw one empty table right at the back. I sat down there and looked around. It was fairly dark except for the stage, which was well lit. There was cowboy paraphernalia on the walls, obviously trying to give a Western appearance to the place. Apart from that, there was nothing exceptional about the Sizzle Saloon.

That is, unless you count the eight table dancers doing their thing in various parts of the room. There were girls of various ages and several different nationalities. Some were in their thirties, some in their twenties, and there were some who I didn't think should be there. I wondered if their parents knew they were there.

A waitress in a low-cut top and short skirt—what else—came to serve me. I asked for a Bud Light. The music stopped, and an off-stage announcer asked for a big hand for the next performer, Annie Fanny. There were a few claps, and she came on wearing a big Stetson hat, a bandana, a black shirt unbuttoned all the way down, short shorts, and cowboy boots.

She strutted around to a few Western tunes, and each time an item of clothing came off. First it was the shirt, revealing a black bra. Then it was the shorts, revealing a black G-string. Then came the boots. That was done sitting down, facing the audience. Most of the time she was wiggling her ample fanny to live up to her name.

When her bra came off, she took her hat off and waved it back and forth across her chest. When the G-string came off, she used the hat to cover that area front and back. Finally, she threw the hat away and used the bandana to cover parts instead. All of this while dancing in some manner to the music. Finally, she threw the bandana away, threw kisses to the crowd, and ran off the stage. She got a good round of applause.

Next it was table dancing for about fifteen minutes. It was still only ten bucks for a table dance. Drinks were expensive, though. It was almost as much for a beer as it was for a table dance. In the past I remembered dancers carrying their small tables with them to whoever had called them over. They had placed a small table at each seating area, so the girls had less to carry. I didn't signal any of them to come over. I waited to see if Bonnie was next on stage.

She was. She came on stage wearing a similar outfit to Annie Fanny, except she had no bandana but carried a lasso. I had never seen such a thing before. Bonnie was the best-looking stripper I had ever seen. She was what you would call voluptuous. She had long, wavy blonde hair down to her waist, big blue eyes, and a red slash for a mouth. She had a large bust and a large derriere, but neither showed any sign of sagging. Her legs were full and rounded. She was perfect there but would probably not make it as a model because they liked them skinnier.

She bounced around the stage, gradually taking things off. She had a lot to bounce, and she made sure everything did. Then after getting down to just her G-string, she whirled her lasso and asked the front row if anyone there would like to be lassoed by her.

About five guys put their hands up. She chose a gray-haired, almost bald old geezer and whirled the lasso over his head. She tugged it a little bit and told him to come on up.

It seemed that he had a little trouble getting up and then getting up the steps to the stage. Bonnie gently tugged on the lasso and brought him face to face with her. He wore glasses, and she told him to take them off. He did so, then she gently grabbed both sides of his head and buried it between her breasts. She moved him from side to side, then let him up for air. There was sweat on his forehead and drool on his mouth. The lasso was taken off, and he was guided back to his seat. A night he would probably never forget.

Back on stage, Bonnie undid the lasso and turned it into a long piece of rope. Then off came the G-string, and she dropped the rope between her legs with one hand and pulled it up the back with her other hand. She appeared to be running it up and down her crotch, but I don't think it was touching. Then she threw the rope away, bowed to the crowd, and bounced off to a good round of applause.

The regular music started again, and the girls looked around for guys signaling they wanted a table dance. I waited until Bonnie came out from backstage, caught her eye, and gave her a hand up sign. There was a slight nod of the head, and she came over.

"Hi, there. I'm Bonnie. Who are you?"

She was wearing a see-through negligee with nothing underneath except a G-string. I told her I was Mitch. She asked me if I was from out of town, and I told her I was a resident. Since the music had already started, she got up on the table, shed the negligee, and started her dance. I call it a dance, but it was virtually a twist and bend and bump and grind routine with a few bounces and the G-string coming off halfway through. She had a great body. There were no spots, tattoos, or anything to mar her terrific figure. I sure got my money's worth.

I had put my card under the ten-dollar bill. I picked them up and gave them to her and started to explain before she could say anything. "My name is Mitch Watson. I'm a private investigator hired to look into the death of a friend of yours, Julie Miller. I'm trying to talk to everyone that Julie knew to get a whole picture of her and her activities and try to figure out who was responsible for her death. Susan Long gave me your name as a friend. I know we can't talk here, but I do need to talk to you. Is there a restaurant or diner near here where we can go for a few minutes after this place closes? Believe me, this is not a pickup of any kind."

I waited and hoped for a positive response. She looked me over pretty good, almost as good as I looked her over. Then she smiled at me and finally replied in a very nice voice, "There is a diner, Dick's Diner, a block from here. You might have passed it coming in. I don't get off here until twelve-thirty, but I can be there at twelve-forty-five."

"Thank you, Bonnie. I won't stay here, but I'll be there waiting for you, then."

She smiled again, said, "Okay," and waltzed away. Would she be at Dick's Diner? Yes, I thought so.

Well, what to do for a couple of hours? I thought about the casino, but I felt like doing something different. Close to the strip joint, there was an amusement arcade on the other side of the street. There were usually more teenagers and early twenties types in there than any older people, but sometimes there were a few my age or older, so I walked over there.

They had some vintage pinball machines and some old-fashioned slot machines for dimes only. Then there were a few "dime falls" where there were many dimes perched near a ledge. Players could put dimes in, and a panel would go back and forth and push them up against the other dimes. With luck a player could put in a few dimes and get more pushed over the edge and into the tray where they could pick them up. Usually, it was the other way around.

I went to the cashier, gave her a twenty, and got four rolls of dimes. After trying the dime falls and putting in twenty and getting ten back, I thought I would try something else. I headed over to the mechanical horses. There were six of them on a glass-enclosed track—white, yellow, red, green, blue, and black. The odds for red and blue were even, green was three to one, yellow was five to one, black was seven to one, and white was twenty to one. I think white came up once on an average of thirty races or more.

I would wait until red had not won at least two races and then bet on it. Sometimes it worked, and sometimes it didn't.

Another system I used was if there had been a long time since the last white win, I would wait another ten races and then bet on it until it came in. I would never get rich at it, but it passed the time and was mildly amusing.

Afterwards, I went back to the casino and watched people lose their money on the roulette wheel. I didn't play; I just watched. At twelve-thirty I headed over to the diner.

There were couples in three booths and two men at the counter. I settled into a booth. Dick saw me and came over. He recognized me from when I was there with Mike. I told him that I was expecting a young lady to join me.

He said, "Good for you."

Wait until he sees her, I thought.

I ordered a coffee and waited. She came in right around twelve-forty-five. She was wearing a low-cut pink sweater and a short, tight red skirt. Everyone turned and looked at her as she walked down the aisle to my booth. I felt the envy of all the guys there that she was coming to see me. Yes, I felt good about that.

She slipped into the booth. "Hi, Mitch. Did you think I wouldn't show?"

"No, Bonnie," I replied. "I just had the feeling that you were the sort of person who means what they say." She smiled at me, and I was starting to feel good about the meeting.

Dick came over, and I asked Bonnie what she would like. She

said that a coffee was fine. She took a sip and then asked, "What can I do for you?"

Lots, I thought, but I played it straight. "Tell me all you know about Julie and any secrets she might have told you."

Bonnie thought for a minute and basically said what everyone else had said, that Julie was looking toward the future, and it didn't seem to include Henry. She wanted to travel and get a new job, meet new people, and live a more exciting life.

I asked Bonnie if there were any secrets that Julie might have only told her. She said she couldn't think of any. I asked her if Julie had mentioned any men in particular that she had seen lately. Bonnie said no, but she said Julie had told her that her nights out with Susan were fun.

I thought about mentioning that Julie was pregnant but decided against it. That news had not yet been released to the public. I thought that, out of respect to Henry, I would keep it quiet for a while.

I asked Bonnie how often she saw Julie. She said not very often, maybe once every two months or so for lunch. It had to be on a Saturday before Julie started doing housework and before Julie and Henry entertained relatives or went to see their relatives.

I asked when the last time was. She thought it would have been about two months ago. I asked her if Julie had seemed any different during that time. Bonnie said she didn't think so.

I couldn't think of anything else regarding Julie to ask her, so I got personal instead. "Susan said you went to university and then quit after two years. What happened?"

"What happened was that I was studying mostly economics, thinking about getting into banking or something similar. I found it to be very dry and mostly tedious. Then someone I know who is an exotic dancer said I should make good use of my body, and there was good money to be made. I went to see a few shows and thought, 'I can do that,' then I went to see the owners at the Sizzle Saloon. They looked me over and asked if I would do a routine that another girl would do first. She would stay and watch me. I was a bit nervous but said okay. It was similar to what you saw tonight. The other girl was not built quite as much as I am, so I thought I would improvise and bounce around a lot. They liked it, thought I would do well, and offered me a contract. I signed on the spot, quit the university, and as they say, the rest is history."

"Yes, Bonnie, sounds great in a way, but the strip clubs will be gone soon to make way for the condos, so what will you do then?"

She looked at me and said, "You had to spoil it all, didn't you? Yes, I know, you brought up the question I have been trying to answer myself for the last few weeks. I'm thinking of moving to Kansas City where I'm sure I can find a place doing the same thing. The money will probably be better there as well. Sooner or later I'll have to face the fact that I won't be able to do this forever and have to change my career. Right now I don't know what I would want to do. How about you, Mitch? Are you going to be able to do what you do now for the rest of your life?"

"Oh, Bonnie, right now I'm not thinking that far ahead. When the C Section gets replaced, it won't affect my work. Hopefully, I have a long time to go before I start thinking of what I should do next." Changing the subject, I said, "Do any of your girls at the saloon have drug or alcohol problems? I think in your line of work some of them might need a shot of something to do what you do."

As soon as I said that, I felt that it was not a subject to bring up, and I regretted it.

Immediately, Bonnie went on the defensive. "We have great girls there. While there may be one or two that use a little something, no one has a problem with anything. Because we strip for a living, you think we are all bad in our lifestyles? Some of them are housewives, and some have good educations. All we are doing is bringing some pleasure to the opposite sex. Don't knock it. I will bet our girls have higher moral values than most private investigators. From what I know, many private investigators are into blackmailing and other criminal activities. Your profession doesn't have a good reputation, you know."

"Wow! I admire you for sticking up for your people that way. I'm sorry for the way I sounded, I was wondering how all you girls got along together. I have no criticism of what you do whatsoever. You are also right about some of the ones in my profession. However, you only hear about the bad ones. A lot of us go about our jobs, helping the people who hire us, sometimes doing something like police work, saving the cops time to do more serious work. One bad apple can give the impression that all the apples are bad.

"Anyway, I like you and what you do and am glad to hear that you're a happy bunch. Sad to hear you won't be around much longer. You have my card. Call me from Kansas City, and I'll come out for the show." With that I gave her a big smile, hoping we were good.

She smiled back and then said, "Let's get back to Julie. Where does the investigation stand?"

I thought of what to say, then decided I had to tell it like it was. "The police and I are working on interviewing anyone who knew Julie in any way. Unfortunately, there were no witnesses—no one saw or heard anything. Some of the people who knew Julie have no alibis because the time of death was around dinnertime, and any single person would be home having dinner. So, not much to go on so far, but we all will keep working on it."

Bonnie said, "How about those guys she worked with at the flower shop? Julie said they were a couple of creeps. Do they have alibis? Are they suspects? Did you question them?"

"To answer your questions, I talked to them, as did the detectives. While I agree with Julie's assessment of them, there seems to be no motive for either of them. I can't discuss if specific people have alibis or not. Unless any evidence is uncovered regarding either of them, they are not likely to be considered as suspects."

"Mitch, do you think the person responsible will be caught?"

"Yes I do. It could take some time, but we will get him or her. I will do everything I can, and I'm good at what I do, not much else maybe, but I'm a good investigator, although maybe I'm not as good at my job as you are at yours."

She gave me a big smile. I thought she was reaching out to grab my hand but then changed her mind. I decided to do something I had not intended to do when I first saw her. "Bonnie, this was never my intention in the first place—please believe me—but how about we go out for dinner one night and carry on our conversation?"

She looked me straight in the eye, cocked her head and said, "We're not supposed to make friends with any customers, but no one said anything about investigators, so okay. How about next Monday? I'm off that night."

I was pleasantly surprised that she agreed. I asked for her address, she gave it to me, and we agreed that I would pick her up at six-thirty on Monday. We left the restaurant together, said goodnight, and walked to our cars. My Mustang was in the other lot, and her Honda Civic was in the Sizzle Saloon parking lot. I thought she should have a much splashier car for the way she looked, but I knew the Civic would be good on gas, and it was as reliable as any other vehicle, so I guess it worked for her.

She drove past me as I walked to the other lot. She waved as she went by. I waved back. I felt like a teenager who had just asked a girl for a first date, and she had said yes. I needed some cheering up, and that had done the trick.

Looking back on the day, what had I found out? First of all, don't wait for the white horse to win. Next, Bonnie Boom Boom Bountiful was really bountiful, and last, I was no further ahead on the case than before.

As I drove home, my mood was upbeat at first from my meeting with Bonnie, but as I gradually turned my mind to the death of Julie Miller, I felt somewhat depressed. It was the lack of answers, the dead ends that left me feeling frustrated. After I talked to that Yuri character from the club and then Julie's university students, what should I do? What leads would there be?

I almost wished that Julie had been involved in drugs, prostitution, human trafficking, or fraud. Those situations nearly always led to many other people and lots of leads. Julie had been a fairly normal person in an unsuitable marriage and needed some escape. It had cost Julie her life. Who was responsible and what the motive was remained unclear.

In the morning I would check with the detectives to see how they were doing. Also, I would call Susan to see if she had the dates on Julie's one-night stands. One last thing, I would see if Henry had been allowed back home yet. Tomorrow was Saturday, so in the afternoon I would visit Greg and Doug. They would be at one of their homes, watching college football.

CHAPTER 26

Saturday morning was windy and cool. In Cairnford it was difficult to predict the weather. We got it all, sometimes when we least expected it.

After breakfast, I read the paper, drove out to the lake, and went for a walk down by the water's edge. It was cooler there, so I turned up the collar on my windbreaker. It was not cold enough yet for my winter jacket, but it seemed like it was getting close. Still, this being Cairnford, we would probably have a few more warm periods before winter finally settled in. It would be November 1 next Thursday. There were a lot of bare trees already.

When I got back home, I settled in my favorite armchair and decided to start calling people. Nowadays, the favorite means of communication seemed to be texting. Young people seemed to do it all day long. My favorite way was face to face. That way, I could tell when a person was lying and sense all their emotions. Very helpful in my line of work. If seeing a person was not possible, then phoning was next best for me. Hearing a person's voice could tell me more than a written note. So, I texted sometimes, but mostly it was a phone call.

I had just settled down, but before I could start, my phone rang. It was Henry. He must have read my mind. He seemed to be in a good mood for a change. He told me that he was home, all the yellow police tape had been removed, and he had his phone and both cars back. The police were holding on to Julie's cell phone and computer for a while.

I told him that was all good news, I was still working trying to get answers, and that I had a question for him.

"Okay, what?" he asked.

"Henry, is it okay with you if, during my investigation, I mention to someone I'm interviewing that Julie was two months pregnant?"

"Why would you want to do that?" I could tell that Henry was not happy with the idea.

"It could help my investigation. It may help a person think in a different way from what they were thinking and bring to light some information that would be helpful. I'm trying every approach to find out who was responsible."

There was a pause. I let Henry think about it. Finally, he came back. "Okay, if it will help, but I'm not happy with it, so don't go around telling everybody."

I thanked Henry, told him I would come around in the near future, and hung up. Okay, one down and three more to go.

I called the division and asked to speak to Detective Puccillo or Detective Finnegan. I was told they were both working but out of the office. Did I want to leave a message? I said I did. She asked which one, so I said Detective Puccillo.

Next, I called Doug and asked him if he and Greg would be watching college football that afternoon and if so, where? He said yes and it would be at his house, so he told me to come on over.

Then I called Susan and asked her if she had the dates of Julie's one-night stands. She said she had figured it out and asked if I was ready to write them down. I told her I was.

"Julie was killed on Friday, October nineteenth. So, I went back to Tuesday, August twenty-first to make it close to two months. There was nothing that night. Julie went home with me. The two weeks before that, August seventh and fourteenth, it was Alan both nights. The week after the twenty-first would be the twenty-eighth, and that was Steve. The week after that was September fourth, and that was Brad. I know you wanted me to forget about him, but I thought you might want that date. Mike was before the time period. He was July thirty-first. As far as I know there were none before July thirty-first and none after September fourth."

"Thanks so much for this, Susan. Yes, I have already eliminated Brad from everything, and Mike is out of it as well. I don't think he was involved in either the pregnancy or the death. So, that leaves Alan, who has no alibi and whom I do not like, but that does not prove he is responsible for anything."

"Mitch, does that mean we are no further ahead, then?"

"It does give us some information we didn't have before, Susan. It may help eventually. Don't forget we're going to try to see Yuri on Tuesday. I'll be at your place at the same time, okay?"

"Okay," Susan said, then we hung up.

I would check up on my email, have lunch, and then head to Doug's place.

CHAPTER 27

Doug and his wife and two children lived in a modest, semi-detached house in the east end of the city. Most of the houses in the area were two-story brick homes with a living room, dining room, and kitchen on the main floor and three bedrooms upstairs. There could be a bathroom on either floor or both floors. Doug's house was one of the few that also had a den. It made the three other rooms a bit smaller than the other houses.

Doug's wife, Martha, met me at the door. She was a lot like Doug, short and stocky with a wide, smiling face. Her brown hair was fairly long, coming down past her shoulders. She was wearing a white blouse and a pair of old blue jeans. Trade in the blouse for a T-shirt, and she could have been Doug.

She ushered me into the den where Doug and Greg were playing some kind of video game that I had not seen before. The den had a hardwood floor with a big red area rug. The red was for the Kansas City Chiefs for whom Doug and Greg both had season tickets. It was over an hour's drive to KC from Cairnford, but they didn't care. They shared the cost of gas, and when there was a night game—there were a couple a year—they rented a hotel room and shared the cost.

One time when Doug was sick and couldn't make it, I went in his place. I enjoyed every minute I was there. Over 70,000 fans in Arrowhead Stadium, mostly dressed in red, shouting and screaming.

I realized what Doug and Greg got out of it.

Greg said, "Come on in, Mitch. Sit down and shut up. I'll beat Doug in a few minutes."

So, I sat down and shut up. They were both on a sofa, and I took the only armchair in the room.

Greg was right. Shortly after, Doug gave up and asked if I wanted something to drink. I knew he always had Bud, so I asked for that. He asked Greg, who said make it two, and then Doug said that he would make it three.

While Doug went for the beer, I looked around the room. The walls were mostly covered with Chiefs pictures and banners. The room was supposed to be cozy, but with so much red, it wasn't. At least neither of them were wearing red that day. They would tomorrow when they watched their team play. Greg was wearing a white golf shirt and black pants. Doug, being Doug, was wearing a brown sweater and an old pair of blue jeans. He handed out the beer, and we settled back.

Greg started it off. "So, you want to talk about the case, Mitch?"

I wanted as many opinions as possible with maybe something new being said that I could follow up on. I told them everything I knew so far, including that Julie had been about two months pregnant.

"Doesn't the pregnancy point to motive?" Greg asked.

Doug joined in. "So far, from what you have said Mitch, that looks like the only lead, so have you pursued it?"

"Yes, guys, I have pursued it, but it is difficult to pin it on anyone, and even if I could, it would not necessarily mean that the person was responsible for her death. Apart from that, we have the problem of when the pregnancy could have happened. Julie seemed to be with Henry and/or his family or her family from Friday to Monday. She worked five days a week and took night courses on Wednesday and Thursday. That leaves Tuesday night. Henry is convinced it happened then, and it is logical. However, according to the time frame established by the medical examiner and Susan's record of who Julie was with, there seems to be only one person eligible. Though I don't like the guy, he doesn't seem like a killer. He is an actor, not on stage but in his manner; he acts in a way that he thinks people would want. I don't think he has the guts to kill anyone, and anyway, there is no way I can prove it."

Greg said, "So, you're back to square one?"

I looked sharply back at him. "Yes, unless you guys have any ideas."

Doug said, "Well, you're the detective."

"What do the police detectives think?" Greg asked.

That reminded me that I had not heard back from them. I would call them again on Monday. Meanwhile, I needed to answer Greg. "I have left a message for them to call me. The last time I talked to them, they had Henry as the only suspect. Their other choice was a random burglar whom Julie saw. I don't believe either of those scenarios."

Doug was sitting there thinking. Finally, he said, "How can you be sure nothing happened over any weekend? Was Henry with her all the time? Twenty-four/seven?"

Fair question, but I couldn't give a definite answer. I did my best. "He wasn't with her when she went shopping for groceries. He was in the house when she did the laundry, the dusting, the vacuuming, and the dishes. He was with her if they went to a movie or a play. He was with her when her sister and husband came over, he was with her when his brother and wife came over, and he was with her when they went to those places, so it doesn't leave much time for anything else."

Greg took a swig of his beer and said, "You're back to square one then. Have you talked to Jack or Tony? Maybe they have some ideas."

I had forgotten that Tony had said he was going to do some

investigating, and I knew that was going to surprise these guys.

"I talked to Tony. He said that he was going to do some investigating on his own. He said that he and Henry were good friends and that he had the time and he wanted to help out. I'm planning to see Jack tomorrow."

They both stared at me in disbelief. Greg said, "No way. Tony has no experience in that field. It could even get dangerous for him."

I said, "I told him that, but he didn't seem deterred. I'll call him next week and see how he's doing. If he can solve the case, then maybe he should become a detective, and I will take up art."

They both laughed at that. Doug said, "The only thing you could draw would be nudes. You could practice by taking pencil and paper down to the strip joint."

I had no answer for that.

Doug said, "Football should be coming on soon. Do you want to stay? How about staying for dinner as well? We are having a roast, and the kids are away at a birthday party, so there'll be lots to eat." I thanked him and asked him to check with Martha.

He did and she said that it was okay, so I watched football and had an old-fashioned English dinner of roast beef and Yorkshire pudding, followed by apple pie with ice cream.

The conversation was general, mainly about happenings in the city. However, at one point, in a silent moment, Doug asked Martha what she would do if she found out he was having an affair. Would she kill him? Martha said she would not, but she would kill the woman. There was an awkward silence after that. I don't know what got into Doug to ask that. I stayed for a while, then left and packed it in for the day.

CHAPTER 28

The first thing I did on Sunday morning after breakfast was read the newspaper. It was my favorite day to read the paper, as it had a travel section and also a games page with a crossword puzzle, sudoku, and other puzzles. First, however, were the news pages.

While looking at the local news, something caught my eye—an update on Julie's killing. It said that detectives from the 9th Division had told the newspaper that an autopsy had revealed that Julie was about two months pregnant. The detectives said that at the moment there were no suspects, but the investigation was ongoing.

I hoped the detectives had talked it over with Henry first. I decided to call him. I asked him if he had seen the morning paper. He said that he had and had seen the short article. I asked him if he had talked it over with the detectives first, and he said he had. He also said that they told him it might help with the case, but he was not sure how. Anyway, he said they seemed to know what they were doing.

Then he mentioned that Julie's body was at Gray's Funeral Home close to where he lived. He said that he was making arrangements with his brother and with Julie's sister. Tentatively, there would be visitation a week from Friday and a church service the day after. When arrangements were completed, there would be an obituary in the newspaper.

He asked me if I had any news, and I had to tell him more or less what the detectives had said, that the investigation was ongoing. I told him I would call him as soon as I had something. I knew that was frustrating for Henry, but I couldn't tell him things were going well when they were not. All the leads seemed to have fizzled out.

I was hoping to see Mindy, the librarian next door to Henry's house, that morning. Then I hoped to see Jack that afternoon. I called Mindy, hoping she was home. She said she was and told me to come over. She said she was alone and that her father was at the firehall. *Even better,* I thought.

I decided to wear a turquoise golf shirt, dark-blue pants, and a medium-blue suede leather jacket. Not that I wanted to impress her or anything. I remember an old friend telling me that if you look sharp, people will think you are sharp. It works for me.

Mindy must have been watching for my car to drive up because she met me at the front door. She was wearing a tight pale-yellow sweater and dark, form-fitting pants. I guess that the saying that worked for me worked for her too. So, we had something in common.

We went into the living room, and she asked if I would like a drink. I said that if she was having coffee, I would have one. Mindy agreed and headed for the kitchen. Shortly after, she came back with a tray holding coffee cups, cream and sugar, and cookies.

We fixed our coffees, I took a couple of cookies, and Mindy started things off. "Mitch, did you see this morning's paper?"

"You mean the part about Julie being two months pregnant? Yes, I saw that. It can change how we look at the case."

"But, Mitch, doesn't that lead to a motive? Now you have a new lead."

"It may lead to a motive, and it may not. The person responsible for the pregnancy may not be responsible for the killing. The two could be quite separate."

Then Mindy asked me a question that stopped me cold. "Mitch, can you get DNA from a two-month-old fetus?"

I stared at her. Why had I not thought of that? Maybe I'd automatically believed that it was not possible.

Mindy broke into my thoughts. "Mitch, did you hear me?"

"Yes, your question has never come up before that I know of, and I was trying to think about that. I'll check with the medical examiner tomorrow. She'll know."

Mindy was excited. "Then if you can, you can get DNA samples from all the male persons of interest that Julie knew and you might have a killer."

"Wait a minute, Mindy, there could be some hurdles along the way. I don't believe that you can force a person to provide a sample under these circumstances. This is not a paternity suit. Also, it doesn't lead directly to a murder conviction. All it will prove is that Julie and someone were intimate. So, unless all the males voluntarily give DNA samples, we could be back where we started."

"Well, you will look into it, won't you, Mitch?"

"For sure, and thanks for the tip." I wondered if the detectives had already looked into it. Something to ask them tomorrow, along with other things.

Mindy was finishing her coffee when she looked up at me. "Are there any suspects at the moment?"

"No, not really, only a few persons of interest."

She looked into her empty cup of coffee as if trying to find the right words to say next. "You know, Dad always looked out the window on Tuesday nights and watched Julie as she went out. He said that she always looked different on Tuesdays. She dressed sexier, and she had more makeup on. I wonder what Henry thought of that."

"Henry just felt that it was a girls' night out, and she was going to have an innocent, fun time. I know it sounds somewhat incredible, but Henry loved and trusted Julie so much, he never thought much about those things.

"Is Henry a suspect? I know you said there were no suspects, but doesn't this pregnancy change things? I know Henry better than most people, and he didn't kill Julie. I am one hundred percent sure." She looked at me with a worried look on her face. "I would hate to think I was living next door to a murderer."

"No way, Mindy. You have no reason to worry." I thought about lightening the conversation up by saying that if she was worried, she could stay at my place. *A little too soon for that,* I thought. I wanted to change the subject, but I had to take one last shot at something that was troubling me. "Mindy, I still can't get over the fact that no one heard or saw anything on the night in question. Can you not hear people talking on the street? Can you not hear cars coming up your next-door neighbor's driveway?"

"Maybe we can, but we don't pay any attention. In this area we pretty much mind our own business. I can only tell you what I told you before. We didn't hear or see anything unusual. In the middle of the night, though, we heard all kinds of police cars and trucks in the area. Most were parked right outside. They woke us up, and we couldn't get back to sleep. I suppose they were detectives, uniformed officers, and what do you call them—oh, forensics I think. I'm not complaining; I'm just telling you the way it was."

Okay, I thought. *Enough about this. Let's start a conversation in a lighter vein.* It was time to have a nice chat with a nice-looking young woman that might lead to some kind of relationship. She was good to look at and good to talk to. Her features reminded me of Ingrid Bergman in *Casablanca.* Same kind of hairstyle, beautiful eyes, and a warm smile. Time to turn on the charm.

I asked her about any funny or interesting things that had happened to her as a librarian. There were not that many. I asked her what exciting things she would like to do that she had never done before. Her main answer was to travel to different countries. *Another Julie,* I thought, but then I thought, *No, Julie and Mindy are two different kinds.* I couldn't imagine Mindy sitting in a bar and flirting with guys.

She asked me about any funny or interesting things that had happened in my job. There were tons of those, some of them too risqué to talk about at that stage. I took up a fair bit of time, and she seemed to be enjoying it all. Finally, she asked me if I would like to stay for lunch. It would be leftovers, lasagna with cherry pie and ice cream for dessert. That, along with her smile and her blue eyes looking at me, meant I couldn't resist.

I told her I would stay on one condition: that I would take her out to dinner next weekend. She smiled coyly and said that would be very nice. So, we settled down to lasagna and cherry pie with vanilla ice cream. A yummy lunch. I said I couldn't stay long after because I had a meeting with someone to discuss the case. I left shortly after that.

♦

CHAPTER 29

♦

When I got in my car, I called Jack to see if he was home. He said yes and asked me to come over to watch some football. I wanted to get his opinion on the case rather than just watch football. Maybe we could do both.

I walked down the familiar path to his front door. It was around the end of October, and most of the flowers were done for the year. Leaves were mostly off the trees. Not a great time of year, in my opinion. Some people would say when the snow came, it made it look better. Not if you're driving in it.

Jack answered the door, and I followed him down to his living room. How many times had I been there? Too many to count. He had the game on the TV when we went in. I asked him if he could turn the sound down for a little while, so we could talk about the main reason I was there. He said okay and muted it.

Jack started the conversation. "Did you see the morning paper?"

"About Julie?"

"Yes, what else?"

I told him almost everything I knew. I didn't mention Brad. I told him that I kept reaching dead ends and asked him if he had any ideas.

"Well, Mitch, if you can find out who impregnated Julie, wouldn't that point to a motive?"

"Not necessarily," I said. "We could be looking for two different people: one responsible for the pregnancy and one for the killing. I have to keep all the possibilities in mind."

Jack asked if it was possible to get DNA from the fetus. I told him I was going to check with the medical examiner in the morning. Then he said, "You have mentioned that Julie didn't want a baby under any circumstances, so she must have been sexually assaulted, right?"

"Yes, Jack, it appears that way, but all of Julie's time is pretty well accounted for. I cannot see when that could have happened."

"You told me her schedule, so it must have happened on one of those Tuesday nights, right?"

"It seems that way, but what is surprising is that she didn't tell her best friend Susan. Julie told Susan almost everything. There are all these things that don't add up. So, I must be missing something, but I don't know what. It's very frustrating."

"You're a good detective, so you will find out. Just have patience. Now, can I turn the sound up?"

"Thanks, Jack, for all your help." I couldn't help but be sarcastic.

"Mitch, you're a detective and you don't have the answers. I'm not a detective, so how am I going to have any answers?"

Jack was right, but I was disappointed. I thought that at least I might get some fresh ideas. So, I started watching the game. I asked Jack where Brad was and how he was doing. He said that Brad was out with his buddies, and he was doing great at the university. "Smart kid, that one."

Yes, I thought, *and a nice young man as well.* Sometimes smart and nice don't always go together, but with Brad, they did.

The early game ended at around four-thirty, and Jack asked if I wanted to stay for dinner.

I told him no thanks, but I would take a rain check. I just didn't feel like it. I was feeling down and wanted to think my way out of it, if I could.

Seeing Mindy had been such an upper and seeing Jack was a downer, mainly because he didn't have any answers and seemed more interested in the football game. I couldn't blame him. How could I expect him to have any answers if I didn't have any? I'd have Jack at my place in a week or two, and we would have a pizza and a few beers—my treat.

For the moment, I would go home, see if there were any leftovers in the fridge, and plan my week. In the morning, I would call Jan and then the detectives and then, depending on what they all said, I would figure out what to do until I picked up Bonnie for our dinner date. I had decided to go to the best Chinese restaurant in town. I had not asked her if she liked Chinese. If she didn't, we would make it Italian. Either way it would be good.

CHAPTER 30

The next morning, I was eating my breakfast at about eight-thirty when my phone rang. It was too early for telemarketing calls.

"Hi, Mitch. It's Detective Beth Puccillo. You called a couple of days ago. We've been very busy, not only on the Miller case but also on other cases as well. So, what's on your mind?"

"Can you check your databases for the following names—Mike Hutchinson, Alan Wilson, Steve Kowinski, and Yuri Moldev—to see if anything pops up?

"Sure, Mitch. We already did Mike, and we did the young man who teaches the courses that Julie was going to. We seem to be following you. Anyway, both were clean."

"Thanks, Beth, can you do this Yuri character today? I hope to see him tomorrow. Apparently, he had a rather nasty argument with Julie at a club."

"Yes. I'll call you later. I have to go. Patrick is calling me."

I thanked her and hung up.

After I finished my breakfast and read the newspaper, I would call Jan. I didn't know when she started work, but the number she gave me was her cell, so it didn't matter.

It was actually around ten a.m. when I called her. She was her usual self. "Well, if it isn't that detective who can't figure out how a girl can get pregnant. I better not go out with you."

I laughed. "Jan, I'm happy to say you don't change. I have a question for you that you should be able to answer. Can you get DNA from a two-month-old fetus?"

"You're a little late with the question. The answer is, it is possible because there would be live cells. The detectives already asked that question, and we have supplied DNA samples already."

"So, Jan, let me be clear on this, if we get DNA samples from all the men she had contact with, we could get a match that would give us the impregnator and possibly the killer. Is that right?"

"Yes, but don't get too far ahead of yourself. First of all, you may not be able to get everyone or even anyone to volunteer a sample. This is not a paternity case, nor will it directly solve a murder case. The DA might have to get involved, and then the persons of interest could get their lawyers involved. I don't know how that would work out."

"Something else is bothering me. This morning, I talked to Detective Beth Puccillo, and she never mentioned this. I need to know what's going on."

"Mitch, you don't expect them to tell you everything do you? They actually don't need to tell you anything."

"Well, they expect me to tell them everything. Okay, I'll have to keep bugging them. Thanks for this, and listen, when I solve this, we'll go out and celebrate. You won't have to worry. I will have figured out by then how a girl gets pregnant."

Jan laughed. "By that time it will be too late for you anyway."

I couldn't think of a good answer, so I just told her goodbye and hung up.

I had nothing left to do until I picked up Bonnie for our date. I was interested in what she thought about her future. In the paper that morning it had said certain businesses in the C Section would have to close down next week as demolition would be starting the week after. They had been advised of the demolition date earlier, but most of them wanted to carry on for as long as possible.

I thought about the death of Julie Miller and how I was no further ahead than when I started. I didn't think that this week would help much. I couldn't see Julie telling any of her three university friends anything that she had not told Susan. Anyway, I would see them later on in the week.

I decided to check my emails to see if there were any job opportunities. There was a good one; it was undercover work. My favorite kind of work. I emailed back, saying to give me a week, and I would see them. I was very interested.

◆

CHAPTER 31

◆

I had a snooze in the afternoon. When I woke up, I had a shower and changed my clothes. I wondered what Bonnie would be wearing for our dinner date tonight. Since it was Halloween in two days, I decided to wear an orange golf shirt, black pants, and a black windbreaker.

Bonnie was waiting for me in the lobby of her apartment building when I arrived right at six-thirty, as we had agreed. She was wearing a white cashmere sweater, tight black pants, and a black jacket. If I had known that, I would not have worn black. As it was, it looked like we were going to a funeral. I would have to brighten things up with a few of my favorite jokes. However, when we started talking, I forgot about the jokes because it seemed that both of us were interested in what the other person was saying.

I had decided on a Chinese restaurant downtown called Shanghai Success. It was upscale, but I didn't need a jacket and tie to get in. I did need a reservation, which I had already made.

The hostess was a young Chinese woman wearing a tight, spar-kling crimson dress split high on both sides. She showed us to one of several alcoves along the far wall, just right for two people. The place was about three-quarters full, with most tables having seating for four.

Although it was called Shanghai Success, most of the pictures and paintings on the wall seemed to feature areas around Hong Kong. I wondered if the place had changed hands, or if they thought most people would not know the difference. Anyway, the pictures brought life to the room. They and the crimson-and-gold carpet brought out the Chinese atmosphere.

Our server could have been a sister of the hostess. They both had a slim, attractive build. Our server didn't have a crimson dress, though. All the servers wore black. I thought if Bonnie or I got up to go to the bathroom, a customer might call out for a drink.

It was a rare Chinese restaurant in that it was not a buffet. It was table service only. After we both ordered a beer, our server left us a couple of menus. My beer was a Coors, and Bonnie's was a Heineken. That surprised me. I didn't think of Bonnie as a Heineken drinker for some reason. I wondered what other surprises she might have for me that evening. I would wait and see. Maybe it was just wishful thinking.

By the time our beers were delivered, we had made up our minds on the menu. We ordered chicken chow mein, barbecued ribs, and shrimp with mixed vegetables. We thought about a couple of other items as well, but we knew the orders would be huge, and we would have a lot left over for doggy bags anyway, so we stayed with the three items.

I started the conversation off. "I saw in the paper this morning that demolition on the good old C Section is going to start next. Will your club be one of the first to go?"

"No, it will not be *one* of the first to go; it will be the *first* to go. We got word on Saturday. This coming Saturday will be our last performance. Rather sad, actually. I'll miss the place and the girls."

"So, what will you do?" I wondered if she had made any firm plans. After all, the employees there had known this was coming for some time. This was short notice on the actual termination though.

"I'm going to Kansas. I have a job there. The place is called the

Harem. It has an Arabic atmosphere to it. A bit different from my place here, but I think it'll be okay. I'll make more money too. I just rented an apartment a short distance away, so I can walk to work if I want to. The area is okay. I think KC is a great place, and I'm going to enjoy myself."

"Good for you, Bonnie. You have a lot of initiative. You deserve some good things happening to you. How long do you think you'll be in the line of work you're in?"

"Mitch, why don't you just say it—how long can I still be a stripper? Anyway, I haven't thought that far ahead yet. If I keep a good diet, I think I can go for a fair bit longer. So, are you going to come over to see me in KC?" "Where would I stay if I went?"

She smiled, and I smiled back. I said, "I thought it was worth a shot."

"Well, my living room in my new apartment has a nice sofa. It would fit you quite nicely." We both smiled at each other again.

"Bonnie, give me your address, so I will know where to find that sofa. When are you actually moving?"

"Monday next week. I start at the club the following Saturday." Bonnie grabbed a napkin and wrote down the address where she would be staying. She put her cell number underneath. I already had that. I would input her address into my cell.

Our three dishes arrived with big spoons and a plate for each of us. We both decided to cover one of the dishes that we ordered, mainly because it would be difficult to get all three on a plate. When we finished the first two, we would go on to the other one.

It was all very tasty, but there was a lot left over, as we had expected. We ordered doggy bags, and I told Bonnie she could take them home with her. I'm not fond of leftovers. She thanked me and said that would be good because it would save her cooking, as she was anticipating a busy week, packing for Kansas.

We each had another beer while eating and then another one

when we had eaten enough. We talked some more about a lot of things. She talked a lot about her coworkers. Some were housewives, and others were university students who wore a lot of makeup and changed their names to avoid recognition. On Fridays and Saturdays, the busiest days, there were part-timers who just came in for those two days.

Bonnie talked with surprising insight on several issues, including politics. Thankfully, we generally agreed on our political points of view. I have always thought that politics is the fastest way to turn friends into enemies. If I feel that the person I'm talking to doesn't share my political views, I don't initiate any conversation on that subject.

We both agreed that our City Hall was a mess and generally wasted taxpayers money. My councilor was good, but I didn't know why some of the others kept getting elected. If you phoned your councilor, with most of them you got a recorded message: "For all Cairnford policies and procedures call [a three-digit number]. For anything else, leave a message." The three-digit number was for a call desk where they would try to find the subject you wanted, and then they would read what it said on the computer. No personal service at all. Just lousy service. Bonnie and I took turns describing stupid things the city had done.

I talked to her a little about the Julie Miller case and told her that I might be taking on another job. She wondered if the case would ever be solved. I said that I thought so, but I had no conviction in my voice. For a moment or two my mind wandered back to the case, and then I realized that Bonnie had asked me a question, and I was gazing into space. I apologized and asked her to repeat it.

She wanted to know if there were any strong suspects. I told her that there were not. I couldn't name names anyway. A private investigator usually has to beware of privacy issues as much as the police do.

I knew it would be good seeing her again, but it was enjoyable to have an interesting conversation with her. I appreciated her much more than just seeing her on stage. I told her I thought she should take some courses in what she might be interested in, and I thought she could go places. She thanked me for my positive remarks about her.

Finally, we got up to leave, and I drove her home. I didn't know what to expect when we arrived at her apartment. Maybe a little loving, maybe a lot of loving. I was ready for either. I was not ready for what she said.

"Thanks, Mitch, for a really nice evening. Look me up in Kansas, and keep in touch, okay?"

I mumbled, "Okay," and then she was out the door, waved, and was gone. I felt that I wouldn't see her again. I drove home feeling sad and empty.

CHAPTER 32

On Tuesday morning the weather outside was cloudy, drizzly, and cool. It didn't lift my spirits. I thought that planning my day might help a bit. After my usual breakfast and reading the newspaper, I would call Beth Puccillo to see if there was any news. I would probably have to leave a message, but that was okay. No point in texting because the number she'd given me was the station number, not her cell. Anyway, as I have stated, I like to hear a person's voice. In my line of work it can really help.

Later I would see if I could get an interview for that undercover job and get that sealed for the following Monday. I was looking forward to that. In the evening I would call Susan and remind her that we had a date that night to find Yuri Moldev. It would probably be my last visit to the C Section, seeing that they would start demolition next week.

I hadn't finished reading the paper when my phone rang. It was Beth.

"Hi, Beth. How is my favorite detective?"

"Hi, Mitch. I thought Frank was your favorite detective."

"Frank is my favorite *male* detective. You are my favorite female detective."

"How many female detectives do you know?"

"You're it," I replied.

She laughed, and so did I. Now it was time for business.

"So, Beth, what have you got for me?"

"We ran a check on the guys from the flower shop—I think I told you that. We also checked out Alan Wilson, Mike Hutchinson, Steve Kowinski, Yuri Moldev, and the fella from the course place, Tom Duncan. They were all clean except for the Yuri character. He has one charge of assaulting a woman on his record. The charge was dropped because the woman wouldn't testify. That's it."

"Did you get DNA samples from the persons of interest?"

"We did and we didn't. We checked out seven. Four gave, and three refused. I can't tell you which was which; the info is too private and personal."

"Two questions then. How can they refuse? Isn't this a murder investigation? Also, did you get a match from any of the samples?"

"To answer your first question, none of them have been charged, and even if there was a match, it would not lead directly to the death of the victim. For all we know, the sex might have been consensual and have nothing to do with Julie's death. Anyway, the ones who refused talked about their freedoms and told us to get a warrant, and they would check with their lawyers. We have forwarded all this to the DA. He can decide how to proceed. To answer your second question, we have not heard back from the lab."

I decided that I would proceed by calling my detective friend, Frank, and maybe he might tell me more. I knew that all the detectives were brought up to date on each other's cases.

I told Beth that I was hoping to see Yuri that night and asked her if she and her partner had talked to him yet. She said that he was on the calendar for tomorrow but not to tell him that. I said I would not. Then I thanked her for the info, such as it was, and hung up.

So, what to do? I decided to call Henry, Julie's sister, Jennifer, and my detective friend, Frank Dobson.

I called Henry first and told him what was going on—not much.

I didn't tell him I was going to get off the case by next Monday. I would tell him on the weekend.

I had not talked to Jennifer since I went to her place the day after Julie's death. When I called her, I told her what I could and said the police and I were working hard to get all the answers, although so far, the leads were not working out. I didn't mention the men Julie met with on Tuesday nights. If Jennifer needed to hear that, someone else could tell her.

I debated whether to call Frank or not. He certainly couldn't give me the information I wanted over the phone if he was in the office. I decided to text him on his cell and ask him if he was out of the office. He texted back that he had a bad cold and he was at home. I felt that I could get him to give me the answers to my questions by actually talking to him rather than texting, so I called him.

"Frank, I need to know which persons refused to provide DNA samples. Beth is clamming up, but I need to know, and no one will ever know that I know or where I heard it. It's not a big deal."

There was silence for a moment. "You know, sometimes I'm almost sorry we're such good friends."

I stayed quiet, hoping he would come through for me.

"Mitch, I'm going to hate myself for this, but here goes. The ones who were contacted, first names only: Henry, Tom, Mike, Alan, Steve, Arthur, and Ryan. The ones who refused were Alan, Ryan, and Arthur. Now, don't ask me anything else until the case is closed."

"Thanks a lot, Frank, I hope your cold clears up quickly. See you soon."

I wasn't sure what it all meant. I knew I was not any closer to solving the case. I felt bad about having to let Henry know I was moving on and that I would be off the case by the weekend.

I was looking forward to leaving the case and working under-cover in a new job. It was not officially confirmed, but the general manager, Brian Watson—no relation--had said in his email that he wanted me for the job.

I wanted to see him first to find out what I would be doing. I decided not to phone him but to email him instead, asking if I could drop in to see him. I mentioned that I was available that day. I hoped he would reply quickly and positively.

What could I do while I waited? I could go in the backyard and rake up the leaves that had been falling for the last month. Not my favorite job. I had just started raking when I heard my cell phone ring in my pocket. Sure enough, it was Brian Watson.

He asked if I could see him at two p.m. I told him I was looking forward to it. I was so happy, I raked the backyard and the front lawn as well.

CHAPTER 33

Watson's Hardware was started by David Watson many years ago. At first it was one small store. Gradually, he opened three more stores in Cairnford. They were spread out—one each in the north, west, and east sections of the city. The main store was downtown.

David was the owner and president. His son, Brian, was the general manager. I headed downtown to see him. The store and offices were located in a large building at the corner of a main intersection a block away from the C Section. The store was on the ground floor, and the offices were above on the second floor.

I arrived there bang on at two o'clock. The store was well organized with five sections - paint, metals, tools, housewares, and builders. There was a small elevator at the back of the store with a sign that said, "OFFICES."

I went in, went up, and got out; it was a small, fast elevator. I went out into a lobby with dark-gray tiling and a large sign that said, "WATSON'S HARDWARE." I guessed I was in the right place.

A receptionist sat at an expensive-looking rosewood desk. She looked to be in her thirties with long, curly black hair, bright-red lipstick, and a smiling face. She wore a black dress with what looked like a pearl necklace. Maybe they paid well at Watson's Hardware. I would soon find out.

Her red lips parted and out came what she must have said several times a day: "Can I help you?"

I told her that I was Mr. Watson, there to see Mr. Watson. I waited for her to laugh, but she didn't. I explained that I was Mitch Watson, there to see Brian Watson.

She had one of those phone sets with many buttons. She picked up the receiver and pushed a button. "Mitch Watson is here to see you." After a moment, she hung up and said, "Mr. Watson's office is the second on the right; you can go on in."

Brian Watson was a big man, a really big man, probably around three hundred pounds and well over six feet tall. He could have been an offensive lineman for the NFL. He was graying and balding on top of a large, round, smiling face. I figured he was a jolly, old soul.

His suit matched the color of the gray walls in the lobby. With his black tie on a white shirt, he looked like an efficient, professional businessman.

He greeted me warmly and pointed to an office chair across from his desk where he sat in a high-back red velvet chair, which added some needed color to the room.

He told me how the company operated. The warehouse was in an industrial/commercial part of the city in the east end. Apparently, taxes were much lower there.

The warehouse was a large facility that held all the inventory purchased by the company. In turn, the items in the warehouse were distributed to the stores as required.

There were a manager, assistant manager, three receivers, three shippers, and three drivers. Also, there were three women to look after the office work required at the warehouse. So, three workers at each position. Hiring me would change that. How would he explain that to the staff? Also, I found it interesting that all the warehouse-type work was done by men and the office work by women.

Maybe that was the philosophy of the GM's father. It had probably always been that way. Of course, it was also possible that it turned out that way due to the type of people who applied for each job. Still, I thought a GM who was not a relative of the owner would have a slightly different gender ratio.

There was an inventory count once a year, and in the last one there had been several discrepancies between what there was supposed to be and what there was. No one in the warehouse could explain it. The suggestion was that there most likely had been billing mistakes. However, none were found. It seemed likely that there was a problem in the shipping area and maybe in accounting as well.

I would be hired as a shipper. The reason given to the staff was that stores were complaining that deliveries were not always coming fast enough. The GM said this was actually true when staff were on vacation or sick.

One of the first jobs I had was in a small hardware store. So, I had some knowledge of the items I would be dealing with.

We decided I would use a different name. I would be Mike Lawson.

I would receive a salary in the same range as the other shippers, so no one in the office would be suspicious. After I solved the problem, I would be awarded a bonus, the amount still to be determined.

The plan was that I would meet the GM at the warehouse parking lot at nine a.m. on Monday. The staff would be notified beforehand that a person with hardware knowledge was being hired as a shipper.

With all this settled, we shook hands, and I walked out of Watson's Hardware with a smile on my face. *Come on, Monday!* I thought. I could hardly wait.

Now I had to think back on the Julie Miller case. Hopefully I would be able to see Yuri Moldev that night and see if it led anywhere. I doubted it.

In the meantime, I would go out for dinner and celebrate, even if it was by myself. Then I would call Susan to make sure we were still on for our last trip to the C Section.

I went to the Wild West Steakhouse, the best steakhouse in

Cairnford, and had a porterhouse, medium-rare. Two vodka martinis made it even better. The only mistake I made was in not taking a cab. I felt like having a few more martinis, but I stopped short of ordering since I was driving. My limit when driving was always two. If only I had a chauffeur.

I called Susan, and she agreed to be ready by nine p.m. I decided to wear all black to intimidate the man I was going to meet. I didn't know what to expect. I found it rather exciting and had mixed emotions about going down to the C Section for probably the last time.

CHAPTER 34

Susan was wearing a pink dress, pink lipstick, and a red brooch on the top left area of her dress. She looked very attractive, as usual. I found it strange that I wasn't that attracted to her. Good looking, nice personality, yet there seemed to be something missing. Perhaps she'd had a bad affair with someone in the past. I think that Julie must have done most of the flirting when they were out together.

We were going to the Game, a sports bar in the C Section. I asked Susan why Julie and she would go to a sports bar. Neither of them were that interested in sports. She said that they just wanted to see what it was like. They didn't like it very much, especially after meeting Yuri.

I asked Susan what started it all off. She said that Julie had been staring at Yuri because he looked like a movie villain. He had a head of thick black hair, black eyes, and a lot of facial hair. On the night she saw him, he was wearing a black denim jacket and black jeans. Susan said he had a scowl to go along with it. I wondered who was going to intimidate whom that night.

Susan said that Yuri had noticed Julie and snarled at her. "What are you staring at?"

Julie said she was not staring at him. He said she was and that it was rude and that she should apologize. Julie said to forget it and turned away from him. That was when he called her a stupid bitch and said she should get out, that the Game was no place for a stupid bitch like her.

Then Susan said that Julie turned around and answered him back, but she didn't remember the words. That was when it got ugly and scary, and Yuri wound up calling Julie a two-bit whore and said that Susan was one as well.

Susan mentioned that they'd finished their drinks quickly and gotten out of there. She said she was glad that the place would be demolished.

The Game didn't look busy, probably because it was a Tuesday night. There was lots of room in the parking lot. We entered through the wooden front doors and then through two swinging doors like in a saloon in an old Western movie.

Once inside, I noticed two things. The first were the wall-to-wall screens, showing basketball, hockey, football, tennis, golf, and horse racing. Baseball had finished two weeks ago, so that was not on. Football games would be replays of the weekend matches. Everything else was probably live. The other thing I noticed was the noise. It was not from the screens but from the patrons shouting and whooping it up over everything they were watching. For a small group, they were loud.

Susan walked in nervously behind me. She leaned into me and said in my ear, "I don't want him to see me. If I see him, can I point him out and go back to your car?"

"Okay," I said. "Stay behind me, look around, and tell me if you see him." We edged our way to a side where we could see most of the room, and then she pointed him out.

"That's him over there, sitting by himself looking at the football game."

I looked over to where she was pointing, and it was easy to see the man she had described earlier. He was on the other side of the room, looking at a screen somewhat ahead and to the right of where he was sitting. He was wearing a gray denim jacket and black jeans.

"Alright," I said as I handed her the keys to my car. "This should not take long. I'll come right out after talking to him."

Susan walked out quickly. I sauntered over to where Yuri was watching the screen. He was so intent on the football game, he didn't even notice me until I sat down opposite him.

He turned around, looked me up and down, and then with a scowl on his face said, "Who are you, and what do you want?"

I answered by putting my card in front of him. Before he could say anything else, I got going on what I hoped would get him involved. "About two months ago, you had an argument with a young woman here. About two weeks ago, she was found murdered in her backyard. I'm a friend of her husband, and he has hired me to investigate. I'm doing that, but at the same time, I'm working with two detectives from the Ninth Division. I need to ask you a couple of questions. If that works out okay, I'll tell the detectives not to bother with you. We just want to eliminate any possible suspects."

He glowered at me. "I don't know what you're talking about. Was it a waitress? I don't have any problem with them. I think they're scared of me, so they're always quick to serve me."

I explained to him what Susan had said and that there had been the two women. One had been staring at him, and he'd wound up calling them two-bit whores.

"Oh, yeah, now I remember. She was staring at me, and they looked like two-bit whores. Why else would they be here? They didn't belong in this place. Those types often come to a bad end."

So much for not speaking badly about the dead. I didn't expect much better from him anyway.

"Okay," I said. "Can you tell me where you were a week ago Friday between five and seven p.m.? If anyone can verify that, then no more questions from anyone."

"Five and seven? That's dinnertime. I would have either been at home or in a restaurant.

"Can you remember which it is? It's important."

"I don't remember what I did yesterday. Let me think for a minute."

I let him think for a minute. So far, he was being surprisingly cooperative. I had to keep it that way.

"Okay, I go to a family restaurant sometimes. I think I did that weekend. I'm not sure if it was Friday or Saturday. Dino's Family Restaurant on Prince Street at Beckwith. Do you know the place?"

"Yes, I do know the place. Do you know who served you?"

"It would have been Indy. She is a Black girl from India. I think her name is short for Indira."

"Oh," I said. "Like Ghandi."

"No," he replied. "I told you, Indira."

I should have known that this character knew nothing about international history. He probably thought that Mussolini was an Italian pasta.

What else could I ask him? So far, so good. I had a lead. I thought that anything more might bring out his bad side, so I thanked him and walked out.

Back in my car, Susan was surprised to see me so quickly. "So, I imagine he wouldn't talk to you."

"Actually, he gave me a lead. I have to check out a restaurant where he said he thought he was that night. Dino's Family Restaurant. I will go there on Friday and see if the same waitress is there. He was quite cooperative. I didn't push my luck by asking him more questions."

"If his alibi holds up, where does that leave us?"

"Unfortunately, square one. I will have to see if the detectives have anything new. I still have those three university students to check out. However, I don't think Julie would have told them anything she wouldn't have told you. Maybe I'll find out something new. I'm going to visit them on Thursday and Friday. Tomorrow is Halloween, and people will be busy. So, do you want to go somewhere else?"

"No. I'm sick of all of this. Please just drive me home, Mitch. When you have anything new, you can give me a call."

I understood the way she felt; it had been a very rough time for her. I didn't know how she would get over it. I wished I could give her a comforting word, but I couldn't come up with anything. It was a silent drive back to her place.

When we arrived, she turned to look at me and put her hand on mine. "Thanks, Mitch, for trying so hard to find out who did this to Julie. Please keep in touch."

I told her I would, then I drove off, feeling somewhat drained, knowing how she felt. There were times when I felt great living alone with the freedom that it gives me. That night, however, it would have been good to have someone waiting for me at home.

CHAPTER 35

It was Wednesday. Halloween. At night when the kids came knocking, I would wear an orange shirt and black pants and hang a figure of a skeleton on the front door.

At the moment, it didn't matter, so I put on a casual white shirt and black pants. After breakfast and the newspaper, I would plan my day.

I felt that I should go back to the flower shop and maybe convince the owner and the driver to give a DNA sample. We would then probably eliminate them as suspects, or maybe not.

Later, I would give Frank a call and see if he had any news and maybe get together for lunch. Afterwards, I might check in on Henry to see if he was getting rid of his depression.

I drove down to the flower shop in the late morning. As I entered the shop, the usual pleasant smell of flowers greeted me.

The two men were not there, and there was a woman at the counter where Julie used to work. I looked at her closely and noticed her thin face and plain-looking appearance. It had to be the daughter her mother had talked about.

In a pleasant voice she asked, "Can I help you?"

I replied, "I am a private investigator helping the detectives who are investigating Julie's death. I have already spoken to your mother, and I'm just going to check with her again."

"Oh, she told you I was working here?"

"She told me when I first saw her that you might be filling in for Julie. I'll go up to see her for a moment."

With that I headed over to the office. Mrs. Bundheim saw me and opened the door as I came up. "Mr. Watson, how nice to see you again. Come on in."

I knew I would have to be careful in what I was about to say. I couldn't let her think that the detectives were telling me everything.

"Hi, Mrs. Bundheim. I see you have your daughter working for you."

"Yes, I had to have someone reliable. I needed someone with experience or someone smart who could learn quickly. I'm still looking for someone for the permanent position."

"Well, I won't keep you. I just wanted to talk about Julie being two months pregnant. Did you already know about that?"

"No, it came as a shock when I saw it in the paper. Julie had said that she didn't want to start a family, so I don't know what to think."

"Mrs. Bundheim, I also heard that the detectives were taking DNA samples from all the males who knew her. Did the detectives come here?"

"Yes, they did. Our driver was going to, but my husband told him not to. He said it was an infringement on his rights."

"That's bad advice, Mrs. Bundheim. The DNA samples would have eliminated them as suspects. Now the police will keep checking up on them and their whereabouts, trying to find a connection to Julie. You should try to get them to change their minds, for their own good."

Okay, there were a couple of little white lies in there. I just hoped it would work.

She said, "I will try, but my husband can be obstinate. Sometimes he has tunnel vision and can't see the whole picture."

We talked about a few other things, including the business. She said it was fairly steady.

I said goodbye to her and her daughter and then walked out of the shop. I had no idea if what I had said would make any difference.

I thought about texting Frank, but I have fat fingers and thumbs, and I am not a great typist. I don't know how teenagers do it so easily, but then they abbreviate everything anyway. They sure get lots of practice.

I had him on speed dial on my phone, so that was what I used. He was on the day shift, working in the office, so we could meet for lunch.

We met at a small diner called Rick's Place, which was near the 9th Division's station house. Maybe it was named after Rick's café in *Casablanca*, but it didn't look Moroccan or much like anything. Mostly, it seemed to be a hangout for detectives and uniformed officers. When I saw that, I was not happy. Anyone seeing us together would wonder what we were talking about. I caught Frank by the arm and pointed to the door.

Outside, I said to Frank, "What were you thinking of with all those cops in there and you talking to me?"

"Sorry, Mitch. I'm so used to going there, I didn't think about that. Okay, you pick a place."

I picked a deli near where I lived. Their corned-beef sandwiches were to die for. With pickles, hot mustard, and cherry pie, all washed down with a beer, it didn't get much better than that.

After we ordered, I got right down to business. "So, what's new on the Julie Miller case?"

"Mitch, could you at least wait until we get our beers? It seems now that all our get-togethers are just to pump me about a case you're working on."

Frank was right. It was wrong to be like that; we were really good friends. I told him that I would wait until our lunch was finished, then I would ask him again.

The lunch was terrific. I asked Frank how he liked it, and he gave it a thumbs-up. Then it was time to use my skill at persuasion.

"You know, Frank, I cannot solve this case without your help. Together with what we both know, we have a chance to avenge Julie's death and put away a killer. Isn't it worth it to share information?"

"So, the end justifies the means? Is that it, Mitch? It's not worth it if I lose my job. I can only tell you so much."

"Okay, then tell me so much."

"Actually, there is nothing much to tell. We're no further ahead. Julie had a very precise schedule. She had very little in the way of activities and not that many friends or relatives for a person her age. Apparently, she was on Facebook and Twitter before she was married, but she quit both shortly after. Do you have any ideas of your own?"

"No. I'm seeing three university student friends of hers tomorrow and Friday. I'll go to a restaurant on Friday to check an alibi, and that's about it. I was hoping something more would come from the DNA tests."

"None of the ones we want to test are charged with anything yet, so the DA does not want to get involved. He tells us to bring evidence. The DNA would be evidence, but we can't get it unless there is other evidence or they volunteer. We have nothing on any of them."

"Frank, you might get a DNA sample from Yuri Moldev. He's the one who had an argument with Julie. I saw him yesterday and am going to check his alibi on Friday. In my opinion, right now we have him, Alan Wilson, and the two males from the flower shop as possible suspects. I think if we can get any evidence of anything on any of them, you can force that person into supplying a DNA sample."

"Yes, but how do you propose to get any evidence on any of them? Right now, they're just plain, law-abiding citizens."

"I know; you had to bring reality back into it. There is not much to follow up on. I prefer a case where there's a good, old-fashioned brawl and chases and being shot at and gangs and crooked politicians and drugs. This has none of that. It doesn't seem to have much of anything."

"You're missing something, Mitch. There is a fetus. That is our only lead at the moment. We need to tie someone to it. You can do that, and you probably have your case."

"Oh, well, the lunch was good," I said and smiled at Frank.

He smiled back, looked me in the eye, and said, "I know you're frustrated, Mitch, and I wish I could help you, but you know as much as we do."

We talked a bit longer about several things and then left. I was in a bad mood. I was right; the lunch was good, but I was no further ahead. Now I was going to see Henry to cheer me up. Fat lot of good that would do me. I wondered if I should go trick-or-treating. That would have cheered me up. I called Henry, and he said to come over. I had almost been hoping he would be out.

Henry saw me pull into his driveway and opened his front door before I got out of the car. He welcomed me in with a question. "Coffee or beer, Mitch?"

I settled for coffee.

He made the coffee, and we settled back in his living room. I made one last attempt to create some leads. "Henry, can you think of anyone who had an argument with Julie during the last few months? Maybe someone at one of the stores she went to? Also, Friday to Monday evenings, was she ever out with anyone other than you or family?"

Henry leaned back and thought for a moment. Finally, he said, "Julie never mentioned anyone having an argument with her. She didn't like arguments. She would always try to avoid them. As for going out on the weekends, I can't think of anyone of either sex that she went anywhere with. We both had a straightforward schedule of what we were going to do each day, and we kept to it."

Boring, I thought. Also, it didn't develop any new leads. I didn't say that to Henry, though. There was silence for a few minutes as I thought of what to say that might produce something to follow up on.

Henry broke the silence. "Allow me time to grieve, Mitch. I don't want to keep thinking about this. I just want to try to relax and remember the good times Julie and I had together."

I was tapped out as far as asking more questions, so I left early and headed home to make dinner and prepare for the trick-or-treaters. I had a box of fifty small packages of potato chips. I couldn't get a smaller box. I usually ate most of the leftovers. Oh well, the packages were tiny. The first kids came at around six o'clock, and the last ones at around eight o'clock. I gave out twenty-three packages. Then I had four myself with a couple of beers. That was my Halloween.

CHAPTER 36

Thursday morning was cloudy and drizzly. It fit my mood. I was nowhere on the case and going nowhere because there was nowhere to go.

I had never wanted to quit after being on a case for such a short period of time. Well, I didn't actually want to give up, but when there seemed like nothing to do, my mind started telling me to get out and do something else.

So, after my usual morning of breakfast and newspaper, I brought up my spreadsheet of all the possible suspects. I don't know how many times I had looked at it. The only two who stood out were Alan Wilson and Yuri Moldev, but even then, they didn't look more than forty percent to me.

It was too bad we couldn't get DNA samples from all the men who had been involved with Julie. I had an idea about that and decided to call the two detectives on the case to see what they thought of it. I was not optimistic.

I called the division and was surprised to hear that both detectives were in. The desk sergeant asked which one I wanted. I said that I would try Detective Puccillo. I would try her any day, but I didn't tell him that.

"Mr. Watson, I presume, what can I do for you?"

Lots, I thought, but I held my tongue. "Hi, Beth. Has there been any progress on the Miller case? Anything new?"

"No, Mitch, nothing. Even if there was, I might not be able to tell you, but nothing new has surfaced."

"It's too bad we can't get DNA from some of the possible suspects."

"We need more evidence, Mitch. DNA is a very personal thing, and you can't go around intruding on a person's private life without due cause."

I was going to tell her my idea, but after what she said, I thought about it and knew it wouldn't go over very well. Instead, I asked her to keep in touch and then hung up.

My idea was to meet Alan Wilson one Tuesday night and sit down with him for a bit. When he went to the washroom, I would take his glass or bottle, put it under my jacket, and walk out with it. I would then take it to Jan and ask her to check for a match with DNA from the fetus.

I wondered if Jan would do it. It would be against the rules. She was only supposed to work on official business. I didn't think the detectives would let her go ahead. Oh well, it would have been fun to try.

So, what to do for the rest of the day? I had the two university students to see that night. Susan had already let me know that they would be happy to meet me.

In the morning, I did odd jobs around the house. In the afternoon, I went to the casino to spend some of Henry's money. I figured I might as well put it to some good use. Surprisingly, I was up on the day, and it put me in a good mood for the evening.

Susan had talked to the two university students and had given me their address. She said they expected to see me at around seven-thirty p.m. Their names were Betty Wansall and Ashley Gibbons. I arrived at their three-story walkup apartment with a couple of minutes to spare.

On the way there, I thought about how the women I had met

in the investigation had all been very good looking. Susan was quite sexy but seemed to have lost her interest in men, Bonnie the stripper and Beth the detective were also good looking in their own ways. Would Betty and Ashley continue the trend? I couldn't wait to find out.

Their apartment building was in a middle-class area just outside the downtown core on the west side. I buzzed their room, number 103, and a female voice said, "Come on down," and the inner door clicked.

Although such buildings were called walkups because there were no elevators, the ground floor was usually a few steps below ground level. So, I actually walked down and then along to 103.

The door opened as I got there, and then I got the shock of my life. The two young women standing there were the opposite of what I had been thinking. One was chubby, and the other was skinny. I mean quite chubby and quite skinny. The one who introduced herself as Betty was the chubby one. Ashley was the skinny one.

They both had fairly straight brown hair, and they both wore glasses. Betty was wearing an orange sweater, probably one she'd been wearing the day before for Halloween. They were both wearing blue jeans. Ashley was wearing a black T-shirt, which she couldn't really fill out.

They both smiled and welcomed me in. The living room was a colorful place. A burgundy sofa, light-brown chairs, light-green carpet, and drapes. Decorations on the walls were mostly university mementos. It was all quite cheerful. They were both cheerful and happy. They were bright, easy to talk to, and made me feel at home during the short time I was there. As they say, you can't judge a book by its cover.

At first glance, I had wondered how Julie could have been happy going around with those two, but their cheerful personalities were infectious.

They asked me if I would like a drink. I asked them what they had and when they got around to saying beer, I said okay. The beer was a lot heartier than I was used to. It went down well, though.

Betty started things off. "So, what would you like to know? What should we zero in on?"

I had already thought about that. "What was Julie like when she was with you? Did she talk about her marriage? What were her dreams for the future? Were there any incidents? Any troublemakers or bad incidents where you can remember any of the people involved?"

Ashley said, "Julie was always happy when she was with us. Remember, it was only once a season, so it was a terrific break from her humdrum life."

"Why do you say she had a humdrum life?"

"The answer to that leads into the next two questions you asked. Her husband, Henry, is a decent guy but is happy with an uneventful life. Julie was the opposite. They never should have married.

"Julie spent most of the time on the weekends with either Henry's family or her sister's family. Five days a week, she worked in a flower shop. How exciting can that be? Two nights a week, she was taking courses. Only on Tuesdays when she went out with Susan could she let her hair down and have fun. So, to me that was a humdrum life."

Betty was anxious to say something and chimed in. "We had fun together. No matter what we did, we were just ourselves. We could say what we liked, and none of us ever got upset with each other. I can't think of any bad incidents. Can you, Ashley?"

"No. I'm trying to think. No. There was nothing, really. There never was a time for anyone to get upset with any of us."

"Yes, but did Julie ever speak of any trouble she ever had with anyone?" I asked

They thought about that. They looked at each other and then thought again. Ashley spoke first. "She did mention the two men she worked with in the flower shop were jerks sometimes. She said she could handle it, though. Also, they were both out a lot of the time."

Betty added, "Yes, there was that, but I think she had it under control. Maybe it could be worth looking into."

I mentioned that I had already done that and didn't think there was much follow-up I could do.

We talked a bit more about their time together with Julie and a bit about their own lives. They both had office jobs, and from the sound of it, their offices were active places with plenty of socializing with their coworkers. So, they didn't think of their lives as humdrum.

Then Betty startled me by saying, "You know, the four of us have nicknames. Do you want to hear what they are?"

I told her that I would love to hear their nicknames, and I had no idea what they would be.

With a big smile on her face, Betty said, "Lisa, who I understand you will see tomorrow, is 'Brains.' That's because she researches all the different events we can go to and recommends where we go. We trust her completely. Julie was 'Flygirl' because she was always on about flying away somewhere. I am 'Joker' because I'm the life of the party, always telling jokes." She laughed at herself.

I could imagine that. Chubby people often seemed to be happy.

Ashley broke in. "Guess who I am?"

I said that I had no idea.

"Orgy," she said, and they both looked at each other and laughed.

I must have looked stunned.

Ashley said, "It's not what you think or would like to think. It's short for organizer. After Lisa recommends something to do, I do the organizing and handle all the details."

Phew, I thought. I had been trying not to think of the other possibility. I could see how they could have fun with their nicknames.

We talked a little more. They asked me if I would like another drink. I told them no thanks.

They walked me out to the front door of the building and waved goodbye. The evening was a very nice surprise. I really liked those young women.

On the way home, I thought about the next day. I would have to bite the bullet and tell Henry that I couldn't do anything more. That would be tough. I would have to figure out a decent way to tell him. I didn't see how I could put a positive spin on it. I would go see him in the afternoon.

In the evening, I would go to the restaurant that Yuri Moldev said he was in on the Friday when Julie was killed. I hoped the same waitress would be on shift, or else it would be another waste of time.

Then it would be on to see Lisa, the last of the university students. Maybe the "Brain" would be able to come up with something that the other girls couldn't. I was beginning to suspect that there was nothing there to come up with, but I had to try every possibility.

At the moment, it was time to head home, have a couple of beers, and then hit the sack. I could still taste that craft beer I'd had at Betty and Ashley's place. I wondered how many of them they could drink in a night. Maybe more than me, I thought. Then I remembered they had a designated driver every time the four of them went out. That was a good thing. Smart girls.

CHAPTER 37

On Friday morning, before I did anything else, I checked the weather forecast on the news channel. The day before, they'd been saying that a large storm was heading our way.

Sure enough, it would start in the early afternoon and continue until near midnight. High winds and heavy downpours were expected. I couldn't let it change my plans for the day.

I planned to see Henry in the afternoon and tell him that I was ending my investigation. I knew it wouldn't go over well, and I was not looking forward to our meeting. I had to do it, though. I would tell him that the detectives were continuing the investigation, but I wouldn't tell him they were no further ahead than I was.

At around dinnertime, I would go to the restaurant where Yuri said he was when Julie was killed. Hopefully, the waitress would be there to confirm or disprove his alibi.

At night, I would see the last university student, Lisa the "Brain." Unless any of that provided new information, my investigation would be over.

At around two p.m. I arrived at Henry's house. It had already started to rain, and the wind had increased over the last hour. It was going to be difficult driving that night.

I got straight to the point with Henry. I went through everything I had done and what I had found out. I also told him that I couldn't see any way of following up on what I knew. The detectives had all kinds of databases they could look through to see if there was any useful information on any of the persons of interest.

To my surprise, Henry seemed to understand. He thanked me for what I had done and asked me to keep in touch with the detectives. I said that I would. He even asked me to stay for dinner. I said that normally I would but that I had to check out one final alibi at a restaurant.

I stayed with Henry for the rest of the afternoon, and we chatted about several things. When I left, I felt sad about the whole thing, empty and depressed. I hoped the trip to the restaurant would provide some useful information and provide a bright side. At the moment, I could use it.

The restaurant was on the east side in a low-income district. The building was on the corner of an intersection with parking around the back. The front was brick veneer with neon Coke and Budweiser signs in the windows.

I walked in and looked around. It was a typical family restaurant. There were booths along the walls and tables in the center. The tabletops were all Formica with a red-and-white pattern set in them.

The weather had reduced the number of customers. It was only half full, which was probably unusual for a Friday night.

I looked around for the waitress that Yuri had said was called Indy and was the only Black waitress there. I think someone classier than Yuri might have been able to come up with a different description. However, his description did help me spot her.

I took a booth in the area she was serving. She came over and handed me a menu. "Coffee?" she asked. She had a slim build and a pleasant, smiling face.

"Yes, and a hot beef sandwich with mashed," I said without looking at the menu. If a family restaurant didn't have that, they were not a family restaurant.

"Okay, be right back," she said, whisking the menu away. She came back with the coffee right away and then the meal a few minutes later. I am always amazed at how fast short-order cooks can be.

I finished everything off and waited until she came back to collect the dishes. She smiled at me. "Can I get you anything else?"

I got to the point quickly. "No thanks, but I have a quick question for you. I'm a private investigator, and a person I am investigating said he was here two weeks ago Friday, and you served him. His name is Yuri Moldev. He is Russian and is about six feet tall. He has black hair and a lot of it on his face too. Do you remember him?"

Indira thought for a moment. "I think I know who you mean, but I don't remember the last time I saw him. It could have been that weekend, but it could have been Friday or Saturday. Those are usually busy days. Many customers come and go, but I do not keep track of them. Sorry."

I gave her my card and asked her to think about it some more and if anything occurred to her, to let me know.

She said, "Okay," then walked away.

A few minutes later, she came back with the bill. I gave her a ten-dollar tip, hoping it might refresh her memory.

So, there it was, another possible lead that didn't work out. I walked out into the wind and rain. I was glad I was wearing a warmer windbreaker, but I never wear a hat, and my hair was blowing all over my face. I was nearly soaked by the time I got to my car.

I had some time before I was supposed to see Lisa, so I drove home, changed my clothes, and dried my hair. One more person to see, and that would end my investigation.

Lisa Peters lived in a condo in a newly developed area at the north end of the city. It was a middle-income or perhaps middle-to-upper-income part of the city.

Betty and Ashley had told me that Lisa was a bank manager and was a prime candidate to be an assistant vice president for the region by the time she was thirty. Her nickname, "Brains," seemed quite appropriate.

I buzzed her unit in the lobby, and she buzzed me in. The building had seven floors, and she was on the sixth. She had the door open for me as I walked down the hallway.

I said hello to a very professional looking young lady. She was blonde, and her curly hair hung down to her shoulders. She had sparkling blue eyes and wore medium-red lipstick, a tight white blouse, and a tight, knee-length black skirt, which made her look smart and fit.

She welcomed me into a classy living room where the predominant colors were silver and black. The hardwood floor had black area rugs, the sofa was black, and the recliner had a silver cover. Another armchair was a light-gray color. The coffee table had a glass top. It was all classy but not my idea of a warm home environment.

Lisa motioned for me to sit anywhere, so I chose the recliner. She asked me what I would like to drink—wine, scotch, vodka, or beer? The atmosphere seemed to suggest wine, probably red wine.

I told her a glass of red would be nice. She said she was having the same thought. I was thinking she probably had that thought often.

She went into the dining room and returned with two glasses of dark red wine. She handed one to me and then sat on the sofa, holding the other one. She spoke first. "I understand you have already seen the rest of our little group. What do you think of them?"

Tough question. While Betty and Ashley were similar in some ways, when I included Julia and Lisa, it made for a very mixed group. It was amazing that they had come together and stayed together. So, I decided to be polite. "All four of you are extremely interesting young women. I can't imagine what it was like when all four of you were together." That was at least the truth.

Lisa smiled. "You know, it was amazing. We got along well and enjoyed our differences as well as the things we liked to do together. We will all miss Julie very much. Speaking of her, that is why you're here, so how can I help?"

I asked her basically the same questions I'd asked the others. There was not much difference in her answers. But at the end, she surprised me. "What about Henry? Is he a suspect?"

I said he was not one to me but that the detectives would have him under some suspicion since he was the husband.

Then she said, "I think he should be the prime suspect. I feel sure that he is responsible for the pregnancy and probably wanted her to end it. They had an argument, he threatened her, and killed her."

Wow, I thought, *that is a harsh statement.* "Why do you think that, Lisa?"

"Because Julie told me her marriage was a mistake, and she wanted out. She said she had not said that to anyone else but knew I would take her seriously. I think you and the police should investigate him thoroughly."

As far as I was concerned, she was wrong, and I couldn't see how we could investigate him further anyway. So again, being polite, I said, "I'll tell the detectives your feelings, and I'm sure they will do everything they can to get to the truth."

We didn't talk much more after that, so I finished my wine, which was very good, thanked her for it and all her thoughts, and bid her goodnight.

Her comments about Henry disturbed me. I tried to remember what Susan had said about Henry when we first got together. It seemed to me that she had mentioned that the marriage was not good, but she had not been as harsh about the situation as Lisa.

Since Susan had been Julie's best friend, from what I had been led to believe, I decided to give her a call and go over it again.

She answered on the first ring. "Hi, Mitch. Have you solved the case already?"

"No, but I just got through a meeting with Lisa, and she was very serious about her thoughts of Henry being involved in Julie's pregnancy and her death. She said that Julie had told her that her marriage was dead, and she wanted out and that Julie had not told anyone else about it. What do you have to say about that?"

"Well, Mitch, I did say something along those lines, but I didn't think, and I still do not think, that Henry was involved. He's not that sort of person, and he loved Julie so much. She could do no wrong as far as he was concerned. I know Lisa is smart, but I think she's wrong on this. So, where are you at on it? Anything new you can tell me?"

"Unfortunately, no. Nothing leads anywhere. I have spoken to the detectives, and they say the same thing. They don't have to tell me anything, but I think there's nothing to tell." I didn't want to tell her I was dropping the investigation, so I just said goodnight and hung up.

CHAPTER 38

Saturday morning turned out to be the opposite of the day before. The rain and the wind had all gone. There was a clear blue sky, and the sun was a red glow high above. It was a little bit cooler but still a lovely day.

All I had on my schedule was dinner with Mindy, the librarian. I had not made a reservation anywhere, so in the afternoon I would go looking at a few restaurants.

After a morning of doing practically nothing, I drove out to the lake. It was a very pretty area, and several restaurants had been built near the water's edge.

Most were on the east side of the lake facing west, which allowed patrons to observe a glorious sunset. Yesterday, though, would have been a complete washout.

As I drove around, I saw Italian, Japanese, Chinese, and Mexican restaurants. Also, there was a steakhouse and a seafood restaurant. All of them had their menus posted on the front windows.

I felt like having a good seafood dinner. The restaurant was called Lakeshore Seafood. Seemed rather contradictory to me. I couldn't imagine a restaurant being called Seashore Lakefood either.

I checked the menu, found some dishes I liked, and went inside to see if they took reservations. They did, it being Saturday, their busiest time.

I tried to remember what time the sun started to go down. It was early November, so I made reservations for two at six p.m. That would allow time to see at least part of the sunset over the lake.

The thing to do now was to call Mindy and let her know I would pick her up at five-fifteen p.m. It wouldn't hurt to get to the restaurant early. I called her, and she said she was good with seafood and was looking forward to seeing me.

So, what to wear? It was a first date and a dinner date, so smart casual was fine, but how smart and how casual? I didn't want to wear any of my usual windbreakers, and I didn't want to wear a suit and tie either. I had two blazers, a burgundy one and a medium-blue one. I chose the burgundy one with a matching open-necked burgundy shirt and light-gray pants.

I picked Mindy up right on time. She was wearing a yellow-print knee-length dress. The print was a design of colorful autumn leaves. Her only makeup was red lipstick, which matched some of the leaves on her dress. The words "glamorous" or "gorgeous" didn't quite fit. Mindy was just a very pretty lady whom I was honored to be with.

It was a fairly quiet drive to the restaurant. I wanted to save as much conversation as possible for before, during, and after our meal.

We were seated in a small banquette that overlooked the lake. The sun seemed ready to start its decline.

The restaurant had all the usual seaside décor, such as ships, sand, sun, and fish in pictures on the walls. Most of the tables had blue-and-white checkered tablecloths.

Our server was a young woman wearing a mid-thigh dress. I figured she was probably a university student, helping to pay for her education. I asked her for the wine list. My choice was a New Zealand sauvignon blanc. It was okay with Mindy, and I asked the server to give us some time before we ordered our meals.

I have always thought that when telling stories about what I have done and where I have been, I should always try to find humorous bits to include. It makes for a more enjoyable and relaxing conversation.

Mindy had not been to nearly as many places or done as much as I had, so it was up to me to keep the evening rolling along smoothly.

I was able to do it for a while, and Mindy listened intently. Then I tried to draw her out with questions like "What countries would you like to visit and why?" So, everything seemed to be going well when it suddenly went wrong.

My phone rang! I couldn't believe it. I was sure I had it turned off. I always hate it when I'm with someone and their phone rings and their response is, "Sorry, I have to take this," leaving me twiddling my thumbs. Politeness and manners seem to be forgotten when it comes to cell phones.

I pulled it out, glanced at it, and saw that it was from Susan. *Why now?*

I said, "Sorry, Mindy. It's about Julie." Then I answered the call. "Susan, I'm with someone now, Can this wait?"

"Sorry, Mitch, but I thought you should know. Your friend, Tony, has been going around saying he's working for you and asking questions of the people of interest. I did tell him a few things initially because I thought it was alright. Now I think he's gone too far, and I don't believe that he is actually working for you."

Not now, I thought. I didn't want to hear any of that at the moment. Actually, I didn't want to hear any of it at all. I was really mad at it. I calmed down enough to tell Susan, "Thanks for letting me know. I'll call him in the morning." That was all I could say. I hung up and stared at the table.

Mindy broke into my thoughts. "Bad news?"

"It was something I wasn't expecting, and it doesn't help anything," I said. "Let's forget it and get on with our evening."

I looked out the window and saw the sun's glow was spreading across the water. I tried to brighten things up. "You know, Mindy, this is just as nice as the sunsets at Key West or the Pacific Ocean." It really wasn't, but I figured she had never been to any of those places.

"Yes, Mitch, it is very, very nice," was all she could come up with.

I couldn't add anything more, so I signaled for our server to take our orders.

We skipped the appetizers. Mindy ordered shrimp Alfredo linguini. I ordered tilapia stuffed with scallops and topped with lobster. Wow, a triple header!

I tried to keep the conversation light, but the mention of Julie had changed the atmosphere. I could feel it, but I couldn't do much about it.

Our orders came, and we ate mostly in silence. I poured us each another glass of wine, leaving probably another full glass in the bottle. I ate everything on my plate including the peppers and a baked potato. Mindy said her meal was very good, but she couldn't eat it all. The linguini would have been filling.

I offered Mindy dessert, and I knew the answer before she said it. "No thanks." I asked her if she would help me finish off the wine, and I got the same response. Seeing that I was driving, I decided to let the rest stay in the bottle. I didn't want to leave right away, but what could we talk about?

How about her father? He lived next door to Henry and Julie, he worked different shifts, and maybe he saw things sometimes that no one else saw.

I asked Mindy what he did in his spare time at home. She replied it was mostly watching TV or reading.

"Did he see or have many conversations with Julie?" I had talked to him before, but I was hoping for some new information.

"No, they never crossed paths at all as far as I know. He might have seen her in their backyard occasionally, as his bedroom overlooks it. If she was sunbathing in a bikini, it might have gotten his attention, but he never would have mentioned it."

Then she seemed to realize what she had said and gave me

an angry look. "Why do you keep asking questions about him and Julie?"

I realized that I had gone too far. I explained again how none of the other neighbors were helpful and that he might have known something that was different.

It didn't work; I could tell. She looked at me suspiciously and said nothing. I'd blown it. Sometimes I'm smart and other times not so much. I signaled the server for the bill, paid it, and we left.

I drove her home with little conversation. She thanked me for a nice evening, got out, and never looked back. I was angry with myself, and I was angry with Tony. I would let it all out on him in the morning. Maybe that would make me feel better.

◆

CHAPTER 39

◆

On Sunday morning, I got up and looked out the window. I could hardly see anything. It was very foggy. We get a few days like that occasionally, usually in October and November.

I did my usual morning routine—shower, get dressed, breakfast, and read the paper. Sometimes I also watched the news to see if anything had happened overnight. Finally, I checked my email.

After all that I phoned Tony. I was ready to blast him for saying he was working for me. I would tell him to stop playing detective.

My call went to voicemail. I left a message to call me back as soon as I could. I thought about texting him, but I wanted to hear his voice. I would give him until early afternoon, and if I had not heard from him, I would try again.

It was the last day of my investigation of the Julie Miller case. I was looking forward to my new job the following morning, working undercover in a warehouse, trying to find out who was behind the items going missing.

I studied the spreadsheet that showed all the persons of interest one last time. Nothing stood out. If the detectives with all their tools and databases couldn't come up with something, I didn't feel so bad.

At two o'clock in the afternoon, I picked up my phone to call Tony again. Before I even dialed, it rang. It was Tony.

When he spoke, it didn't sound like Tony; his voice was desperate.

"Mitch, I'm scared. I found out something that you should know. I think the person knows that I know. There could be someone following me. I don't want to get you into danger. Meet me tonight at the 'ghost' at seven o'clock. Don't be late. I can't hang around." *Click.* He had hung up.

I hadn't said a word. Tony didn't give me a chance. I was stunned. Now I was confused and getting angrier. There were too many questions in my mind.

Why would he not tell me what he knew over the phone? How could he have found anything out that I couldn't? I was a trained and experienced investigator, and he was an artist. Maybe we should change jobs. The problem was, I couldn't draw a straight line. In school, art was my worst subject.

The "ghost" that Tony referred to was an unfinished condo in a valley on the south side of the lake. The developer had run out of money, there were legal contract issues, and it had been left with just the framework of three stories completed. Fancy bricks had been brought in and stockpiled near the building. They were supposed to start adding them to parts of the completed area to show potential buyers how attractive the finished product would look. At least, that was the plan.

The original boarding that had been up when the building was started had become dirty, broken, vandalized, and just plain ugly. It was replaced by a wire fence, which was not very efficient at keeping out trespassers.

In different areas the wire had been cut, and large holes were quite apparent. Teenagers met there, usually at night, and amused themselves by hurling bricks at the concrete. The result was an area that looked like a bombed-out site from the Second World War. The dysfunctional city council couldn't come up with a solution. They didn't want to spend anything to clean up the mess.

Normally it would take me about thirty minutes to drive there.

However, in the fog, I figured at least another fifteen minutes. I left my house at six-ten and arrived at the "ghost" at six-fifty-five. I parked at the curb. There were no other vehicles around. At least I couldn't see any in the fog. I also couldn't see the building, but I thought I knew exactly where I was. If I walked at a right angle from my car, straight ahead, I should come to about the middle of the east side.

The fog was much thicker there. In London, England, it would be called a pea-souper. It was an extremely thick pea-souper.

I could barely see anything in front of me. Walking with my right hand stuck out in front of me and my left hand touching the wall, I started to feel uneasy and had a growing sense of foreboding.

I was cursing Tony under my breath. This was crazy. He should have thought of any place but there. I made up my mind that as soon as I saw him, I would tell him to follow me back to the car.

It was a relief to touch the wall, but the sense of foreboding would not go away. I tried to think positive, but there was nothing positive about that place.

Inching my way along the wall, I reached the northeast corner and called out to Tony that I was there and that I would wait a minute for him.

He didn't answer. I waited for what I thought was about two minutes and then started walking along the north wall. It was not warm, but I started sweating. I could feel it in my underarms, my face, and my hands. I felt even worse than before. I had been involved in attempted muggings, domestic disputes that turned violent, and had even faced people with guns, but I had never felt like that before. It was the fear of the unknown, but I had never thought it would get to me like that. I had to grit my teeth and get tough, which wasn't easy when I couldn't see a foot in front of me, and I didn't know what lay ahead.

I came to the northwest corner and called for Tony again. I waited another couple of minutes, but nothing happened. Two more walls to go, then I was getting out of there.

I came to the southwest corner and did the same routine with the same result. By then I was three quarters of the way around the building. One more length of the building, and I was going home to have a few stiff drinks. Maybe I would call him when I got home, and maybe I would not. Thinking of those drinks buoyed my spirits. Maybe I would have more than a few.

I turned the corner, looking ahead, when I tripped over something. I was halfway back up when I thought I heard something behind me. I tried to turn, but then I felt a terrific blow across the back of my head, followed by sharp pain and then total blackness.

CHAPTER 40

There was a white blur in front of me. Where had it come from? I strained my neck, trying to get a better look, but it hurt my head, so I gave up.

A female voice came from the blur. It said, "Finally."

What did that mean? I couldn't think. I was too tired. I closed my eyes.

I have no idea how long it was before I opened my eyes again. This time there was no blur. I was in some kind of a room, but what kind, I didn't know.

There was the sound of machines in the background. Maybe I was in a factory—why would I be in a factory? I could see I was lying in a bed. Where was I? I started to realize that I knew nothing.

Then it seemed like out of nowhere a woman in a white outfit came and stood by my bedside. I turned my head and saw a middle-aged woman with gray hair peering down at me.

"Mr. Watson, I presume. I'm Nurse Ellen. I am so glad you're awake. We have been waiting patiently for this."

I wondered who "we" were.

Nurse Ellen continued, "The doctor is on the other side of the unit. I'll bring him over."

Okay, I had one answer. I was in a hospital. Where it was and how I got there, I didn't know. Hopefully, the doctor had all the answers.

A short, middle-aged man wearing a white hospital coat over a blue shirt and gray pants came into the room and approached my bedside. He was Asian with a small build and graying hair.

"Mr. Watson, I'm Doctor Hakiota, and you are in Cairnford General Hospital. You have suffered a severe concussion. Another fraction of an inch, and you would have had a broken skull, and you would not be here. You would be in the morgue. You are a very lucky man."

I wondered if I could talk. I tried and found I could. "That's funny, Doctor. I sure don't feel lucky. I feel just the opposite. I hope I never get this lucky again."

That felt good. The fact that I could still come up with a smartass remark made me feel that at least part of me had not changed.

Dr. Hakiota ignored my comment and continued. "Here is what will happen. For today and tomorrow, you will be monitored closely. All you need to do is sleep, which is the best medicine for you at the moment. The machines you hear in the background are tracking your blood pressure, your heartbeat, and other vital signs. In a couple of days, we will start a food program other than the intravenous. Just liquids at first, like soup and juice. Then afterwards, pudding, Jell-O, and the like. If we gave you a roast-beef sandwich now, you would be nauseated and unable to eat it.

"Speaking of that, here is a warning for the future, which will be repeated before you leave. Do not do anything that requires exertion. Do not worry, do not study for long periods, avoid arguments, and do not get excited. Also, do not use cigarettes, alcohol, or caffeine. On those three items, I suggest you never use them again.

"If you do anything that I have mentioned, one or more of the following bad events could happen—headaches, nausea, panic attacks, fatigue, and depression. None of those things are likely to happen here; the danger is when you are starting to feel better and want to do more. You'll have to be very careful to not overdo it.

"Depending on how you come through this week, I hope to have you up and able to take a few steps in the hallway next week. If that progresses, then we can see about sending you home. By the way, Mr. Watson, do you have anyone at home who could look after you for a while?"

"No, Doctor, I do not."

"Very well. We will have to contact a health agency to have someone with you twenty-four hours a day for the first couple of weeks after you're released. Anyway, that's all in the future. Progress is usually slow in these situations, but your vitals are good, and you're reasonably fit, so we shall see. If all goes well along the way, I suggest you may be ninety to ninety-five percent recovered in six months. But you may always have some symptoms, depending on your lifestyle."

"Thanks, Doctor, for all the info. It's made me feel a lot more confident about my future. Let me ask you, what day is it?"

"It is now Wednesday afternoon. You were found Sunday night. That reminds me, there are two people who wish to see you. They are two detectives from Division Nine. I told them not today or tomorrow but maybe the day after that. Apart from them, no other visitors.

"Mr. Watson, we have seven doctors and numerous nurses working different shifts in this unit. Therefore, you will not always see Nurse Ellis or me. However, all the medical staff will have up-to-date medical information on your condition. You are in good hands here."

I thanked him again, then they both left, but the nurse was stationed right outside my door.

All that info helped my spirits. However, not having cigarettes, alcohol, or caffeine in the future was bad news. Especially alcohol and caffeine. We would see. If I completely recovered, maybe I could slowly start back on them again.

Meanwhile, I had to do everything the good doctor said and do everything in my power to get back to where I wanted to be. Whatever it took.

CHAPTER 41

The next two days went pretty much the way the doctor had indicated, the boredom only interrupted by tests and scans. I started eating again, and everything went down well and stayed down.

I didn't keep track of the days, but I think it was Friday that the detectives were allowed to see me. The doctor told them that they had just ten minutes to talk to me.

Beth was wearing a light-blue pantsuit, and Patrick was wearing a navy-blue suit. Both of them looked smart and professional, as usual.

Beth spoke first. "I won't ask how you are because you wouldn't be here if you were okay. However, the doctor said that you're improving, so I hope you will be out of here soon."

"Yes, well, the sooner the better, but it is nice to see you both again. Can you tell me what happened?"

"We were hoping you could tell us," Patrick replied. "Why were you there in the first place?"

I told them about Susan's phone call telling me that Tony was investigating on his own and saying he was working for me. Then I told them about his call to meet him at the "ghost" and described how I'd tripped and when I was part way up, got hit on the back of my head.

The detectives looked at each other. "What did you trip over?" Beth asked.

"I don't know. It was so foggy. There was a lot of debris around, and I was looking ahead, trying to find Tony."

The detectives looked at each other again. Finally, Beth said, "I hate to tell you this, Mitch, but you fell over Tony's foot. He was lying on the ground to your left, and you tripped over his shoe. Tony is dead, Mitch. He had a fractured skull."

I was stunned. My heart started beating faster, and I didn't feel so good. A dizzy feeling crept over me. The nurse was at the back of the room. I called out to her, "Nurse, would you please get the doctor? I don't feel so good." She looked at the vitals on the board behind me and rushed out of the room.

The detectives were concerned. Beth said, "What is it? I'm so sorry to have to tell you that news."

I told her that I was not prepared for it, and it seemed to have shaken my system.

The doctor came bustling in and asked what happened. I told him that I had received bad news and, in my condition, it had shaken me up. I knew my heart was beating faster, and I was worried, even though I knew that would only make it worse.

He glared at the detectives. "That's it. Leave now," he said in a stern voice.

Beth said, "So sorry, Mitch. We will talk to you at a later date."

They left with the nurse and the doctor glaring at them.

The doctor looked at the numbers on the board behind me. "Mr. Watson, please calm down, and try not to think about what you just heard. Think about all the things you're going to do once you're out of here. You have been doing so well, so let's keep it going. I'll give you something for now. You can see, though, why we are not allowing visitors."

With that he went over to the nurse and talked quietly with her. She left and came back with a couple of pills for me and said they might make me sleepy. They did, and when I woke up, the daylight was gone. The night nurse was on, a young Jamaican woman called Rina. I asked her if I could have something light to eat. She said sure and came back with a tuna sandwich and a glass of apple juice. It hit the spot.

I lay there thinking about what I would do when I got out, as if I were in prison. The doctor was right; it kept my mind off other things. After a while I went back to sleep again.

CHAPTER 42

The rest of my time in the hospital went pretty much the way the doctor had said it would. By the end of my first week there, I was eating solid foods and had started walking around a bit. I did exactly as I had been told. I didn't worry, think hard, or concentrate on anything.

The doctor again mentioned all the things that might happen. Apparently, there were many of the same symptoms in concussions, but they could vary quite a lot with different people.

The second week I was moved over to another part of the unit because I was not critical anymore. I was allowed one visitor at a time. Henry, Jack, Doug, and Greg all came at different times. An insurance-claims manager whom I had done some work for dropped by too.

I was told Tony's murder and my concussion had made the headlines in the newspaper. It had all been connected to Julie's death. The investigation was ongoing. Of course, that meant there had been no progress.

I had a surprise visitor. It was the man I had been going to work for the Monday after the weekend I was meeting Tony. He said he had been shocked to see it in the newspaper but that he'd had to get someone else for the job. I told him I understood.

My favorite visitor was Jan. She brightened up the room. We told jokes, but she told me to not laugh too hard. Jan and the detective were the only two women who came to see me. I was disappointed.

At the end of the second week, Henry came around to pick me up and take me home. A woman from a health service was there to meet me. She said there would be someone there night and day for at least two weeks.

Her name was Agnes. She was a portly woman in her fifties, a real mother hen. She said that three people would rotate. Life was going to be different, I realized. *Oh well,* I thought. *I'll just have to get used to it.*

The first thing I did when I got in was phone my sister in England. I told her what had happened and that I was on the road to recovery. She wondered if she should come over. I told her not to, but when I was well enough, I would go over there, probably in the spring.

I followed all the routines and the therapy. After two weeks there was just one person from the health service there in the daytime. After two weeks of that, it was only two times a week.

I could do most everything for myself, excluding hard labor. I walked a little farther each week, still quite slowly, though. I was taking medication and had to go back to the hospital on occasion for checks and scans.

Days became weeks, and weeks became months, and I could feel myself gradually getting stronger, all the bad symptoms subsiding.

After four months I still had not had coffee or alcohol. I decided to try decaffeinated coffee. I wanted to get back to my old lifestyle, minus some of the unhealthy things.

I walked and walked and walked. By then I thought I knew all the side streets within a five-mile radius.

I started thinking about Julie and Tony but decided to wait until six months had gone by when, hopefully, I would be back to at least ninety percent of my former self.

The next two months were quite boring. I was starting to feel that I could do anything again. However, I was doing nothing other than continually getting fit. Nothing wrong with that, but I was itching to get going.

It finally happened. Six months to the day of my concussion, I phoned Henry and told him I was ready to get back to work. He was ecstatic. He said he'd been waiting for this day. I told him I had been too. I said that he would be the first person I would talk to, so that meant it would be the first step in solving two murders. I spent the day planning who I was going to see and what I was going to do. Then I was confident that I would find the answers. *Bring the world on,* I thought. I was ready for it again.

CHAPTER 43

Henry had sold his house. He had already been a rich man, and now he was richer. His brother sold his house as well. Now, Henry, his brother, and his brother's wife had moved into a new, three-bedroom townhouse. It was smaller than what either of them had had before, but it had all the modern conveniences and was in a central, residential part of the city.

It was May 2019, and spring had sprung. The flowers were in full bloom, the tree branches were full of leaves, and the city had taken on a new look. Spring was an uplifting season.

It was a leisurely, twenty-minute drive from my place to Henry's new home. It was located in what the city liked to call a revitalized area. There were four short streets with townhouses. They all had small front and backyards.

A small business was at the end of each street. I saw a pastry shop, a drug store, a hardware store, and a dry cleaner as I drove by. New trees had been planted on each street. It was a nice area, but a big comedown from Henry's former property. I could only assume that there were too many memories of Julie there.

He saw me coming through his big bay window and greeted me warmly at the front door. He told me that his brother and his sister-in-law were out.

Henry showed me into the living room. I was surprised to see the furniture from his old house. I guess he needed some old memories. Anyway, I liked the furniture; it was comfortable and looked more like furniture than some of the new stuff coming out.

We settled in, and Henry asked if I would like coffee. I told him maybe later. We talked about the new neighborhood and what it was like living there. Then I got down to business. A few months before when Henry had visited me at home, I'd asked him about Julie's funeral. It had been held when I was in the hospital, so I couldn't attend. Henry had been reluctant to talk about it. Probably it was too soon for him to think about it. Now, six months later, I figured he should feel more comfortable discussing it.

I asked him who came to the funeral. He said that Julie's father had left the country. There were bad goings on between him and his two daughters, and Jenny didn't want him at the funeral. Their mother had remarried and was living abroad, but she came to the funeral.

Henry told me that his brother and wife, Julie's sister and husband, the poker players, Susan, university friends, the instructor from the travel classes, the two detectives, the flower shop owners but not the driver, some neighbors, and a few others he didn't know were there.

I asked him if there was anything unusual that stood out about any of the people he didn't recognize. He said there were two women who were very emotional, even more than family members. One was middle aged and wore a veil, so he couldn't describe her very well. The other one was a young woman about Julie's age who was clearly very upset.

I asked Henry if he'd had a chance to talk to either of them after the funeral, but he said they'd both left immediately when the funeral was over.

It seemed to me that this was two leads to follow up on, but how? Then I thought of the visitor's book and wondered if they had signed it. Henry said there were no female names that he didn't recognize.

That meant that they didn't want to be identified. Why not? I would have to find out.

We talked a bit more. I wanted to know about Tony. What did Henry know about him, and what could Tony have seen that got him killed? Henry didn't have a clue. He was as shocked as everyone.

Gradually, we got away from Julie and Tony and talked about the city and the changes that were taking place. Henry said he was in a more comfortable frame of mind, and he was even looking at volunteer job opportunities. I wished him well, told him I would keep in touch, and then let myself out.

CHAPTER 44

That had been a good first step. New leads to follow up. I thought about the two women at the funeral. It occurred to me that maybe the detectives had noticed them and had talked to them. My next step was to give them a call.

The desk sergeant said that the detectives were both out, but he would tell them that I had called. I was regretting that I had not become more familiar with either one, especially Beth, so they would let me phone or text them directly.

I realized I had not been downtown or visited the C Section for six months. I wondered how the demolition and rebuilding of the area was progressing. I decided to find out.

A lot had been done in the six months that I was recuperating. The demolitions had all been done, and new buildings, including several condos, were in different stages of completion.

There were several empty stores. They would be filled by the time people started to take up residence in the condos. For the moment, it was an incomplete picture.

As I exited the area, I noticed that on the north and east sides, farther out, some of the old tacky stores had started to appear. I wondered if the muggers and drug dealers had returned. Those types were like roaches and bed bugs. Clear one area, and they popped up in another.

I drove around aimlessly for a while, taking in all the places I had frequented in the past. Mostly it was same old, same old, but that was okay. Cairnford had some nice areas—streets, parks, malls, and plazas. It was good to get out and around again.

I thought about lunch and wondered if the restaurant where I'd taken Mindy would be open at that time of day. I drove to the lake and had a look. Yes, it was. I didn't know why I wanted to go there. We hadn't had a great experience, but it wasn't the restaurant's fault.

I ordered water, decaffeinated coffee, and lobster rolls. Very nice but not filling, so I had strawberry shortcake for dessert. It sure beat anything I had been making for myself at home.

By early afternoon I was back home when my phone rang. I figured it would be one of the detectives. I was hoping for Beth, but it was Patrick. I asked him if they would be in the office for the rest of the day and, if so, if I come down and talk to them for a while. He said, "Okay."

Beth and Patrick were at their desks in their usual smart business attire. I thought maybe I should wear a jacket and tie sometimes when I met them. Maybe I would get a little more respect. We got along reasonably well, but I didn't recall any time they'd gone out of their way for me.

We exchanged greetings and then Beth said, "What's on your mind, Mitch?"

I told them that I was back on Julie's case, and I was also investigating Tony's killing. I asked them if they had any new developments.

Patrick spoke up, "No, not yet."

That was too short and abrupt for me. I was starting to get angry. "So, are you regarding them as cold cases already?"

Beth noted my attitude. "No, Mitch. They are just inactive at this time. There are no new leads to work on."

"Well, Beth and Patrick, this is my first day back on the job, and I already have two leads that you should have already investigated.

You were both at Julie Miller's funeral. Henry said there were two women there that no one knew, and they were very emotional. Why were they there? How did they know Julie? Did you ask them?"

The detectives looked at each other. Finally, Patrick answered. "Yes, Mitch, I know who you mean. However, they both left right after the funeral. We didn't have a chance to talk to them."

A sudden thought hit me. "Did Julie have any pictures of university friends stored at her house when you first investigated?"

They looked at each other again. They did that a lot. Again, it was Patrick who spoke. "There were a few pictures from her past. We looked through those and at what was on her laptop and her cell phone. Nothing stood out. We returned everything to her husband."

I found their answers annoying. "You know what I'm getting at. Did you think of going back and seeing if the young woman at the funeral was in any of the pictures?"

If they looked at each other again, I would mention it in a sarcastic way, but Patrick just looked at me and said, "The woman at the funeral was of average height and weight and wore a black hat and coat. Tears were streaming down her face most of the time. I don't know how we could identify her from a picture from the past."

I felt like being snarly, but I still needed their help, and I would probably need it again in the future. "So, you didn't go back to check on anything. Let's talk about Tony then. What can you tell me about that investigation?"

"There were fewer leads there than in Julie Miller's case," Beth said. "He had few friends and hung out mostly with fellow artists. Apparently, Henry Miller was someone he respected, and he was nosing around trying to investigate Julie Miller's death. He must have discovered something, but we don't know what it was. That's the most I can tell you because that's all there is."

"Can you at least tell me where Tony and the other artists hung out?"

"Yes. It was at a coffee house on Gordon Street called John's Java House. Downstairs it was mostly for coffee and pastries. Upstairs they had some of their paintings on the walls, and customers could purchase them."

"Thanks for that. I know where it is. I'll follow up on the women at the funeral, and I'll visit the coffee house. If I find anything interesting, I will let you know."

That was nicer than I wanted to be. I was frustrated with their lack of information and their lack of concern about it. I knew they had all kinds of other cases on their hands, so I would have to go along with what I had. With that in mind, I got up to go, said, "See you," and walked out.

I called Henry and asked him if he knew of any photographs that Julie might have stored away anywhere. He said that some of her personal things had been thrown out, some had been recycled, and some had been kept. He would take a look.

I told him I would call him in the morning.

It was my first day back on the job, and it felt good. I didn't have much to go on, but it was a start. I needed some relaxation, so I headed for the casino. I figured I would play some blackjack and call it a day. I got up seventy-five bucks and quit before I gave it all back. Yes, it was not a bad day.

The next morning, I called Henry at nine a.m. sharp and asked him if he had found any pictures. He said he had a few and asked why I wanted to see them.

He was right. I had never bothered to tell him why I wanted them. Henry was going to have a fit. "Henry, you need to look through them to see if you recognize the young woman from the funeral who was very emotional."

"Mitch, you have to be kidding. She was all in black."

"Yes, I know. She was wearing a black hat, black coat, was of medium height, medium weight, and had tears rolling down her cheeks. I know all of that, Henry. Still, there is a chance you may recognize her, and we have to follow every lead no matter how small and unlikely it may be."

"Okay, then, are you coming over now?"

"I'll be there in thirty minutes. See you then." I hung up before he could offer any arguments.

When I got there, Henry had the photos lined upon the dining room table. He said that he had been through them, but he didn't recognize anyone as the woman from the funeral. That was not good enough for me.

"Let's go through them again."

Henry groaned and then agreed.

There were photographs from Julie's last year in high school. Then there were some from classes of the two years that she'd gone to university. There were several other pictures that were older and were probably family members from the past.

I had Henry go through each photograph and each page of photographs. I pointed out several young women who were around average height and weight. "Maybe, but I don't think so" was the best he could say about three young women from the university pages.

I had an idea. "Henry, you said that Susan and those three other girls that Julie hung out with were at the funeral. Let me take the photos with me, and I'll see if I have better luck with them."

He was fine with that. I thanked him and headed out. My next step was to start investigating Tony's death.

CHAPTER 45

I had been to Tony's apartment one time before, shortly after Julie was killed. Traffic was good at that time of morning, and I got there about fifteen minutes after I'd left Henry.

I buzzed the superintendent, told him who I was, and asked if I could come in and talk to him about Tony. He buzzed me in.

He looked like nearly all the supers I had met. Solidly built with a protruding belly, thick arms and legs, and gray, thinning hair. A black sweater and blue jeans completed the picture.

He invited me into his apartment, which I found to be similar to Tony's. About the only difference was that there was no art on the walls or anywhere else. He said it was a two-bedroom apartment, and the second bedroom was his office.

After I was seated and had declined a drink, I asked him what he knew about Tony.

"There's not much to tell," he replied. "He always paid his rent on time, and there was no loud music and no problems with any of the other tenants, so from my point of view, he was an ideal tenant."

"What about friends, people who came to see him?" I asked.

"I don't know who they were. If anyone came to see him, he would buzz them up. I wouldn't get to see anybody."

It seemed like another waste of time, but I tried one more thing. "When he came to pay the rent, did he talk about anything? I'm thinking particularly about the last two months he was here."

"No, he didn't talk much. Sometimes he would say he was off to see his friends at the coffee house. That's the one where the artists hang out."

I asked him about the people in the apartments on each side of him; perhaps they might know more about Tony.

He told me that on one side the family had moved out last month. On the other side was an auto mechanic who would not be home until the evening. I asked the super if he would contact him and ask him if it was okay if I came over that evening. He said he would.

I asked if he could think of anything else, but he said no he couldn't. I thanked him for his time and left my card in case anything occurred to him. *Extremely doubtful,* I thought.

I had nothing to do that afternoon, so I decided to go home and take a nap and then plan my next moves. Hopefully, that night I would be able to see the person in the apartment next to Tony. Then I would visit the coffee house where the artists hung out.

In the meantime, I made a list for the following days. I needed to see Susan and have her look at the photographs. Also, I needed to revisit the three other university students she hung out with.

I wanted to spend time with Jack and share my thoughts with him just like the good old days. Also, there was Frank, my detective friend. We had not talked for a long time. I thought he might be able to give me more information than the other detectives had.

It was also time to think about the house. It was May, which meant it was time to put the spring flowers in. We had at least two big nurseries in Cairnford, but I was thinking of the flower shop where Julie had worked. They didn't have all the varieties of the nurseries, but there would be enough for me, and it would be interesting to see what the owners and the driver had to say at that point.

Satisfied that doing all this would keep me busy for days, I lay down on the sofa, closed my eyes, and waited for the afternoon to turn into night.

CHAPTER 46

It was just before seven p.m. when the super called me. He told me that the person who lived next to Tony was Archie Davis. Archie said he would see me, and I should buzz his number when I arrived.

Half an hour later, I was sitting in Archie's living room. He was tall and thin, maybe in his forties, with a receding hairline and a slightly protruding stomach. He asked me how he could help.

I asked the usual questions and got the usual answers. That is, until he said, "I didn't think Tony was gay, but now I'm not so sure."

I felt a ripple run through me. This was entirely out of left field. I asked him to explain what he meant.

"There was one time when I was coming in, and Tony was going out. He had someone with him who was definitely gay. He was a big guy with blond hair. I could tell by his gestures and his voice that he was gay. Him and Tony seemed to be on good terms."

I was shocked at that. Tony was certainly not the macho type, and I suppose he could have been regarded as somewhat effeminate, but I would never have considered him to be gay or to have gay friends.

Archie didn't tell me anything else that was significant, so I thanked him and went on my way. It was time to visit the coffee house. Tomorrow I would visit the gay bars.

The coffee house was on the edge of downtown, situated in the middle of a commercial block. It was a solid brick building with a neon sign over the door, stating it was John's Java House.

I stepped inside, and immediately to my right was a medium-size room filled with people drinking coffee—at least, I assumed it was coffee. Some were eating pastries and talking to each other.

The patrons seemed to be mostly between twenty and forty years old. The dress was casual, actually very casual, with T-shirts or sweatshirts and jeans worn by the majority. It was predominantly a male clientele with only a few women to be seen.

I was told the artists' hangout was upstairs, so I headed there. The room was of a similar size to the one below, but the walls were adorned with many paintings. The majority were scenic ones. There were also some still life paintings and portraits. Prices were usually attached.

There was a counter there just like on the floor below. An elderly man reading a book was sitting behind the counter. I approached him and introduced myself, saying I was a friend of Tony's and that I was investigating his death. I asked if there was anyone there who had been friends with Tony that I could talk to.

He looked around the room. "Probably Dennis Thatcher is your best bet. I think Tony talked to him the most."

Dennis was a thin man with facial hair and glasses. He was sitting at a table at the back of the room, talking to a younger man who looked like he could be his son. Their facial features were similar.

I went over and introduced myself, then told them why I was there. Dennis said the younger man was his nephew, Tyler, who had been curious about the place and had come for a visit.

I asked Dennis what he and Tony had talked about. He thought for a minute and said, "Mainly two things—art and politics. Tony sure didn't like our local government. I don't think anybody does, but they get voted in all the time."

I knew the problem, and I wanted to put my two cents in. "It's name recognition. As soon as an election is over, they are out all the time, attending local events and handing out their cards. They spend more time trying to get elected than anything else. The incumbent has a considerable advantage when the next election comes."

Dennis reached over and shook my hand. "We are all on the same page here; I can tell."

"Dennis, did Tony say much about what he was doing over the last couple of weeks he was here? Anything he was working on that was not related to art?"

"Yes. He vaguely mentioned he was snooping around, seeing if he could find out much about Julie Miller's death. He said he was a good friend of her husband. It's terrible; first Julie, then Tony, and finally, you got concussed. Don't the police have any ideas who was responsible?"

"No, Dennis, they are not active cases. Leads have run dry. They have other violent crimes to try to solve now. Our police force is stretched too thin. Not enough cops for all the crime we have. Again, blame it on the politicians for not putting taxpayers' money where it is needed most. So, Dennis, did Tony say where he had been or who he had seen?"

"No. He didn't go into any details. If he had found out anything, he didn't tell me."

Tyler, who had been quiet so far, said, "Mr. Watson, do you think Tony found out something that got him killed? And if so, how come the police and you didn't find it out, considering you are all experienced investigators?"

I wished he had not asked that question, mainly because I didn't know the answer. "All I can tell you, Tyler, is that he got lucky and then got very unlucky."

As soon as I said that, I realized it was somewhat insensitive. It was not a time to be making comments like that.

However, all I got from Tyler was, "Yes, I guess so."

We talked a little more about not much in general. I thanked

Dennis, said goodbye to him and his nephew, and left John's Java House.

I was going to go to the gay bars to follow up on the comments made by Tony's neighbor about a possible gay friend. I didn't feel like going there that night, so I would go home, have a couple of beers—I had started taking the odd drink again—turn on the TV, and maybe go to sleep wondering what Tony had found out that I couldn't.

CHAPTER 47

The next morning, I awoke as rays of sunlight were trying to pierce the slits in my well-worn drapes. Someday I would have to do something about that. Maybe I would switch to blinds. Anyway, that was someday.

After my usual morning activities, including breakfast, I turned on the TV and went to the weather station. It was going to be a nice, warm May day.

I thought of spending a day with Jack, maybe even going golfing together, but I had no idea what his schedule was. Some days he did fitness classes for seniors, usually in the afternoon. Some evenings were for his senior clients. Some days were free.

Maybe I would get lucky. I called him and got lucky. He said that he just had one student in the evening.

We decided that in the morning we would sit outside on his back veranda and drink coffee and have a long chat. I would try to get a tee time in the afternoon at either an eighteen-hole, par-three course or a nine-hole regulation course. I got a par-three course with a two-thirty p.m. tee time. That way we would be back in time for Jack to be with his client, and I would go to the gay bars.

Jack had planted bulbs in the fall. Daffodils and tulips were welcome additions to the backyard. They brightened the place up.

It was still a bit early to put annuals in. It was safer to wait until later in May to avoid any frosty nights.

I told Jack what I knew about the two deaths. It was not much. He wanted to know what the police were doing. I told him not much either. They were not exactly cold cases, but they were not active cases.

Jack thought I should just give it up and do what I did best, which was working on adultery or fraud cases. I told him that I was going to persist. Detectives, whether public or private, get luckier the more they persist.

Talk turned to our usual subjects—sports, politics, and some items from the past. We both enjoyed talking about these things, and we agreed on most topics.

The morning went well, and so did the afternoon. It was a great day for golf, not too hot and not too cold. We played five bucks a hole, and at the end of the day Jack was up ten bucks. It was a great day, and I needed that. Then it was on to the evening and the gay bars.

The two bars were on the edge of the former C Section. City council had decided to let them stay. There was never any trouble, and the police said they were two of the safer places in the area.

They were about a block apart. Louie's Bar and the Rainbow Club had been there for some time. Louie's was called Left Foot Louie's until Louie discovered that "Left Foot" was a derogatory term used in England years ago for gay men. So, he changed it to Louie's Bar.

I headed there first. I hadn't been sure what to wear. Anything except pink. I didn't want to be considered a patron. So, blue shirt, dark-blue pants, and a windbreaker.

Louie's was a red brick building with "Louie's Bar" displayed in lights over the large front window. When I entered, there was no one to greet me. I looked around the room. It was about three quarters full.

There were booths along one side wall and tables spread out across the room. It looked like they had Formica tops. Easy to wipe clean. There was a wooden floor and no carpeting.

What brightened the room were pictures on the walls on both sides. They were mostly scenes of the four different seasons. I recognized the styles of some of the artists I'd seen the day before.

Most patrons were drinking beer. A few were munching on bar-type food like nuts and pretzels. There was recorded music playing softly, and a few couples—male couples—were dancing together in a square area to the right of the bar.

There were two bartenders, one young man who I thought was gay and an older man with gray hair whom I was not sure of.

I approached the older man. He looked me up and down and then said, "Son, you need a new roadmap. You are completely lost here."

I smiled and told him I was looking for a really big man with blond hair.

The bartender told me he knew who I was looking for. He said his name was Ronnie Fairweather. He mentioned that sometimes he came into Louie's, but he was usually at the Rainbow Club.

I thanked him and dropped him a ten spot. I didn't have to because I knew I would never be there again. However, it is good to let people know that you will pay for information.

I drove the block to the Rainbow Club and parked in their lot. It was fairly full, so I figured business was good. It had seven different colors in its sign over the front entrance.

As I walked in, I was greeted by a young man in a purple jacket over a purple shirt and wearing black pants. He greeted me politely and asked me if I wanted a table for one.

I looked around the room. It was bigger than Louie's place. There were booths on both sides of the room plus tiny alcoves for two people. On the walls were different paintings, all with a rainbow in them. A bit much, I thought.

The chairs were wooden with cushioned seats. The tables seemed to be a kind of wood veneer. I thought a lot of money had gone into the place. I had no idea who the owners were.

Another difference from Louie's was that there were a few female couples there. There was also a stand for a disk jockey, but he was either on vacation or on a break.

I turned to the young man and told him that I was looking for Ronnie Fairweather, a big man with blond hair. He motioned me to an alcove on the far wall. I could see the man, who was talking to a much older man. I weaved my way through the tables, ignoring a lot of curious looks.

Ronnie Fairweather was indeed a big man. He could have been a football lineman. He had a big, round face with no facial hair and a thick head of curly blond hair. He was wearing a black polo shirt and gray pants.

I introduced myself and told him who I was and why I was there. I said I was sorry to interrupt, but it would only take a few minutes, and it was quite important.

The man who was with him smiled at me and said he would come back later. I took his place and looked into the big blue eyes of Ronnie Fairweather.

He spoke first. "So, how can I help you, Mister Watson, is it?"

"Yes, but please call me Mitch. I understand that you brought Tony here, or maybe it was the other bar. I didn't know Tony was gay. That was a surprise."

"Tony wasn't gay. I was at that café where the artists hang out, and I met him there. We talked a lot, and I liked the man. He seemed to be effeminate, and I thought he might be one of us in waiting, if you understand that. So, I invited him to our club. It was then that I noticed he was quite uncomfortable here, and I realized that he was not one of us and never would be."

Okay, I thought, *that settles that.* "Thanks for clearing that up. Now I need to know what Tony told you about his investigations into Julie Miller's death."

He thought for a few moments. "He said he was interviewing people who had any involvement with her. He said he was excited about this. He also mentioned that if he couldn't make it as an artist, he would like to become a private investigator like you."

If I had known that I would have tried to discourage Tony. I hadn't gotten any real information yet, so I decided to try again. "Thanks for that, but did he tell you who exactly he had been speaking to? If so, did he tell you what he found out?"

I waited while he thought that through. "No, he never mentioned any of that."

With that, the interview was over. He asked if he could buy me a drink. It was nice of him to offer, but I was starting to feel uncomfortable. I stood out like a sore thumb. So, I thanked him for the offer, was gracious in my comments, said goodbye, and walked out. My summary of the experience was that I didn't have any criticisms, but I definitely didn't want to join.

CHAPTER 48

The next day was another mild May day, with sunshine and a clear blue sky. If the weather kept up, I could see if the nurseries had any annuals, and I could spruce up the front of the house with some flowers.

Instead of visiting a nursery, I decided to do what I had been thinking, which was to go to the flower shop where Julie had worked and get my flowers there. I didn't want to see the owners again, but something new might come up in conversation.

I also wanted to visit Jenny to see if she recognized the two women from the funeral in any of Julie's pictures that I had.

Usually, it was the evening before I could interview anyone on a case because most people worked during the day. That was changing a bit with more people working from home. However, Jennie was a housewife and would probably be at home most of the day.

I gave her a call, and she told me to come over in the morning because she was going grocery shopping in the afternoon. I told her I would be there at about eleven.

When I arrived, she invited me in and asked if I would like tea or coffee. I thanked her but told her I was fine.

I could see that Julie's death must have had some depressing effects on her. She wasn't wearing any makeup, and I noticed some lines around her eyes that I had not seen before. There was sadness in her face.

I spread the pictures on the coffee table and asked her to look them over carefully to see if anyone resembled either of the women from the funeral.

She looked them over and then turned to me. "Since they're school and university pictures, I'm sure the older woman isn't there. As for the other one, I don't think so, but it's hard to tell. I'm so sorry, Mitch. I really wanted to help." Tears welled up in her eyes as she continued. "I just want it all to be over. I keep thinking of Julie and what happened. I can't stand it. I want it all to go away." With that she leaned against me, put her arms around me, leaned her head on my shoulder, and sobbed uncontrollably.

I held her gently, not saying anything. I didn't know what to say. I could only imagine what she was going through.

She gradually pulled away, wiped her eyes, and reached around for tissues on the table. She looked up at me with red-rimmed eyes and said, "I'm sorry, Mitch. I couldn't help myself."

I had to say something. "I understand. I completely understand." It didn't seem like enough, but it was all I could think of. Sometimes I could come up with sharp comments. That was not one of those times.

I picked up the pictures and asked her if she was going to be alright. She said she would be and that the grocery shopping would keep her mind busy.

I gave her one last hug, told her I would let her know when anything new turned up, and that I was sure I would find out everything. Then I let myself out, not feeling that good about rekindling memories that she was trying to forget.

I needed cheering up. Six months earlier, Henry would have been the last person I would have wanted to see. However, he had changed somewhat and seemed to be out of his depression. Maybe changing residences had been good for him.

So, I called and asked him if he wanted to go out for lunch. He said sure and asked what I had in mind. I told him I felt like fish and chips. He said fine and that there was a place about a block from his place called McGregor's Fish & Chips. He gave me the address, and I told him I would meet him there in about twenty minutes.

Traffic was light, and I made it there in about fifteen minutes. I parked in front and waited a few minutes until I saw Henry coming around the corner. I got out and waved, and he hastened his step, then we went in together.

It was a small place. There was a counter at the front with a middle-aged Asian man and woman behind it. It made me wonder what had happened to McGregor. The rest of the room had five tables down each side with seating for four. One couple was seated at a back table. I assumed that most of the business was takeout.

We took a table near the front. The woman came over, and we both ordered halibut fish and chips. Henry ordered a Coors Light, and I had my usual Bud Light.

Henry was wearing a white turtleneck sweater and black pants. He looked quite good. I was wearing all blue. No jacket because it was unseasonably warm. Henry looked good, but he must have been very warm in that turtleneck. I don't know if he was trying to impress me or what.

We had some mild, bright chatter until our orders came. I had a couple of questions for Henry, but I wanted to wait until we had finished lunch because I thought he might get upset. We finished the fish and chips, which were quite good. Our beers were down to less than half, so I decided to go for it.

"Henry, did Julie have any aunts?"

He looked at me quizzically. "We had carpenter ants once if that's what you mean."

"No, Henry, not that kind. Aunts as in aunts and uncles. I'm still trying to find out who those two women at the funeral were. I'm thinking that maybe the older woman is an aunt on her side of the family."

"That's funny, Mitch. No aunts that I know of. Maybe in some far-flung part of the country or even another country but none that I know of."

"I would like you to help on this, Henry. Would you do an ancestry search and find her family tree? I would, but you know her background better than me." I knew what was coming next.

"Mitch, you know I'm no good at that type of thing. Anyway, the computer is Julie's, and I've never been on it. You're looking at the wrong person for this."

"You can do it on your cell phone," I said. "Type in something like 'heritage' or 'ancestry,' and you can take it from there. Organizations that do this sort of thing can trace things back for years. They might ask questions that I wouldn't know the answers to, but you would."

"No, I can't do it. Why not try Jenny? She's Julie's sister, and she would know even more than me."

"I just came from her place, and when I left, she was upset just thinking about Julie. I can't ask her right now. What about your brother's wife? She'd be good at it. I suppose she'd have to get some answers from you, but it's worth a shot."

"I think you're really reaching on this, Mitch. I don't think it will work. Just leave me alone about Julie. I'm gradually putting everything in the past and feeling much better lately. Now that I'm talking to you about this, I feel like I'm going to have a relapse."

I gave up on the one, but I had another question. "Okay, let's forget about this for the time being. I have another idea anyway. I want to put a one-page ad in both newspapers, asking the two women to tell me what they know about Julie. Also, anyone who has any information at all. They can remain anonymous. The women were emotional, so I'll appeal to their emotions. Will you pay for this? I think this is where the answer lies. I think we can finally get closure."

Henry looked at me and didn't say anything. I waited. Finally, he said "Okay, Mitch, if you think it will do any good. I'm so tired of this. I just want it to end."

Just like Jenny, I thought. Alright I understood. I couldn't criticize either of them. I had never had to go through what they were going through. Maybe I would go back to Jenny in a few days to see if she would do a history chain. Okay, maybe more than a few days.

That night I would see Susan again. It had been a long time. The last time I had talked to her was the night before I got concussed when I was out with Mindy. Susan had never come to see me when I was in the hospital or talked to me after. I had phoned her earlier about seeing her with Julie's pictures, and she said that was fine. We settled on seven-thirty p.m. I hoped for some good news. After all, Susan was supposed to have known Julie better than anyone. We would see.

CHAPTER 49

I headed out to Susan's place at seven o'clock. I made my way leisurely through traffic that had gradually thinned out. No reason to rush, but my Mustang always seemed ready to blast off.

Susan greeted me at her front door. "Hi, Mitch. How are you? It's been a while. How's your head? Did you get over your concussion?"

I told her I was okay and about ninety-five percent recovered. As I spoke, I looked at her, and she seemed different from the last time I'd seen her over six months before. I didn't know what the difference was, but she was not quite the same.

She was wearing what she had worn the first time I saw her—a green top and tight khaki pants. I remembered that quite well.

I asked her if there was anything new in her life. She hesitated and said, "No not really. Same old, same old."

We went to her dining room table, and I spread out the pictures. I told her to take her time and think about the young woman at the funeral and then see if anyone matched her at all.

She looked them over carefully, sometimes to study one in particular. Finally, she said there was one that might be her. It was one of the university students. The young woman appeared to be about nineteen or twenty.

There was nothing unusual about her. She had long black hair down one side of her face and the rest down her back. She had a

THE MAN WITH THE AXE

round, pretty face and was wearing some makeup, including a red lipstick that stood out.

I asked Susan why she thought the person might be the one at the funeral. She said she thought she had seen her before at the university, and she thought it could be her. That was the best she could do.

I made a mental note of the young woman. I wanted to give her a name. Was there anything appropriate? I couldn't think of anything. So, I decided to use the alphabet. The first female name that came to mind was Abigail. Okay then, I would think of her as Abby. Now, all I had to do was find out who she was.

Susan asked if I would like a drink. I thought about it and then told her, "No, thank you. Not tonight."

I wanted to talk to Susan to find out what was going on in her life, but I didn't know how to start the conversation. Finally, it was Susan who asked if there was any new information on either of the killings.

It seemed like that was all we could talk about. I told her there was not much new, but I was following up on the two women, as they were the best leads that I had.

I tried to remember what we had talked about when we went on those trips to the bars to find the men whom Julie had met.

I asked her lamely how her job was going. She said it was okay, but someday she would look for something else. So, I asked her what she did for fun these days. She said, "Not much."

I assumed that she was not in a talkative mood, so I decided to ask her one last thing. Would she contact Julie's three university friends to see if they could meet at one location and look at the pictures? She could text me back, and I would confirm. Also, sooner rather than later.

I told her it was good seeing her again, and I would let her know of any new developments. I let myself out and decided to go straight home because there was nothing else for me to do.

Traffic was steady. I was on Rockford Road, a main artery going east and west in the city. It would take me about twenty minutes and then through a couple of residential streets to get home.

I had been gone for about five minutes and was watching the traffic patterns behind me as well as those in front of me when I got the feeling I was being followed. I had been followed in the past, and I had followed people in the past, so I knew what it was like and how it was done. It made me feel nervous and excited.

I checked the rear-view mirror. The traffic was steady. Rockford was a four-lane street with two lanes each way and no parking. At main intersections there was an additional left-turn lane.

I was in the inside lane. There was a Mustang like mine right behind me and an SUV right behind him, but beyond that I couldn't tell. They were mostly SUVs in the outside lane.

The streetlights had come on, and the vehicles had their head-lights on. It was difficult to make out what the vehicles were except the one beside me and the one directly behind me.

The Mustang made a quick turn into the outside lane. That lane was the fastest, because cars in the inside lane slowed to make right-hand turns. Replacing the Mustang was an Acura with tinted windows. We went less than a block, and the Acura slowed to let in a small Hyundai Accent.

If I were following someone, that was what I would have done, stay two or three car lengths behind or even go in the other lane for a while. I figured the Acura was the one following me, so I needed to find out who it was.

Up ahead was a long bridge where there were no intersections. Traffic became more spread out. Beyond that on either side were residential developments. On my side of the road, the side streets were named after trees such as pine, ash, oak, and birch.

Just before the bridge, I whipped into the outside lane, made good speed, and after passing two cars on the inside, came down off the bridge and made a quick right turn onto Oak Street and then another quick right onto Locust Road. I drove past the second house, then reversed into their driveway and waited.

It only took about twenty seconds before headlights appeared around the corner. As the vehicle approached the second house, I drove out in front of it, causing it to brake abruptly. I grabbed my gun from the glove compartment and ran to the car's driver's-side window.

The window came down, and I looked into the face of Albert Grove, private investigator, commonly known as Bert or Berty.

We had taken the PI course at the same time. We were not close, but we were okay with each other. I put the gun away, and Bert spoke first.

"Well, if it isn't Cairnford's top PI, who was so smart he almost had his head bashed in."

"Good to see you too, Bert. Why were you following me?"

"I guess Susan never told you she was having trouble with an ex. First phone calls, then emails wanting her back. Then he started coming around. Susan wanted to get a restraining order, but she wanted physical evidence that he had been there. So, she hired me. She would have probably hired you, but when it started you were still convalescing.

"You were in your car about two seconds after you came out of the house. It's dark, and I didn't get a good look at you, certainly not for a camera shot either, so I thought I would follow and either get a good look or even approach the person. Unfortunately, it turned out to be you."

So, that was what had been bothering Susan. I'd known there was something. Those kinds of guys made me sick. I hoped they would get the restraining order quickly.

Bert and I talked briefly about our current cases and how they were doing. In my case, there was a lot of interviewing and not much in the way of results yet. Then, since we were holding up the cars that had just turned in, we wished each other good luck and drove off.

I had just about made it home when my phone rang. It was Henry. *What now?* I thought. I let it ring as I went into my house and made myself comfortable. Then I called him back. "What's up, Henry? Did you get that historical list yet?"

"No, that's not why I'm calling. I had a thought about the middle-aged woman at the funeral. You know what? I think she looked like Doug's wife. Do you think that's possible?"

"You mean our poker-playing buddy? Didn't his wife go to the funeral with him?"

"No, he went with Greg. You know he goes more places with Greg than with his wife. I mean, don't you think the two women look alike?"

"How would I know? Remember, I was not at the funeral. I had a headache at the time. Anyway, why wouldn't she go with her husband if she was going to go? Also, she wouldn't have known Julie as far as we know, so why should she be there and be so emotional?"

"I don't know, Mitch. You're the detective. It's up to you to figure it out."

This was starting to sound like a broken record: "It's up to you to figure it out." First I needed some relevant information. It seemed crazy to me. Wouldn't Doug recognize her there, even if she wasn't close to him and was all covered up? I thought that Henry's idea was a long shot and probably not worth looking into.

I thought it over some more. I would see if I could get myself invited over for dinner and somehow talk about the funeral and what Doug's wife had been doing at the time. The worst thing that could happen was that I would get a free dinner. I decided to call Doug the next day.

CHAPTER 50

The following morning after breakfast, I made a list of who I wanted to see and what I wanted to do. My list included the flower shop, Doug, the university students, Jan, Henry (to follow up on Julie's history), and newspaper ads.

I felt that the two women I was trying to trace held the key to both killings. Susan picking out one that she thought was possible helped. If the other three young women picked out the same, it would really be a step forward. Susan had said she would get back to me when they got back to her. So, I had Henry and Susan to wait for.

I would go to the flower shop that morning and phone Doug right before dinner that evening. On Friday night, maybe he and Martha would go out for dinner. I didn't think they went out much, but I would give him a try.

It was a bit cooler that day, so I wore a light windbreaker over my usual golf shirt and pants as I headed out to the flower shop. I wondered if Mr. Bundheim and the driver would be there. I couldn't see the owner going out every day to drum up business. Maybe he was just fooling his wife sometimes and going to strip joints. After seeing his wife, I wouldn't blame him.

When I walked in, I saw a young woman at the table who had not been there the last time. She was in her early twenties and had a nice, trim figure that looked nice in a blue sweater and short black skirt. I could imagine the driver trying to stay longer in the shop each day.

She smiled at me as I came in. "Hi, can I help you?"

"No thanks. I'm here to see Mrs. Bundheim. I see that she's in her office. I'll pop in to see her." I smiled at her as I walked by, not giving her a chance to ask if Mrs. Bundheim was expecting me or anything else.

I didn't need to knock on the door, as Mrs. Bundheim opened it when I approached. "Mr. Watson, how nice to see you again. Have you recovered fully now?"

"Very close, thanks for asking. Your husband and the driver both out this morning?"

"Yes. They are out doing their jobs. Well, I hope so. I see you met my new assistant when you came in. That is Felicia. She just finished university. I do not think she will be here long. She is overqualified. I trained her, and she learned quite easily, and she smiles at all the customers, so I would like to keep her for a while. So, what can I do for you today?"

"I haven't seen you since my friend Tony was killed, and I wondered if you or your husband knew him. Did he ever come in here?"

"No, he never came in here, and we didn't know him at all. The newspapers said he was an aspiring artist. A shame he was killed before he became famous."

"I asked because he was doing some investigating on his own, which I didn't know about, so I wondered if he had visited the places that I did. He found out something that got him killed, but I don't know what it was."

"Well, it was nothing from here. I never heard of him before he was killed."

She said that as if she were annoyed I was asking her about it. Too bad. I was just doing my job as well. I wanted to ask her what she and her husband were doing the night Tony was killed, but I thought that would get me nothing but hostility.

I asked her how the shop was doing and when most of the spring flowers would be in. She said by the end of next week. I decided that I wouldn't buy anything there. I thought it unlikely that I would ever go there again. I didn't want to stay any longer. I bid her goodbye, walked out of her office, and smiled at Felicia as I walked by, wishing her a good day. "Same to you," she said as I walked out.

Doug would be at work. I would phone him in late afternoon when he was home but before he started dinner. Then I would see If he would invite me over for dinner. I would practice what I wanted to say to him and how I would say it, so it would be natural for him to invite me.

In the meantime, it was just household chores for me that afternoon. I needed a maid and a gardener. I was not good at chores.

CHAPTER 51

I called Doug at five p.m. I knew he would be home by then. He sounded excited to hear from me. "Hey, Mitch, how are you? It's been a while."

"Hi, Doug. I'm good. I wanted to talk to you about Julie's funeral and a few other things. Oh, I just realized it is almost dinner time. I better let you go, and we can talk after. I don't know what to have tonight. Maybe I will get takeout somewhere."

"Mitch, hang on, I have an idea. Just a minute."

I heard him talking to his wife, Martha. Then he came back on the line. "Mitch, why don't you have dinner with us tonight? Martha says we are having meatloaf, and there will be lots to go around. What do you think?"

"Doug, that is very nice. Tell Martha I appreciate it. So, yes, I will be over. I will leave in a few minutes. See you then."

I hung up before they could change their minds. I left right away, because it would be rush-hour traffic and slower than usual. I wouldn't want them waiting on me before they could serve dinner.

Martha met me at the front door. She looked different from the last time I saw her. I couldn't figure out what it was at first, but the I noticed her hair was cut much shorter than before. It didn't improve her overall appearance.

She was wearing a plain blue blouse and blue jeans. I suppose there was no reason to dress up for me.

Martha asked about my concussion, and I gave her the usual answer. She said that she could put dinner on the table right away if I would follow her into the dining room.

I followed her in and saw Doug and the two children sitting at the dining room table. It looked like they had been waiting for me, so they could start.

Like Martha, Doug was wearing jeans and a black sweatshirt that made me think it was what he'd been wearing at work that day. People didn't dress up to work on cars and trucks.

The children were nine-year-old Norman and seven-year-old Nancy. Both had short brown hair, brown eyes, and round, smiling faces. Nancy was wearing a frilly white top, and Norman was wearing a red soccer shirt that showed the name of the team's sponsor, Spangler Chevy, where Doug worked.

Doug welcomed me, said it had been a long time, and then introduced me to the children. They were polite and shook hands with me. I thought that was very nice.

Martha brought out the dinner. There was meatloaf, green beans, and mashed potatoes with gravy. Very basic but also very tasty.

I wondered how the children would do with the green beans. I know that some children are finicky over some vegetables. Those kids ate everything with no complaints. I thought that showed well on the parents.

My doctor told me one time during a routine checkup that fruit or vegetables should be served at every meal. They contain vitamins that people need. He said that if people took more during their younger years, they wouldn't need all the prescriptions they took in their later years.

We had apple pie and ice cream for dessert. So, meat, vegetables, fruit, pastry, and dairy, all in one meal. No wonder everyone looked so healthy. They could give lessons to many other people.

Martha asked me if I would like coffee. I said yes, and then Doug and I retired to the living room. The children went to the den to play video games.

Doug and I sat at opposite ends of the sofa. Doug looked at me quizzically. "So, Mitch, you said you wanted to talk about Julie's funeral. Well, what about it?"

"Did you notice two women who were there a bit apart from the rest and also apart from each other? They both seemed quite upset."

"It was a funeral. People do get somewhat upset and emotional. That would be normal. I didn't notice anything unusual. If there was anyone there I didn't know, I wouldn't have paid them much attention."

Alright, I thought, *now to get to the heart of the matter.* "What about Martha? Maybe she noticed them."

"Martha wasn't there. She said that she didn't know Julie and thought that only family and friends should be there. She really didn't know Henry either. She only saw him when he came around on poker nights twice a year."

That gave me pause for thought. Could Martha have been there all covered up and away from Doug? If so, why? How would she have known Julie?

Martha came in with a tray with coffee cups, cream, and sugar. We all took what we wanted and sat back.

"Martha, Doug tells me that you didn't go to Julie Miller's funeral. I would have thought that you would have gone together."

"I didn't know Julie at all. Never met her or spoke to her. I didn't really know Henry either. Anyway, Doug went with Greg. Doug goes out with Greg more than with me." She looked pointedly at Doug when she said that. I didn't think she was joking. Doug just shrugged and kept quiet.

I wondered if I should mention what Henry had said about Martha, that she could be the middle-aged woman at the funeral. I wasn't sure what the response would be.

It became quiet. Obviously, Doug and Martha had finished with that topic of conversation and wanted to move on. So, it came down to whether I believed Martha was the woman or not. If I believed she was, then I had to mention what Henry had said. If I didn't believe that Martha was the woman, I'd move on.

"How are the kids doing at school?" I asked. Martha said that they both had higher-than-average marks. Norman was a striker on his soccer team and scored lots of goals. Nancy was into arts and crafts.

I asked Doug how he thought the Kansas City Chiefs would do that year. He took a long time explaining why in some areas they would be good and other areas they would have to improve. However, overall they should be a contender for the Super Bowl.

Martha looked bored.

I finished my coffee. We talked some more about the city and a few other things. Then I got up and said I had to go. I thanked them for the dinner, saying it was great, and I meant it.

Doug said it was too bad we couldn't get back together for our poker games without Tony. I told him maybe he should try the two guys who sat next to him and Greg at the Chiefs home games. They had all been together for many years. Doug said that this was a good idea, and he hadn't thought about it.

We shook hands, said goodnight, and I was on my way. I believed it was not possible that Martha was the woman at the funeral. Nice try, Henry, but after being with Doug and Martha and listening to them, I was sure that Martha was not involved.

On the way home, my phone buzzed. It was Susan texting that "Brain," "Joker," and "Orgy" would meet me at Brain's condo at seven p.m. on Monday to look at Julie's pictures and asking if I would confirm that was okay.

That was the first thing I did when I got home. I was hopeful one or more of them would pick out the young woman whom Susan thought might be the one. Also, maybe they had some thoughts about the older woman.

Tomorrow was the weekend. Maybe Jan would be off work. She didn't usually work weekends, but she was on call and sometimes had to finish work on something she had started earlier in the week.

I valued her opinion. I felt I was getting close. I needed a bit of luck and a break. *Just keep persevering*, I thought. *You'll get the answers.* That was enough for the day, though. Maybe Jan and nothing else on the weekend. That would be okay.

Tomorrow morning, I would create a one-page letter to be printed in both newspapers, asking the two women from the funeral to contact me. I would do that before anything else and ask the newspapers to run it for two days.

CHAPTER 52

CATCH A KILLER

I am Mitch Watson, a private investigator. I am investigating the murders of Julie Miller and Tony Marino. I am making progress, but I need help from two women who were at the funeral of Julie Miller. These two women were alone and stayed apart. They didn't sign the book of attendance at the service.

I believe that both these persons have knowledge of something to do with Julie Miller's death. Please not let a murderer walk away free.

I think that each of you was a witness to something that happened in the past. What happened then is relevant now. With your help I can solve these crimes.

I am not interested in who you are or what you are. I just need to know what you know about an event from the past that could have some bearing on Julie Miller's death.

At the end of this notice, I will give four ways to contact me. They are by email, text, phone call, and postal mail. I believe that postal mail with no return address will help keep you as anonymous as you wish to be. An alternative would be to purchase a cheap burner phone.

Get this situation off your mind, so you can live a worry-free and happier life. Also, if you contact me, it will help bring closure to the family and friends of Julie and Tony, who were struck down in the prime of their lives by the same person.

CHAPTER 53

On Saturday morning, I hoped Jan was available. I needed her insight and her humor, and looking at her helped a lot too. She was a bit heavy but in the right places. I gave her a call.

"Hi, Jan. Are you free today?"

"No, I'm never free, but for you I'll be cheap."

"This isn't really a social call, Jan. I want to talk to you for a while about the cases. When I've solved them, we'll go out and celebrate."

"By then you'll be so old that you won't be good for anything."

"Well, if I am that old, you will be too, and we could have a lot of fun trying."

"That's great, Mitch. Something to look forward to."

"Okay, enough chit chat. How about you come over to my place for lunch and some intelligent conversation?"

"That's okay with me, Mitch, but who will be there for me to talk to?"

She was in some mood today. "See you at twelve o'clock, okay?" I said.

"Can't wait," she said, then hung up.

I wasn't sure if she was going to come or not. I would do hamburgers and hot dogs on the barbecue. If she wasn't there at twelve, I would put a notice on the front door saying I was in the back to come around.

The time came, and I had just gotten up to get out the barbecue supplies when I heard her car roll up. That was good; she could help carry stuff out.

She got out of her car, and right away I could see that she was determined to make it a social call—actually, a very social call. She was wearing a tight crimson sweater and a short, tight black leather skirt. Her lipstick matched her sweater.

I met her at the front door. She spoke first. "So, was it worth the wait?"

"Yes, you look great, Jan. Maybe we should have lunch later." I meant it.

"You will probably need all your strength. Let's have lunch."

I wasn't sure how much of it was our usual banter or if she was serious at all. Dressed the way she was, it seemed serious to me.

I asked her to help carry out the food and the barbecue tools. We decided on beer, and I pulled out a couple of cold Buds. With our arms loaded, we headed out to the backyard and put everything on the picnic table.

We didn't say much as I cooked. Then we ate a hamburger and hot dog each along with a couple of beers each. It was a mild, sunny day, perfect for a backyard barbecue.

When we finished our second beer, I decided it was time to get serious, at least from my point of view. "Jan, remember back when you came up with three possibilities after we found out that Julie was pregnant? I came up with a fourth. I would like to examine them again."

"Yes, I remember. What were they again?

"Julie in no way wanted a baby, so we said that either something went wrong with that plan, Julie didn't tell Susan everything, Susan didn't tell me everything, or Julie was raped. If it was one of those, then which one? If it wasn't one of those, what could it be?"

"I think the most likely situation is that Julie was raped," Jan said. "The only problem with that is when did she have the time for that to happen?"

"Yes, I think you're right. Julie was so adamant about not getting pregnant that I can't see anything going wrong with the plan. I think Susan told me everything she knew. Obviously, Julie had not told Susan everything, but knowing that, how does it help? Also, what about a fifth possibility?"

"You have a fifth possibility, Mitch?"

"No, I'm just saying what if there was one?"

"I can't think what it would be."

"We don't know everything yet. It would help if we had more information on the two women at the funeral."

"What two women? What are you talking about?"

I suddenly realized that I had not mentioned them to Jan before. I told her the whole story, emphasizing that the women must have known Julie, or why else would they have been there?

Jan thought it over, then she turned to me and said, "That is a real mystery, Mitch. As you say, if they knew Julie, why did they not want to be recognized or known to anyone else?"

"Well Jan, that is the sixty-four-thousand-dollar question. If we can answer that, then maybe we can answer everything else. That is why I put this ad in the papers starting Monday." With that, I showed her a copy of the ad, which I had brought out with me.

"You think someone will answer? That idea of sending a reply by postal mail was brilliant. Nobody thinks of that anymore. It sure gives you a better chance of somebody answering."

"Jan, that is the nicest thing you have said to me all day."

"Then maybe we should change the subject while you're ahead."

I was reluctant to change the topic, but I didn't know what else to say about it. I wondered if I should just relax with Jan and see if she had anything else in mind. I decided to ask about her job.

"Jan, how can you relax and enjoy yourself when you see dead bodies all the time? Not only do you see them, but you also cut them up. Maybe you should be a butcher. At least they would be animals, not people."

"Actually, every dead body is a mystery. How did that person die, and what was the cause of death? You have to come to a scientific conclusion. For one thing, it helps investigators find out what happened. Also, you're looking at a body, and you have to realize it is just that. They can't be hurt anymore. In a way, you're helping bring closure to them and their family."

"That was a good explanation, Jan. Although I still think you have to be a special kind of person to do the job you do. I enjoy beating up a bad guy and seeing blood all over him, but cutting up a corpse would turn me right off."

"It takes all kinds of people to make a world, Mitch. Some people like and can do some things, and other people like and can do other things. It would be a boring world if we were all the same."

The conversation seemed to have exhausted both of us. There was silence for a while. Finally, I looked at Jan, sitting there in her tight sweater and short skirt, which looked even shorter when she was sitting down. She saw me looking at her. *It's now or never,* I thought. I asked one question "Where?"

She looked at me in surprise, then smiled. "Well, not the table, the floor, or the sofa, so that leaves only one other place, doesn't it?"

"Yes, follow me." I led her to the bedroom.

I was like a teenager on his first attempt. I couldn't help it. It had been a long time since the last time.

Afterwards as we lay there, Jan turned to me and said, "Mitch, I have a riddle for you."

"Okay, what is it?"

"Why is your lovemaking like the Kentucky Derby?"

"I don't know. Tell me, why is my lovemaking like the Kentucky Derby?"

"It's the fastest two minutes in sports."

I laughed so hard I almost fell out of bed. Jan laughed at her own joke. She was really funny at times. It seemed it was always when she was making fun of me.

Later on, I asked her to stay for dinner. We had Chinese. Then later on, we made love again. It was not the Kentucky Derby the second time around.

She said she couldn't stay the night. She had things to do at home. So, I told her okay and that when I had closed the two cases we would go out and celebrate. She kissed me goodnight, smiled at me, and let herself out.

I was no further ahead in the investigation, but I didn't feel bad about it. Actually, it was the best I had felt in a long, long time. I didn't remember the last time I'd gone to bed with a smile on my face.

CHAPTER 54

I did nothing for the rest of the weekend. That is, nothing to do with the investigations.

Having a house was great, but there always seemed to be more to do in terms of maintenance than if I lived in a condo or an apartment. I didn't know of any other private investigators who lived in a house. Maybe there were some owners of agencies who lived in houses, but not many of us lone rangers did. Some of us spent more time in our vehicles than in our residences.

So, I worked in and around the house for a while. It was a break from thinking about Julie and Tony and trying to figure it all out. I would see the university students on Monday evening, and hopefully they might recognize someone from Julie's pictures.

Monday morning and afternoon passed uneventfully, and I arrived at Betty and Ashley's apartment at seven-thirty p.m. I buzzed their apartment, and they buzzed me up. Betty met me at the door and invited me in.

All three of them yelled out, "Hi, how are you? Nice to see you again," as if they had been rehearsing. We all laughed together.

They had all dressed up for me. Their dressing up was different from my idea of dressing up. They all wore Cairnford University T-shirts, blue with gold lettering. Of course, they all wore blue jeans. Anyway, I liked it and told them so.

Ashley said they were all going to have a beer. They had been waiting for me to arrive. Would I like one? I told them that I would have what they were having.

It turned out to be Miller beer. It seemed appropriate since we were going to be looking at Julie's pictures. I wondered if that was their plan. Betty said it was a coincidence; they just drank Miller sometimes.

She brought out the beers, opened them, and we clinked bottles as we all said, "Cheers." I thought I should go there more often. I liked the atmosphere.

I laid out all the pictures on the dining room table. I had numbered them at the bottom. I gave the three girls a piece of paper each and asked them to write down the number of anyone they thought resembled the young woman at the funeral.

I didn't want anyone to say anything out loud and maybe influence someone else. After everyone had finished, we could go over their selections to see if there were any matches.

They took their time, and I noticed there were hardly any numbers being noted. Finally, they were all done, and I took their notes.

Lisa said she didn't recognize anyone. She was sorry because she really wanted to help. Betty picked out two and Ashley one. However, the one that Ashley picked out matched one of Betty's selections. It was also the one that Susan had thought was possible.

I asked the two girls about the picture they had picked and why they picked it. Ashley said she thought the girl was a cheerleader for the football team. They both said they went to the football games. They were not sure it was her, but they thought it was possible.

Lisa said she didn't go to football games, and it was hard to recognize and connect someone from five or six years ago to someone at a funeral. Then she went into the living room, sat in an armchair, and buried her head in thought.

We followed her into the living room, and Betty interrupted

her. "Is the Brain's brain working overtime to try to come up with something?"

Lisa looked at her, clearly irritated. "I'm onto something, and you broke my chain of thought. Shut up for five minutes, and let me think this out."

We all walked back into the living room. I looked at Betty and asked her why she had picked out a second girl. She said that the person vaguely looked like someone else she knew, but the more she thought about it, the more she was changing her mind. She said to forget it.

I picked up all the pictures and kept the one they had picked out on top. I asked them if they knew the girl's name, but they didn't. They said she had not been in any of their classes.

Lisa called us back in again. She said that she had been thinking about the older woman at the funeral. She said she had seen her face when the woman had lifted her veil to wipe away the tears. She thought the person was the dean of the university.

We all looked at her in surprise. I asked her if she was sure, and she said she wasn't, but the woman did look like her.

I asked Ashley and Betty what they thought. Neither of them remembered seeing the dean before, so they didn't know. Lisa said she had seen the dean at occasional university events.

Lisa thought the dean's name was Mary Deacon or something like that. I thanked her for taking the time to concentrate and come up with a good lead. The girls had been quite helpful.

Ashley asked, "What are we going to do now? Would you tell us some exciting stories from the past? Are there any juicy adultery stories?"

My mind was too busy thinking about how to proceed with the new information, so I turned the tables on them and asked how their love lives were going.

Betty giggled and said they flirted around a lot, but nothing much ever came of it. I thought that was too bad because, although they were not physically attractive, they were both fun to be with.

Lisa was a different story. She had the looks and the personality, so I asked her if there was romance in the air.

She smiled and said she was working on it, but it was an office situation, so it was a bit tricky. She had to be very careful in those situations.

We chatted some more and then I said I had to go. They wanted me to stay and have another beer, but I had too much on my mind.

I thanked them for everything and said that I would keep in touch, then they all gave me a hug before I left. Julie had such great friends. I knew they would miss her immensely.

CHAPTER 55

Tuesday was cooler and raining. Time to wear a spring windbreaker when I went out. I was not sure where to go or what to do. I wanted to visit the university and see the dean. I wondered if she would see me. I would call to see if I could get an appointment. I needed to see her and ask about the funeral. Also, I was wondering if she could tell me who the cheerleader was.

The university would be closing for the summer holidays soon. It always finished earlier than high school. They would be into exams already.

I got the main number and asked for the dean's office. A middle-aged woman answered. "Dean Deacon's office. Miss Sedgewick speaking."

I gave her my name and said that I was a private investigator and that I was investigating the murder of a former university student.

"Just a minute please."

I waited and waited. After a few moments, she came back on the line. "The dean will not be speaking to any private investigator on any matter."

Click. She hung up.

I would find a way to see the dean, but first I would like to have more information, hopefully from a person who answered the newspaper ad.

So, what to do now? I was getting close. I could feel it. Getting the last information would be tough, but I would get it.

While I was thinking about it, Henry phoned. Did he have information? Did he want something, or was it a social call?

I answered. "Hi, Henry. What's up?"

"Hi, Mitch. Maybe you could do a favor for me today, and I will make lunch for you. How does that sound?"

"It depends on what you want me to do."

"Would you pick up a loaf of sliced white bread for me? My brother and his wife both eat brown bread. You can get it wherever you want, but if you go to the bakery where Julie used to go, you can also pick up a dozen lemon tarts. We all eat those here."

"Where is this bakery, Henry?"

"In the small plaza on Browning at Doncaster. It's run by a Swedish family. It's called Nordgren Bakery."

"Okay, it's a bit out of the way for you now that you have moved. What time do you plan on having lunch?"

"How about noon?"

"Okay with me. I'll see you sometime after eleven-thirty."

With that, we hung up. So, it was something he wanted me to do, rather than giving me information. I had some news for him, though, so he would be pleased about that.

The bakery was in a small plaza in a residential area. I counted eight stores. There was pizza, fish and chips, the bakery, a hardware store, a dry cleaner, a shoe store, a barber shop, and a liquor store.

Norgren Bakery was one of the middle stores. It had a small sign over the front window. Through the window I saw tables with various pastries, but I didn't see any lemon tarts.

Inside the store, the front counter had some of the pastries I had seen through the window. Behind the counter were shelves with various kinds of bread. Behind that was the bakery area. Along the side of the store were tables that would seat four customers. I believed most of their business was takeout.

A motherly looking woman stood behind the counter. She had graying blonde hair tied into a bun at the back. I saw the beginning of wrinkles around her blue eyes, which looked at me from her round face. She smiled at me and said, "What would you like?"

I smiled back and said, "One sliced white loaf and twelve lemon tarts if you have them. I don't see any available."

"Oh, we have them. They are in the back; they just came out of the oven. We do two dozen at a time. No one usually orders as many as you want, but I can let you have them."

"Thank you. I also need some information. I'm Mitch Watson, a private investigator, and I'm investigating the death of Julie Miller, who I believe was a customer here."

"Yes, I knew Julie. A lovely person. Terrible thing that happened to her. Are you the investigator who took a bad knock on the head when the man who knew Julie was killed?"

A bad knock? It was a lot more than that. "Yes, I took a really bad knock on the head. Can you tell me if you ever saw Julie in here with anyone else?"

She thought for a moment. "No, I don't think she came in with anyone, not at least while I was at the counter."

"Oh, is there someone else behind the counter sometimes?"

"Yes, my daughter comes in to help on Saturdays. It's our busiest time. She works the counter while I help my husband in the back. Ingrid is in her last year of university. She is doing exams right now."

"I need to talk to her, Mrs. Nordgren. It is Mrs. Nordgren, isn't it?"

"Yes, that's me. She won't be back in the store until Saturday. You can talk to her then."

"Mrs. Nordgren, that's not good enough. This is a murder investigation. We need the information as soon as possible. I'm working with the police on this. I can have the detectives come to your home to interview your daughter. I need to talk to her on the phone today or tonight."

So, I lied a little. Sometimes the end justifies the means.

"Mr. Watson, really? Can't this wait until Saturday? She is at the university now, and she studies in the evenings. It's important to her."

"So is a murder investigation, Mrs. Nordgren. Two people have been killed, and I was brutally attacked. All of that is very important. It may only take a few minutes on the phone. I can tell a lot by a person's voice about what they know and how truthful they are. Of course, I know your daughter will be quite truthful.

"Please give me your home phone number unless you both have only cell phones. I prefer a land line because if she doesn't recognize my number on her cell phone, she may not answer. If that were to happen, I would have the detectives there first thing in the morning before she leaves for the university."

"Oh, this all seems so silly when she might not know anything and even may have never seen Julie with anyone. Anyway, we always cooperate with the law. I will give you my number, and you can call at seven-thirty tonight, okay?"

"Perfect, Mrs. Nordgren. Thank you. Now, may I please have a sliced white loaf and a dozen lemon tarts?" I smiled at her as I said it. She gave me a half smile back. That was all I could expect.

I left the bakery suspecting that all I would get out of it was a loaf of bread and a dozen lemon tarts for a friend.

Henry was happy to see me. He made lunch for us, which included various sandwiches and the lemon tarts for dessert.

After a couple of cups of coffee and some talk that included me telling Henry what I had learned about the women at the funeral, I told him I had things to do at home and that I needed to get going. I thanked him for lunch and then left.

I didn't do anything at home. I just thought about what the girls had mentioned about the pictures and what Lisa had said about the dean. Also, I wondered how I would get to see her.

First, though, was my phone call with Ingrid, during which she would say she either knew nothing or she had some information for me. I would soon see which way it would go.

CHAPTER 56

I called at the time I said I would. Ingrid answered the phone. I could tell it was her because her voice sounded younger. "Hello, is this Mr. Watson?"

"Yes, it is. Is this Ingrid?"

"Yes, mom said you wanted to know if I ever saw Julie Miller with anyone in the bakery. Well, yes, I did one time."

My heart beat a little faster. "Tell me what you saw and heard. Please describe the person. This is extremely important."

"She came in with a man whom I didn't see at first. He must have zipped in and gone to a table. She ordered two coffees and a couple of pastries. I never would have noticed anything at all except I took an order past them to the next table, and as I headed back, I heard the man's voice. It seemed he was having a bit of an argument with Julie who shushed him. I glanced over as I walked by and saw the side of his face; that's all. I couldn't really describe him or identify him. Sorry."

"Ingrid, thank you so much for what you have told me. I have an idea. I have a detective friend who is an artist who can create a drawing of a person based on what someone tells him. I need you to come with me to the police station and tell him what you can, and he will make a drawing. Don't worry that you only had a glance; he can lead you along, showing you different types of eyes, noses, chins, and so on. Tell me when we can do this. It should be as soon as possible because this is a murder investigation. Then I will find out when the detective will be available."

"Oh, Mr. Watson, I don't think I'll be able to be of any help. I saw so little, and it was over six months ago. In any case, I won't be available until next week after exams are over."

"Ingrid, the detective, Jim Hadson, is extremely good, and we have to try this. I will see if he is on days next week and schedule a time. Is early in the morning okay with you?"

There was a pause. I could feel her mulling it over. She wanted to help, but she thought that she really didn't know enough. I waited.

"Well, Mr. Watson, if you think so, then let's get it over with. First thing Monday morning next week if that will work."

"Thanks, Ingrid, I'll call the station now. They'll have his schedule for next week. I'll call you right back. Thanks again."

I got a reluctant "Okay," then we both hung up.

I called the station and asked if Detective Hadson was in. The desk sergeant said I had just missed him. I asked him for the schedule for next week, and he told me that Jim Hadson was working days and usually came in at about eight a.m. to do reports and go over the upcoming day. I asked the desk sergeant to leave a message for Hadson, saying I would see him with a young woman and that I would ask him to draw a sketch based on what the woman said. I left my phone number in case Hadson wanted to ask me about it.

I called Ingrid back and told her I would pick her up Monday morning at seven-thirty a.m. I heard her gasp, and then there was silence. I asked for her address. Then she asked if we couldn't do it later. I told her we couldn't. We left it at that. I thought that whatever we came up with, I owed that young woman, though I didn't know how I could make it up to her.

Now I really had nothing to do until then unless my ad was answered. Each day I went over everything I had found out. Too many pieces of the puzzle were still missing. I needed a good response to the drawing I was going to see, and I needed a reply to the ad. The next few days went by very slowly.

Monday came around. It was back to mild weather again, a bit cloudy but fairly nice. It was cool first thing in the morning, so I wore my burgundy spring windbreaker over my white golf shirt and black pants. I didn't know if Ingrid would be impressed or not, but I was comfortable.

I picked up Ingrid, who was sleepy, at seven-thirty a.m. She was wearing a blue-and-gold Cairnford University jacket over a white blouse and blue pants. She looked tired and unhappy.

On the way to the 9th Division's headquarters, I explained to her what the detective would do. I hoped it would make her feel more comfortable. From the look on her face, it didn't work.

We arrived at close to eight o'clock. I looked around for Jim Hadson and found him at his desk in a corner of the room. We had a history. It involved a lot of bantering. Fairly good natured, but you wouldn't know it if you heard us talk.

We walked over to his desk, and he looked up as we approached. "Well, if it isn't the poor man's Sherlock Holmes. I haven't seen you in a while. I like your new assistant."

"Ingrid, this is Jim Hadson, the poor man's Vincent Van Gogh. Jim, this is Ingrid Nordgren. Ingrid got a glimpse of a man talking to Julie Miller in her mother's bakery. She only got a glance, so she doesn't think she can help, but I know you can bring out details from a person that they don't realize they have."

Jim got up, took out what looked to be a purse from his top drawer, and said to Ingrid, "Come with me to the interview room, and you can help me draw a picture. Mitch can wait in the waiting area."

So, we went our separate ways. The waiting area was a row of seats right inside the main door. No magazines or anything else to read. No one else was there. I took out my cell phone and checked my emails. None of the detectives that I knew were there, so I just sat and waited.

It was about a half hour later when they emerged. Ingrid didn't look that much happier. Jim's expression was unreadable. I saw him ask her to sit at his desk and then he came over to me.

"Well, Mitch, we couldn't do very much. I got everything out of her that I could. She said he didn't have any facial hair that she could see. However, she kept repeating to me that she only got a glance. His nose was ordinary. He didn't have a pointed chin, a square chin, or a backward chin, so just an ordinary chin. Really nothing special about anything. Here is my original drawing; I've made copies."

I looked at a side of a face that could have been any ordinary person with no outstanding features. I was disappointed, but I should not have expected more.

Jim saw the look on my face. "Look, Mitch, that was the best I could do. Next time bring me someone who has seen something."

"Okay, Jim, I know you did the best you could. Let me collect Ingrid and drive her home."

"Before you go, understand that I have to give copies to Detectives Finnegan and Puccillo. They're the lead detectives on the case."

"Yes, of course. I'm not sure what they'll make of it, but I have no problem with that."

I thanked him again, picked up Ingrid, and then left. We were quiet on the way back to her house until she said, "Did I do okay? Will it help?"

"Ingrid, you did the best you could. I will study it and see where it leads. I really appreciate your help. Now you can go and have a good sleep."

"Thanks, but it's a little late for that now."

We were quiet the rest of the way. As she got out of the car, I said, "Thanks again, Ingrid, I'll let you know what happens."

She closed the door, waved, and was gone.

I stopped at a McDonald's on the way home and got a medium double cream. I would read the newspaper, drink my coffee, and look at the picture again, although there was not much to see. I did all that and didn't know what to do next.

I brought the picture out again. I had seen other sketches that Jim had done, and something looked different. What was it?

Then I saw it. Other sketches usually ended with a bit of the neck or no neck at all. After all, they were supposed to be sketches of faces. This one, though, had a neck, then a panel of shading, then a small, darker line. What was that about?

I called Jim. The desk sergeant said he was out and that he couldn't give me his cell number. I asked him to leave a message for Jim to call me back. He didn't call back, so I did nothing the rest of the day.

The next morning, I called him shortly after eight a.m. "Jim, I wanted to ask you something about the sketch."

"So, what do you want to know?"

"You usually end a sketch at the bottom of the face, maybe a little neck. On this one you have a broad, shaded band at the bottom of the neck and a darker kind of fringe. Were you just getting fancy, or does it mean something?"

There was silence. I thought maybe he had hung up. "Mitch, did you ask her what he was wearing?"

"No, why would I? It was all about the face; she hardly even remembered any of that."

"Well, Mitch, great detective that you are, she did remember what he was wearing. It was the only thing that stood out. It was one of those red baseball jackets with a black fringe. I know you call them windbreakers, but almost everyone else calls them jackets. The red caught her eye. Actually, his face never caught her eye at all. So, no, I was not getting fancy; I was just trying to help you out. You need more help than you think."

"Why didn't you tell me that when you handed me the picture?"

"Since she told me about it, I thought she must have told you about it."

That was enough talk. "Okay, Jim, thanks. I can take it from here." I hung up before he could start the conversation again.

I looked at the sketch again, and a chill came over me. I'd seen that jacket on someone before.

♦

CHAPTER 57

♦

It had been a week since I had put the ad in the paper. There had been no replies. Not even crank calls. I was happy about that but unhappy that the cheerleader had not responded.

I was thinking that I should go see the dean of the university. I was sure she would have her own parking spot, and I would wait and confront her as she went to her car at the end of the school day. However, I would wait a few more days to see if there were any replies to the ad. I couldn't wait too long because soon the university would close down for the summer.

I didn't know what a university dean would do during the summer —have a vacation, I guessed. Three months was a long vacation, though. There were probably city events to attend and social functions as well.

It was a Tuesday. If I had not received any replies by Thursday, I would pay the dean an unannounced visit.

I called the 9th Division and asked to speak to either of the two detectives working the case. The desk sergeant said they were both in, whom did I wish to speak to? I told him to take a wild guess. I heard him call Beth, saying there was a call coming through.

"Hi, Mitch. I hear you've been busy. What's up?"

"Did Jim give you guys copies of the drawing he made of the man who was seen talking to Julie? If so, what did you think?"

"We got copies, but we can't tell much from it, and we couldn't use it in court. I think you and the young woman were both trying to be helpful, but I don't see it doing much good. Even if we could identify the man, it doesn't mean he's the killer or even the person who impregnated Julie Miller."

Yes, I know that, I thought. That was why I had done nothing about it. So, I lamely asked her if they had any new information. She said they did not. I asked her to keep in touch and then hung up.

The postman usually came at around four in the afternoon. I think our street must have been the last one on his routine. I didn't get much mail. Mostly ads and bills. Even the bills had dropped off because most of them were paid directly through my bank or credit accounts. So, I didn't usually wait in anticipation for him to come.

Now, though, if I was home in the afternoon, I started looking out the window from three-thirty on. I also kept checking my phone and email. If it had been me who wanted to reply and not leave anything that could be traced, I would have used postal mail. However, I wasn't sure if young people even knew there was such a thing. Everything seemed to be digital. It was as if nothing could be done without it. I was hoping that the young woman would contact me one way or another.

I started looking at how it all started the night that Julie was killed. As I went through the sequence of events the way I thought they had happened, I had a sudden thought.

I called Henry, hoping he would answer. He did, saying it was too late for lunch. I told him that was not the reason for my call. I asked him if, since that fateful night, he had noticed anything else missing other than the jewelry.

He said that not until he moved had he noticed anything but that when he was going through all his clothes, he'd noticed that a jacket was missing. I asked him if he had called the police about it and he said he had not; he didn't think it was worthwhile.

I knew why it had been taken.

The afternoon went by, and at around four-fifteen I saw the postman start on our street. He got nearer and nearer, and I fully expected him to walk by, but he came straight to my mailbox at the side of my house. I rushed over like a kid going to get a new toy, and there it was—a white envelope with no return address.

I tore it open and began to read what amounted to three full pages of a story that made me sit back and read it over and over. In between times, I was putting the pieces in the puzzle that had started where the young university student started her story. All the pieces fit. Now all I had to do was see someone and make two phone calls. I remembered Jan and I talking about four possibilities. Well, there was a fifth one. *The plan had changed.*

◆

CHAPTER 58

◆

Two days later, I walked down the garden path that I had walked so many times before. I wouldn't walk it again. Some flowers had been planted. It always looked well kept.

Jack opened the door. "Hi, Mitch. What brings you out so early? Come on in anyway."

"Hi, Jack. Is Brad home?"

"Brad? Why do you want to see Brad?"

"I don't. I was just wondering what everyone was doing."

"He's out looking for a job. His university days are over now. It's too early for a beer. Do you want a coffee?"

"No thanks." I had to get to it. I couldn't pussyfoot around. I had to get it over with.

"Jack, I know you killed Julie. You also killed Tony, and you almost killed me."

His face went white, and I saw a look of fear in his eyes that I had never seen before.

"I will tell you the story," I continued. "Some of it is guesswork, but with what I know now, all the pieces fit. You can correct me at any time. It all started several years ago when you raped Julie in the university gym."

Jack almost yelled in my face. "Hey, wait a minute. She led me on. You know what a tease she was. A man can only take so much, then he can't stop. It was more like she seduced me."

"Jack, if a woman seduces a man, she is more likely to yell *yes, yes, yes* than scream *no, no, no*. You see, you didn't know this, but there was a young woman in the female locker room next to the gym at the time. She answered my ad in the newspapers. She was a cheerleader on the football team that you coached. She had hurt herself, a mild ankle sprain, so she was moving around slowly and was still there when everyone else had gone.

"Those walls at the university are thin—you know that, Jack—and you can hear people in the next room if they talk loud enough or if they scream. So, she knew it was Julie; Julie was in a couple of her classes. She thought it was you, but she was not sure. You were quieter; you were not screaming. However, she knew your voice from you yelling at the football players.

"This young woman was scared; she didn't know what to do. She waited a week before she saw the dean and told her what she had heard. The dean said she would investigate and get back to her. She did, two days later.

"The dean told the young woman that Julie had told her not to say anything about the incident. Julie said she would deny it. The dean also said that Julie made her swear that she would never under any circumstances say anything about the incident in the future.

"I saw the dean last night. I waited in the university parking lot and approached her car. I told her she could talk to me or to the police. It would be about withholding evidence of the rape of a murdered person.

"She got in my car and broke down while telling the story to me. She had held it for too long. She basically told me what the young woman told me. The dean said that Julie didn't want any examinations or people knowing what had happened and getting stares all the time. She didn't want anyone to talk about it.

"When Julie was killed, the dean thought about going to the

police, but she told herself that what had happened at the university had nothing to do with the killing. She kept telling herself that until she believed it. Anyway, she thought she was just doing what Julie had told her to do.

"She worried that if it got out, she would lose her job. She only had one year to go before retirement. I told her that was not my decision. When I left her, she was a broken woman.

"So, the incident was forgotten, but Julie had not forgotten, had she, Jack? And as luck would have it, she found an unusual way of getting back at you. She was lucky enough, or as it turned out in the end, unlucky enough to meet Brad on a night out for her and a night out for him.

"In the chit chat at the nightclub, he told her about you. He's very proud of you and wanted to impress her by telling her what a great guy his dad was. Julie was a smart young woman, and she put her mind to work to think out how she could take advantage of the meeting. She came up with a fantastic idea that might work and might not.

"You don't know this, but I have already talked to Brad twice about that night. One of those times was yesterday. You see, the first time, I asked Brad if he had worn a condom because Julie was very strict about that. He just said yes. The second time, yesterday, I asked him if there was anything special about the condom. He thought for a moment and then said there was, and how did I know?

"I asked him what was special about it, and he told me that Julie told him she had a special one for him and went into the washroom with her purse. She told him to turn out the lights and put it on. He said he didn't notice anything special about it; he was too excited anyway.

"What it was, and I'm just guessing, but I'm sure I'm right: Julie made a couple of pinprick holes in the end of the condom with something pointed in her purse. I'm saying a couple, but maybe it was only one. Whatever she did, it gave her a chance and it worked. She got pregnant, and she must have been thrilled because now she could really get back at you and start her new life. So, what exactly did she want, Jack?"

"The bitch said that she would tell everyone that Brad raped her, and even if he was not convicted, it would smear him for the rest of his life. She wanted me to pay for the abortion and five thousand dollars a month for a year to keep quiet. I couldn't afford that. I don't have that kind of money."

I said, "I know you and Julie met in the Nordgren Bakery. The daughter of the owner saw you both and said you seemed to be arguing. She had a poor description of you, but I got the police artist to draw a sketch from what she told him. I could tell nothing from the side of a face that was drawn. However, you were wearing the red-and-black baseball jacket that you have. The bakery girl saw it and told the artist, and he put the top part in his drawing. You were the only person in my investigation that I ever saw wear that jacket.

"Anyway, after that, obviously, you didn't change her mind, and on poker night you decided to meet her after Henry left for my place. So, tell me what happened at the house."

Jack looked like he was going to throw up. He cleared his throat and started. "Yes, I waited until Henry left. He always left early, and he was always the first to arrive for poker. I knew I had lots of time. I was going to scare the crap out of Julie and tell her I was going to kill her. I planned to put my hands around her neck and tell her that was what it would be like. I would do anything for Brad.

"She kept saying, 'Don't be silly,' as if she didn't take me seriously. Then I saw the axe. I thought this was even better—I might even cut her a bit. I said I would kill her and ran toward her. Again, she said, 'Don't be silly,' and ran toward me. Just as we came close, I tripped and fell forward. With the momentum, my hands came down and the axe caught her right across the neck. It was terrible, blood everywhere."

"Let me tell you what I think happened next," I said, "and correct me if I'm wrong. You had blood all over your shirt and jacket. You took them off and grabbed a jacket from Henry's closet and put that on. Then you thought to make it look like a burglary, so you took a jewel case from Julie's room. You put the bloody clothes and the jewel case in the trunk of your car and headed to my place for the poker game. How am I doing so far?"

"Right on, Mitch. You were always good at figuring out things."

"Afterwards, you didn't know what to do with those things in your car. You couldn't put them in your garbage because Brad gathered up all the garbage and put it out each week. You couldn't take the chance of him finding out. So, for the time being, when Brad was out the next day, you dug up that first plot in your backyard and buried them there. Right again so far?"

"You're too frigging smart, Mitch. Now you're starting to get annoying."

"The pieces all fit, Jack. You don't have to be a rocket scientist to figure this all out. Anyway, what you didn't count on was the weather. Remember, we had that bad storm with all the rain and the high winds? Then the next day, Tony came over to see you and get your opinion of the whole situation. He was going to check everyone he knew.

"Then you made your big mistake. You invited him out on your back verandah to have a drink with you. That's where we always went. You should have noticed before he got there that the storm had uncovered something you had buried. What was it, a bloody shirt?"

"Yes, it was the part of the front of the shirt, not much but enough for him to see what it was. I wondered what he was looking at, and then I saw. He pretended to look around as if he hadn't seen anything, but I knew he had. Then he finished his drink quickly, said he had to go, and went.

"I didn't know what to do. I figured he would tell you. I didn't think he would do it over the phone but maybe meet you somewhere. So, I followed him from that time up until that foggy night when you guys met at the ghost.

"I didn't mean to kill him. I wanted to hit him hard enough so that it would affect his memory, though if it did kill him, well, I would be sorry, but I would do anything in order that Brad wouldn't be brought into any part of this.

"Then I heard little noises, and I knew it was you. It sure was foggy, but I couldn't take a chance that you could see me, so I hit you hard, hoping to just knock you out for a while. Sorry about the concussion."

He was sorry about the concussion? Sorry? He had been my best friend for most of my life, and he was sorry? I stopped for a moment, trying to understand. I didn't understand. Everything was so unreal. I looked at Jack. He seemed to have regained his composure, as if now that he had told everything, it was all going to be alright. I had to get my head around this.

What else was there? Not much. One thing though. "Jack, is all that stuff still in your backyard?"

"No. One day when Brad was at the university, I put everything in a large black garbage bag and headed out to a park near the lake. It had one of those large garbage bins where people put picnic leftovers and other garbage. I put it in there, so no one could trace it. So, everything is gone. Now everything is okay, and we can get on with our lives, Mitch, just like before."

I had that unreal feeling again. I didn't know how he could talk like that. I had to end it now. I looked at him. This was it. The end.

"Jack, you don't know this, but I'm wearing a wire. The police are right outside. They'll be coming right in, and I'm going right out."

With that I got up and started toward the hallway.

Jack leapt up. "Mitch! Mitch, don't do this! Mitch!"

I didn't stop walking. Coming down the hall together were

Detectives Finnegan and Puccillo. Right behind them were my friend Frank Dobson and the first detective on the case, Surmansky. Behind them were two uniformed officers.

Finnegan shook my hand and said, "Well done, Mitch."

I gave him the wire and the attachment. Beth shook my hand too. "Nice going, Mitch. I was rooting for you."

I said, "We should keep in touch."

She said, "Maybe."

Maybe from a woman to a man always meant *no* to me.

Frank gave me a hug. "You continue to amaze me with your persistence and maybe a bit of luck as well."

"The more persistent I am, the luckier I get," I replied.

Detective Surmansky said, "You hit the jackpot. You should come work for us. You could be my partner."

"Maybe, if it worked for women, it could work for me."

I nodded to the two uniformed officers and walked out. The last words I heard were, "You have the right to remain silent, you have the right to . . ." It tailed off as I walked to my car.

I should have felt happy, jubilant, and wanting to celebrate. Instead, I felt empty and sad. I drove home, not wanting to think about it. First thing I did when I got there was pour myself a shot of bourbon, and then I started thinking about it. I should not have done that, but I couldn't help myself.

I started thinking about all the times Jack and I had been together, and I felt worse and worse. I could feel myself breaking up. I don't remember ever crying in my life before, but the sobbing and the heaving started. I couldn't stop. I shouted out, "You bastard! You bastard, Jack!" and flung my glass against the wall. It shattered, and I felt a bit better. I poured myself another shot. My hands were trembling, and I felt sick to my stomach. I kept telling myself, *Mental toughness. Mental toughness.* I needed mental toughness in my line of work.

I called Henry and told him. He was shocked but thankful it was all over. I asked him to call Jenny and anyone else he could think of. I couldn't talk to anyone else that day.

I couldn't shake the low feeling that I had. Mental toughness would have to start tomorrow.

EPILOGUE

Two Months Later

Jack, his lawyers, and the district attorney came to a plea-bargain agreement. The lawyers were hoping that the tape wouldn't be admissible because Jack didn't know he was being taped. The judge ruled that it was admissible because there was no coercion and that Jack had willingly given all the information about his involvement in both killings.

It was then that the lawyers and the DA agreed to the plea bargain, which would drop the murder charges if Jack would plead guilty to two counts of manslaughter. The DA agreed that it would be difficult to convict on murder charges when there was no evidence of a weapon having been taken to the location of either of the killings.

In my case, the DA wanted me to testify against Jack on an attempted murder charge. I argued that I didn't want to testify and that I just wanted it all to be over. If there was a trial, it wouldn't be for a year or more. The courts were always way behind in hearing cases.

Jack was sentenced to eight years for Julie's killing and ten years for Tony's killing. The judge said that the first one could have been accidental, but Jack had admitted he wanted to kill her. Also, the manner in which she died was so terrible, a manslaughter charge was still justified.

So, a total of eighteen years, but the judge said that Jack could be paroled after twelve years. It didn't seem like enough, and I thought that Jack got off lightly, but at least it was all over. However, the memories would live on for several people, including me.

As for my personal life, the good news was that I had a new job. The insurance company claims supervisor, Keith Smith, whom I had worked for before, called me and said he had a ton of work for me. He said that frauds were on the increase, with several incidents of people claiming damages from incidents that were either staged or exaggerated. I was happy doing that kind of work. It often involved stakeouts, but I was okay with that.

The next good thing was that Jan and I went out to celebrate. We went to three different nightclubs, and we drank all kinds of stuff. I even tried dancing. I fell down twice and told everyone I was breakdancing. We told jokes, all kinds of jokes, and we laughed at them all. We were like noisy teenagers on their first adult night out.

I don't remember much about how it ended. Seems to me that Jan called for an Uber. I remember falling into the backseat.

I know that Jan was talking to the driver. I was not sure what she said, but then I felt her hand in my pants pocket. I wondered if we were going to do anything in the back seat, but then she pulled out my house keys and gave them to the driver.

After that, I remember little. I know that Jan got out first. She must have paid the driver by some method. When we got to my place, I think the driver got me out and must have walked or dragged me up to the door and let me in.

All of that was very blurry. The next thing I knew was when I woke up. I was flat out on the bed, and I still had my shoes on.

I had no idea what time it was, but the sun was coming up. I had a terrible headache, just like when I'd had the concussion, but at least at the hospital they had painkillers.

I had some pills I could take. As I stumbled to the washroom, my stomach turned over, and I reached the toilet just in time. I must have thrown up everything I'd eaten the night before.

I grabbed some Aspirins and Alka Seltzer from the cabinet and took two of each. Then I stumbled back to bed, this time I took my shoes off.

I dozed a bit, but the headache lingered. Overall, I felt lousy. It was too bad because I'd had such a good time the night before, and now I was paying for it. I had thought that the symptoms from my concussion were all gone. However, I had not had that much to drink since that fateful night.

I didn't go back to sleep. It was afternoon by then. My head was a bit better, but I still had a dull headache. The nausea was gone, and I felt a little empty but not hungry.

I felt very thirsty. I slowly drank three glasses of water, and thought I should get something to eat. I heated up some beef broth, had that with a slice of toast, and started to feel a bit better. If only the headache would go away.

Again, I took a couple of Aspirins. I tried to watch TV, but I couldn't concentrate. I went for a walk, hoping to clear my head, but all it did was make me feel tired.

I ordered a chicken dinner. I felt that at least I could eat that. I did, and there were no after-effects. Then I watched TV on and off without paying much attention and then took two more Aspirins and went to bed. A truly wasted day.

The next day, I felt somewhat better. Jan called, wondering how I was. She said that I had been in no condition for anything when she'd left me.

I told her that I'd had a rough day. That was an understatement. Then I surprised myself by saying we should do it again, but this time I would take a maximum of three drinks, only go to one place, and do a little less dancing. She agreed.

A few days later, we did exactly that, I felt much better and stayed over at her place. That time was even better than the time before.

The last bit of good news was that Doug, Greg, and I had assembled a new poker group. Doug and Greg had convinced the two guys who sat next to them at the Chiefs games to join us. I got my claims supervisor who I worked for to come in. He said he really enjoyed poker.

Henry said he didn't want to play anymore. Too many memories. I told him I understood.

There was just one rule for the poker group. The main game we used to play involved the king of diamonds as the wild card. Doug, Greg, and I all said that was in the past. Never again would we play the Man with the Axe.

◆

ACKNOWLEDGEMENTS

◆

Marilyn Smith, Colleen O'Reilly, Dan Smith, family members whose knowledge and technical skills were very helpful.

Dinesh Dattani, who pointed me in the right direction and then kept on giving advice.

Sandy Hebeler whose medical knowledge I relied on.

Keisha Francis, who read my book while I was writing it and inspired me to continue right up to the finish.

Kayla Lang, James Stewart and all the other good people at Friesen Press who made it all happen.

The Man With The Axe was a team effort and I thank them all immensely.